Summoner of Sleep

A.I. Winters

Literary Wanderlust | Denver, Colorado

Published in the United States by Literary Wanderlust LLC, Denver, Colorado.

www.LiteraryWanderlust.com

ISBN Print: 978-1-942856-80-1
ISBN Digital: 978-1-942856-85-6

Printed in the United States of America

Dedication

For Mike Young, fellow horror lover, champion of my writing
since day one, and an amazing friend.
This one's for you.

"Only fate is to blame."
—Gustave Flaubert, *Madame Bovary*

Chapter 1

Ryder

A figure appeared from the mist and ripped a thread from the center of his forehead. He screeched in agony, but then the end of the thread morphed into a black oozing mass. The figure squished the thick sludge in his face and laughed. Blinded, he wiped the burning slime from his face and ran. Eyes surrounded him. Thousands of eyes. Eyes like white, shining gems looking at him from above, below, and upside down. Eyes in black heads. Eyes that followed him as he flew through the emptiness. Out of breath, he peered over his shoulder at the eyes that had now transformed into clocks. Their chimes and rings echoed through the darkness. His pulse throbbed in his ears as he searched for a place to hide in the barren landscape. In an instant, the sky blackened with metal parts. Cold steel gears and sharp spokes pelted and serrated his flesh into ribbons. He choked on wallowing tears and slipped on his own blood. The clocks multiplied and descended upon him.

—

Ryder Ashling's body burned like a bonfire, but he refused to let go of the quilt wrapped around him.

"Explain the meaning of this right now." Julie's gaze slashed back and forth as she scanned the pile of clocks tangled in the sweat-soaked bed sheets.

"I already told you. The clocks came back from my dreams with me."

"Tell me the truth. You and I both know that there's no way in hell clocks just appear out of thin air like that and end up in our bed in the middle of the night."

"You think I just put them there?"

"Yes."

"You're crazy," Ryder said.

"Oh, I'm the crazy one? Who's afraid of something as stupid as a clock?"

"I told you about my nightmares before we got married. Why are you so surprised?"

"You told me you dreamed about clocks, not that they came back with you."

"I know...I know," Ryder said through his clenched jaw. "This has never happened to me before though. Can't you just cut me some slack?"

"No. And you better do something about it." Her face and throat flushed as she darted out of the bed.

"What do you want me to do?" He wiped the sweat from his brow with the quilt. "You know I've tried everything to stop the nightmares. Hypnosis, drugs, alcohol, sleep deprivation, meditation. All those disgusting sleeping concoctions make me queasy. You know that nothing works."

She crossed her arms with a scoff. "I've put up with your blood-curdling screams waking me up at all hours of the night. The welts, bruises, and scratches on your skin each morning. The sleepwalking. Getting phone calls at two in the morning from neighbors asking me to pick you up from their lawn. And now this. I can't deal with this shit anymore, Ryder." Julie strode across the bedroom.

"Where are you going?"

"I'm going to live in the guestroom. When you stop playing these asinine jokes on me, then I'll come back to bed."

"Wait. I already told you. I'm not playing a joke on you. This is real. Please believe me. You're my wife for Christ's sake."

Her wicked glance shot him dead, then she slammed the door so hard their wedding picture sprung from the wall and broke.

For the next hour, Ryder's cries echoed through the cold vaulted hallways of the Ashling house. He had cried two other times in his life. Once when his beloved beagle Bologna died, and once when his stepdad smacked him around for writing poetry. Tears poured from his eyes as he turned and stared at the mound of ticking clocks in his bed. He was too afraid to touch them, to believe they were real.

A sharp pain ached in his gut and Ryder rushed into the bathroom and gagged into the sink, but nothing came up.

His hands struggled to grasp the medicine cabinet handle, but he rose from the depths of despair to ease it open.

What concoction will numb my pain tonight?

His gaze zipped to a little brown vial with a tag wound around the neck that read CURE.

Was this new or old? Who cares?

Ryder palmed the vial, closed the medicine cabinet, and caught a reflection of his haunted face. The Botox hadn't done a damn thing and neither had his weight gain powder.

He sighed and examined the contents of the vial in the light, then uncorked it, and took a generous whiff.

Like an ancient diaphanous entity summoned from the past, the pungent scent burned the delicate membranes inside his nostrils. Luminous colors, exotic tastes, and mesmerizing sounds enveloped him—a merry-go-round for the senses. It was pure glory in a bottle for a fleeting second, until a bone-freezing shock swept through his shaken body.

His limps started to stiffen as if rubber coursed through his veins.

"J-Julie? Help. Julie."

His cries fell like stones into the silence of the house.

His legs were like two wooden boards that tipped him into the wall. Ryder grasped for anything he could to keep himself standing—the bathroom curtains, the shelf, the molding, but then it spread to his arms. They were stuck directly in front of him and he couldn't move any of his joints or fingers. He plummeted to the floor as everything disappeared into darkness.

—

Ryder sat up and bit back a scream in the morning light. A puddle of blood surrounded him on the tile. He touched a sore spot on the back of his head and winced.

He stood and steadied himself against the cold bathroom countertop. There were no signs of welts or scratches from the clocks on his skin and he could move his joints again.

"Julie?" He stumbled about in such a state that if his wife saw him, she would accuse him of being drunk—this time, not rightfully. "Julie? H-help me."

Outside the birds chirped with cheerful melodies, taunting him.

He staggered into the bedroom, but an echo followed. He skimmed the barren room, the dusty shelves, and empty closets.

"No. You couldn't have." Ryder snatched a letter addressed to him on the bed. *I'm leaving. I'm sorry*, it read in black Sharpie. He flipped it over.

"That's all you have to say to me? You didn't even have the decency to sign it?"

Bitch.

He clenched his fists so tight his knuckles went white, and he threw the crumpled paper at the bed. Then he jerked back, fell against the wall, and slid to the floor like a loogie into the gutter. Tears welled and dropped down his cheeks. Now he cried for the fourth time.

"I can't believe you left me for good." He wallowed. Her blissful, toothy smile shot through his memory. He loved that smile. "I never thought you'd get the nerve. I gave you everything. You never had to work a day in your life. All you did was sip margaritas by the pool and go to yoga classes, you bitch."

Earlier in the week, she took him to see a psychiatrist. The psychiatrist had diagnosed him with *chronomentrophobia*— fear of clocks. It was a rare phobia, incurable, and characterized as a fear of time passing too quickly. The disappointed look on Julie's face weighed heavy in his mind.

More tears splashed onto the floor. His head spun and he lurched back to the bathroom, knelt over the toilet, and vomited, wiping away the sweat on his face in between heaves.

He stood with a swimmy head, hunched over the sink, and cupped water in his hands beneath the running faucet. He wiped the residual water from his purple, cracked lips and turned off the tap, as he stared at his inflamed eyes in the mirror, which looked light gray rather than their usual tar-black. The soft, tender spot underneath his ribcage ached when he inhaled.

He slammed his fist on the porcelain. "Why don't I have normal dreams like everyone else?" His skin crawled at the engrained image of disembodied eyes following him that transformed into clocks. "You're such a fucking disgrace. Can't even keep your wife."

Ryder balled his fists. He squeezed them tighter. The thin skin burst from the pressure of his nails. Blood pooled in his palms and dripped on the tile. "Stupid dreams." He punched the mirror. Glass shards burst into a glittery explosion.

Woozy, Ryder groped the window frame, looking half-dazed out the upstairs window. Outside his neighbor skulked about. Ryder had caught old, pudgy Claude Wick spying on him through his bathroom window on more than one occasion.

He was a garrulous neighbor, and their conversations started amicably, but they always turned toward Claude's dead wife—a person whom Ryder never met. Claude liked flannel shirts and a smelly pipe after dinner, and detested noise, mess, and weeds. They were natural enemies.

He glanced at the small mirror installed in a discreet location outside the window which aligned with the enormous clock in the middle of downtown.

Crap. Seven-thirty. Time for work.

For a second, Ryder was tempted to call in sick, but he hadn't missed a single day of work since he started at the firm eight years ago, and he would be damned to let anything affect the promotion he labored so exhaustingly for. He refused for all those sixteen-hour days to go to waste; for all the nights he'd slept at the office and caught hell from Julie to be for nothing; for his rivals who threw him under the bus to reap his reward. He closed the bathroom curtains, washed, and went to the walk-in closet, and changed into a suit, not bothering to spend the extra time matching his tie to his sock color.

Ryder headed down the hall, trying not to notice more missing items, and stopped at the top of the staircase. As his pale hand slid over the cool banister, the blood from his palm mingled with the wood polish and gave off a most peculiar metallic pine scent. Vomit rose in his throat and he swallowed it.

"No."

The stairs were huge beneath his feet and the distance to the kitchen took forever. A small brown vial without a tag sat near the cookie jar on the counter. The dazzling confetti of green and gold liquids swirled with a hypnotic invitation.

"What the—?" Ryder hurried toward the vial and picked it up. "Julie? Are you messing with me?" he called and spun around, but silence met his ears. He returned his attention to the vial. "I'm not making the same mistake," he said—about to set it down, but then his eager fingers popped the cork independently from his brain.

Euphoria followed, but only for a minute. The substance once again encased him before tendrils of panic and pain trembled through his helpless, rubberized body. The world stopped. Every cell in his body deflated.

"Noooooo," he screamed through his constricted throat. He fell to the floor.

—

Ryder's eyes flew open. The sun streamed upon him and the blue jays chattered from the garden.

He pulled himself up, stood with the aid of the kitchen countertop, and glanced out the window. His gaze darted to one of his mirrors positioned outside the kitchen window. He wouldn't have believed it was six o' clock in the morning had the automatic sprinklers not kicked on at their programmed time right then.

Ryder spun around. An overturned vial lay on the kitchen floor and his chest tightened.

It happened again?

All signs indicated an entire day had passed.

Three new vials now waited on the counter.

Too afraid to touch them, he studied them at a distance for comparison. They were the same size, shape, and color, had no discernible markings, and there were no indications of their origin—just the brilliance of their mesmerizing colors that swirled inside them, illuminating the little that remained of his sanity.

Ryder picked up the vials with his sleeve, threw them in an empty grocery bag, then headed to the car.

—

He entered the damp apothecary shop adjacent to the town's pioneer cemetery out of breath. He slammed the door behind him and then cringed. Vern Wick glanced up from behind the counter amidst the thick, incensed air.

There was little organization in the shop: hundreds of dusty bottles lined the shelves, velvet satchels of herbs kept company with wide-potted plants, and colorful soaps made into the shapes of pie slices; he could get lost for hours just examining all of it, but Ryder wasn't interested today. He'd been coming to the local apothecary each week for the past two years and if anyone could help him identify the substance in his CURE bottles, it was Vern.

"Ah, Ryder. Welcome," said the apothecarist. He rose from the chair. Although Vern never traveled, his tanned, hydrated skin made it look as if he had just returned from a vacation. Vern glanced at his watch. "I'm surprised to see you here since you're normally at work during this time. Did I forget about an appointment?"

"No." Ryder fixated on the watch. "Could you put that away please?"

"Oh, right. I always forget about my watch, but I didn't know you were coming in today." Vern fiddled with the strap and stashed it under the counter.

"Well, how did the latest blend go?"

"Doesn't matter." Ryder slowly dumped the vials upon the counter, his palms slick with sweat. "Are these your bottles?"

Vern squinted. "No."

"I thought Julie might've purchased them from you."

Vern shrugged.

"Then I need to know what's in here."

Vern's bony fingers reached across the counter.

"Careful." Ryder stopped his hand. "Just holding it made me open them and when I did the contents made me lose consciousness—twice."

"I will. But I need to examine them closer."

"Use a rag or something to hold them, okay?"

Vern's wiry eyebrow arched, but he retrieved a handkerchief

from under the counter and picked up one of the sealed vials. He held it up to the light. Just the sight of the whirling glittery world inside it made Ryder giddy, and he balled his fists before he shoved his hands deep into his pockets.

"Did you have those dreams of yours?"

"No. It's bizarre. But now there's a new complication. When I woke the other day there were clocks in the bed with me. I don't know how or why."

"Hmm."

"I don't know where the vials came from. They just appeared."

"They appeared in your house?"

"Yes. One yesterday and then more after Julie le—"

The smile vanished from Vern's face. "You don't look well. Do you need to sit? I'd hate for my best customer to become ill in my shop."

Unable to make eye contact or swallow the lump in his throat, Ryder said, "Please just find out what's inside."

"I'll do my best."

"How long do you think it'll take?"

"I'll need to send it to the lab, so about a week or two. I don't quite see the rush, though. What matters is that it made you sleep well. That's been our goal this whole time, right?"

"Yeah, it's just—" Ryder tapped his fingers on the counter. "Please call me the minute you find out, okay? It's urgent."

"I will."

"You believe me, don't you?" Ryder asked.

Vern cocked his head.

"You believe me that I have the nightmares about the clocks attaching themselves to me and ending up in my bed, don't you?"

"It doesn't matter what I believe. What matters is you getting well," Vern said with a wink, then gathered the vials.

"Okay then. Well, don't forget to call me the minute you find out. I don't care if it's in the middle of the night. I'll answer."

The old man nodded. "I will."

Ryder turned with a grin and jingled the car keys in his pocket. He stared out at the city glinting in the distance.

"Yes. I understand now," Vern said. "It's crystal clear."

Ryder looked over his shoulder. "What'd you say?"

Blood was everywhere: blood gushing from Vern's ears and mouth, blood on the counter, blood drenching his sweater, blood coating the floor.

Ryder screamed, rushed to Vern, and grabbed his arm.

"No. It hurts too much," Vern shrieked. "Don't touch me."

"What's wrong? I can't help you if I don't know what happened."

Vern groaned and jetted out the door like he was on fire. He flew through the busy intersection and ran straight into the woods across the street, disappearing into the trees.

Ryder stood breathless at the threshold, his suit and hands crimson. He caught a questioning glance from a man at the bus stop.

"Hey, what did you do? Did you hurt that man?"

"Shit." Ryder lowered his head, strode to his car, and got in.

The man yelled and ran toward his car. "Stop right there." He waved his arms. "I'm calling the police."

Ryder started the ignition. The man jumped and shouted in his rearview mirror, which drew even more attention, so he slammed on the gas.

The roads seemed longer and narrower on the drive home.

What did Vern mean when he said that he understood? That everything was crystal clear? Had he been talking to him or someone else? Had there always been a tree at that intersection? Was that a new deli or an old one?

Shapes and colors passed in a blur, and somehow, he made it home.

He turned off the car, exhaled, and sat in the driveway with closed eyes.

What a rotten day.

"I saw you," a voice said.

Ryder jolted and got out of the car. "Hello?" He glanced around. Someone's eyes were on him. Someone watched him and saw the blood splatter on his hands and clothes.

Shit. They would blame him.

He looked at one of the positioned mirrors, noting that several hours had passed, but the drive to the apothecary was only a few minutes and he hadn't been at the shop for that long.

With shaky hands, Ryder found his house key and ran to the front door, where a bright orange paper the color of construction cones was taped over the peephole. His eyes narrowed.

I'm being evicted? But I'm rich. I always pay the mortgage on time.

Drops of perspiration slid into his eyes and burned them. Ryder tore the notice down and threw it in the bushes. The door screeched open and he stumbled inside and collapsed on the hardwood floor, his legs jelly.

A new vial sat atop a sofa cushion. His gaze darted to the coffee table. Another. Then to the stairs. Another.

—

For days, Ryder sat in his favorite armchair and stared out the window, sometimes going the whole day without food. Showers stopped. Shaving stopped. So did teeth brushing. It didn't matter.

He called Julie too many times to count, but she never answered. His wedding ring became loose and fell into the heating grate. All the while, vials appeared out of nowhere, beckoning him to partake in the unknown contents within, but he refused to open any more.

They popped up inside the fridge, in cabinets, on chairs, in his bed, on top of the toilet, and sometimes jammed in the toes of his shoes. After he'd gather all the vials in a garbage bag using a broom and dustpan, he'd turn around and more would be there...waiting, multiplying. He double and triple-checked all the locks and windows in his house, but always found them secure.

A week later Ryder gave up trying to gather and discard the vials. The repossession men broke down the door and took everything but his car since the title was in his former client's name. They also left the filthy chair he refused to move from. He listened to the men joke about what a poor slob he was and make cracks about him. Didn't they know he was someone important? They even repossessed his phone, so there was no way to contact his wife. Could he still call her that? It was a good thing that they took his phone though. He couldn't stand listening to the voicemail from work again explaining how they had let him go and that Ernest got his promotion. The only good news was that he had saved some money in a secret bank account.

The police would remove him from the premises soon. He wouldn't go without a fight and prayed they'd arrest him. Maybe then the vials couldn't follow and he could rest in the solitary pleasure of a dark, cold prison cell. What a blissful fantasy.

Chapter 2

Claude

Claude gritted his teeth and covered his ears. He couldn't believe it had been a year since he had moved into the exuberant Queen Anne next to the Ashlings and the screams still hadn't stopped. Not once.

Ryder seemed like such a normal man who was charitable and accomplished, and Julie always smiled and waved. They were a stereotypical Barbie- and Ken-type couple who wanted a family and a golden retriever, but that didn't explain the horrors that went on in the Ashling home each night. How was he supposed to enjoy his retirement with constant screaming?

He didn't mean to spy on Ryder from the upstairs window. It just so happened that his bedroom window overlooked Ryder's master bathroom, and within a few weeks, Claude could set his watch to the times of his neighbor's screaming episodes. The bathroom light flicked on around 1:30 a.m. every night after a blood-curdling shriek. There was a sleepwalking incident two times a week. And three times a week there was an additional dream around 3:45 a.m. consisting of panicked yells and loud thumps that sounded like toppling furniture. Claude wondered how much the couple had spent on new furniture each month.

At first, Claude thought they were night terrors until he overhead Julie on the phone. Her voice wafted through the open parlor window as he tended to his roses at the edge of his lawn.

"I can't take it anymore," she sobbed. "Ryder's dreams of phantom clocks. Claims they attack when he's asleep...now, the clocks are appearing in the bed...it's all insane. It just can't be possible. The psychiatrist said his disorder could be dangerous. That he's capable of violence."

After overhearing the absurd conversation, Claude noticed that Ryder didn't wear a watch and there were tiny mirrors positioned outside all the windows too. If Julie's claims were true, Claude was living next to a psychopath.

Curiosity consumed him, and he looked forward to studying Ryder each night readying for bed as he gulped various concoctions and pills. And as time progressed, Ryder consumed a meager diet of nothing more than black coffee and oranges. All of it intrigued Claude but enjoying the quiet of the day when Ryder was at work was what Claude looked forward to most in his retirement.

Then, two months ago, Ryder started coming home from work for lunch and to nap on the living room sofa. The screams sounded at 12:45 p.m. on those days, with an added dream sometimes at 1:15 p.m.

"Ahhh. Oh, God. Ahhh," Ryder screamed like a broken record.

Claude's ears cringed at the screeching. He knew two things from that moment forward: he had spent his life savings on a wonderful home where he could not relax, and the only way to achieve peace and quiet was to move away from the Ashlings and to his family's old cottage in the woods. There and only there could he live out his tranquil days completing puzzles and smoking a pipe by the fire, but he needed to sell his house first.

Circumstances were not so easy though. As if premeditated, whenever a potential buyer dropped by announced or not, Ryder's screams sent them running.

Ryder's dreams now affected Claude so much that he no longer slept. Although he still maintained a regular diet, coffee was the one thing that eased his nausea, and the pounds fell from his plump frame so fast that his glasses slid down his nose every time he exhaled.

All these occurrences made him conclude that Ryder's condition might be contagious, and he would be damned if those wretched dreams would affect him as well.

The interminable screams became such a nuisance that he took one full week to devise the perfect stratagem to alleviate both of their suffering.

Somehow, some way, he'd stop Ryder's dreams and he'd fight his insomnia. That was when he stumbled onto a peculiar plant called *Trem Autem Somno* listed in one of his brother's medicinal herbology books—Latin for Summoner of Sleep. The claim was that this powerful and unique plant could prevent all dreams. "A complete and total numbing," it read.

There were no accounts of the plant being grown and used for centuries, and even then, accounts of its use were spotty.

Although his brother was an expert in herbology, Vern grew cross with Claude upon even mentioning the name *Trem Autem Somno*. Vern warned that the plant was "tainted and dangerous."

Claude didn't mention his plan to stop Ryder's dreams using the plant, and instead contacted his brother's intricate network of international apothecaries for more information.

Discouraged that not one of them knew how to access *Trem Autem Somno* or where it came from, each reacted like Vern, citing that not enough was known and it was dangerous. But Claude continued to take matters into his own hands.

In college, he had befriended a petite woman with high-piled coppery hair named Belinda Chase who majored at the top of her class in chemistry and botany. He kept a close friendship with her over the years, hoping to take her on a proper date one day once her husband passed, but the timing still wasn't right. She was happy to oblige his request to unravel the riddle of *Trem Autem Somno* though.

It took Belinda four days to inform Claude that the plant could be traced to one location in the world—a foggy mountain town nestled in the Sierra Mountains called Marble Woods. There was a single account in a history book of a hermit discovering the plant, growing bushels of it on his property, and then disappearing.

Claude was so excited by the lead that he didn't waste any time pulling out his maps. Unable to locate Marble Woods, he headed to the library and spent hours in their archives, wondering why Marble Woods didn't appear on any of their maps either. The only explanation that the librarian could provide was, "the country is riddled with small mountain towns. Some are so small they aren't known to folks who don't live there."

Claude contacted city planners, architects, cartographers, historians, and anyone who might help him, but no one could. He left messages, wrote letters, met dozens of people, but still, nothing presented itself on the whereabouts of Marble Woods or how to obtain Summoner of Sleep.

Devastated, Claude planned to meet Belinda at his favorite café to discuss their findings over breakfast, but Belinda never showed despite her predictable punctuality. He had forgotten his cell phone at home, so he used the café's phone to call her laboratory. There was no answer, and her voicemail was full.

He worried about her, and to be safe, he went to check on her.

He drove to the outskirts of town and arrived at the laboratory several minutes later. He hated the hospital-like appearance of the building, which made him think of his deceased wife who died in one.

The front door was unlocked, so he let himself in and walked down a long corridor checking the name plates until he found her office.

The door skirted open to reveal hoards of torn books and broken furniture, flickering lights, and mounds of shredded paper. The lab's phoneline was severed and some of the buttons were ripped out of the phone. The most alarming thing though was a trail of blood leading out the broken window overlooking the woods.

He skimmed the room and checked for any signs of life.

"Belinda?"

Claude's spine tingled. He didn't move as he listened to the ticking of the wall clock. He took a shaky step backward, exited through the office door, and closed it.

He speed-walked out of the building and to his car, locked it right away, but still took the time to look over his shoulder.

She dug too deep.

He wailed like a caged animal. "Poor Belinda. My dear, sweet Belinda. I always loved you. My dear Belinda."

His face grew hot. His sausage-like fingers pulsed, and his wedding band dug deeper into his flesh. His heart raced so fast that if he didn't take his blood pressure medication soon, he'd end up in the emergency room again, but he had left it at home on the coffee table.

Claude started the car and did his best to calm his thoughts.

The trip took forever, and his fatigue prevented him from opening the medication bottle at home. He plopped down in his favorite chair and struggled with the stubborn plastic top for a few minutes, pried it open, and then gulped the pills without water. They wiggled down his esophagus and he sighed.

He pressed the light on his blinking answering machine on the table next to him.

"I have what you're looking for," the message said.

Claude's breathing problems and his duty to call the police

and report what he had seen at Belinda's laboratory ceased. "Finally," he said with a smile.

—

Claude went through considerable trouble to obtain the plant and paid for it both monetarily and emotionally. The first transaction took place out of town under the veil of night when his war injury flared up the worst.

He never glimpsed whom he dealt with. All he knew was that the seller called himself *Achilles*. And when he returned home exhausted with the vials in tow, he forced himself to remember why he was doing this.

At first, it was to get enough money to move away, but his neighbor was helpless. Claude had drudged through a lonesome existence for such a long time and endured the pain that came with it. Ryder's struggle presented a prime opportunity to save someone from a solitary life like his. Helping Ryder gave him purpose again. It was his duty, his rescue mission.

Multiple times a day he performed the laborious task of sneaking into Ryder's home and placing Summoner of Sleep vials where Ryder would find them, hoping he'd either confuse them with his existing sleeping remedies or be so intrigued by their mysterious appearance that he would gulp them down. And it worked.

To Claude's amazement, the nightmare episodes ceased after one exposure, and he could now think without screams interrupting his thoughts.

Everything was fine until he witnessed Ryder rush home one day, park his car askew in the driveway, emerge with a crazed look in his eye and bolt into the garden. He appeared a minute later muttering about Vern and blood. Claude peaked through one of his telescopes from the downstairs window. Something red stained his neighbor's clothes.

Was that blood? Hadn't Julie said that Ryder could be dangerous?

Troubled, Claude left his home and ventured to Vern's apothecary where he discovered a similar scene to that of Belinda's laboratory—blood trailing into the woods.

—

There was no sign of Ryder for two whole days, and the uncomfortable lump in Claude's throat grew to a monumental level. He paced in front of the window and thought of his missing brother and Belinda. He needed answers, to crack the riddle. He watched the house day and night, leaving his station to shave and urinate, but he didn't see so much as a light or hear a sound. This made him even more unsettled than the screams.

He had to go into the house and investigate.

When it turned dark, he crept across the damp lawn in his slippers, skirting the bushes and vines like a cat burglar. He pressed his face against Ryder's living room window, but it was black inside. Then he grasped the sticky knob of the back door.

It swished open.

Claude crept inside and found the light switch on the adjacent wall. He wavered for a moment, fearing that once he turned it on, he might find another trail of blood.

What if there was nothing at all, and this project would end?

Claude inhaled with a wheeze and flicked on the light, which revealed a body in a fetal position in the middle of the hardwood floor surrounded by dozens of empty Summoner of Sleep vials.

The stench hit Claude hard and he plugged his nose.

Ryder's skin was blue and covered in bulging purple veins, a mound of crusted foam had settled at the sides of his mouth, and his own filth covered him.

Claude wanted to cry, but he made himself approach the body and crouched down next to it.

"What have I done to you?"

His head fell to his chest and his glasses slid off his face and hit the floor, but he didn't care. As he knelt, his hand grazed

Ryder's cold arm. Claude wept. There were no words for what he was other than a cold-blooded murderer.

Guilt raced through his body, but then Claude thought he sensed something beneath his hand. Was that a pulse?

Claude wiped his tears. "Oh, thank God." He shook the body. "Come on, Ryder...wake up." He didn't stir. Ryder's blue cheeks bloomed bright red from Claude's repeated slaps. "Wake up dammit."

Ryder lay silent and still. He was still under the influence of Summoner of Sleep and it might take hours for him to awaken.

Claude went home to retrieve his best flannel blanket, a pair of pajamas, and some extra slippers. He then changed Ryder's clothes and swaddled him in the warm blanket.

For hours Claude sat next to his unresponsive neighbor, checking his pulse and adjusting the blankets every so often.

It must have been two or three o'clock in the morning when a violent shock erupted in the corpse-like body.

"Yes." Claude let out a joyful squeal and flung himself next to his neighbor, cradling his delicate head in his big, flabby arms.

"J-Julie?" gurgled Ryder. His eyes eased open and panned up.

Claude smiled and tilted Ryder's head back so close that he smelled Ryder's dank and rotten breath. Ryder's onyx eyes locked on his. Claude reached for a glass of water and held it to his neighbor's indigo lips.

"Here. Drink something."

Claude poured half of it down Ryder's throat, but he spat it out and knocked the glass away. The water rained across the pajamas and the glass spun across the floor.

A violent tremble permeated Ryder's sallow limbs. His pulse grew stronger. He stared straight up at Claude. Mouth open, lips parted. Frozen.

Claude stroked Ryder's translucent skin and whispered, "Hello, Ryder. It's okay. I'm here. I saved you. They're gone now."

Chapter 3

Ryder

Ryder repeated the phrase in his head. *They're gone now.* For the life of him, he had no idea what happened or what exactly was gone now. The world was so dark and blurry he couldn't even understand who had spoken, just that the person sounded out of breath like someone had punched them in the gut.

The cold night air and a nauseating potpourri scent whirled toward him.

All his energy melted into the floor. He tried to wiggle his fingers and toes but couldn't. His gaze flickered around the room.

A clock ticked in the background.

Was this hell?

As he lay there taking in the faint light from the room, a shadow hovered above him. It was too big to be Julie. Too plump to be Vern. Perhaps it was his stepfather coming to finish what he had started all those years ago? He would never forget the argument about his sleepwalking when he was a boy, which got so heated that he knocked Ryder out in one punch. The next thing he recalled was water smacking into his face and opening his eyes to discover his stepfather laughing, repeating, "Can't you take a punch, you sissy?" His nose broke in two places that day, and his sunken eyes remained dark purple for weeks. Recalling the pain of his nose breaking and the dreadful smell of dried blood and backed-up snot inside his sinuses sickened him.

Then everything got mixed up and blurry again. The memory melted away and a violent tremor shot through his body. He shouted a flurry of loud, inarticulate curses, his inner voice yelling at him, "Go back to sleep, you fool."

The shadowy figure leaned forward, right in his face.

"I'm so glad you've come back," the voice said. "How are you feeling now that you're awake?"

Ryder came out of his trance and saw the muddy brown eyes in the gray light, the wavy squirrel-colored hair, and the bright red capillaries sprayed across the nose and cheeks of his dumpy old neighbor, Claude Wick.

"W-what are you doing h-here?" Ryder mustered the strength to say.

"I'm here to help you."

"G-get out."

"You don't understand."

"You're t-trespassing." Ryder kicked off the flannel blanket and too-big slippers.

"Don't move so fast. Your body has had quite a shock."

"No."

"Please. Let me first explain. I introduced you to a special plant. *Trem Autem Somno*. It means Summoner of Sleep. Those vials. I put them in your house."

"You did w-what?"

"I put vials of Summoner of Sleep in your house. It can change your life. It already has."

"S-Summoner of Sleep?"

"Yes, but I grew worried when I didn't see you for a few days, so I came to check on you and I'm glad I did."

"Days?" Ryder's eyes bulged.

"Yes. You've slept the entire time. The good news is that *Trem Autem Somno* is meant to stop your nightmares. As I've monitored you, I haven't heard any screams. There are no marks on your body either. Maybe you're cured now."

Drool poured from the sides of his lips and tickled his chin. His body vibrated and stung, which prevented him from getting up from the floor.

"You're in a state of shock right now, but I believe that soon you will realize the tremendous benefit of Summoner of Sleep," Claude said. "You will be able to live a normal life again with the power of this special plant. You just need to consume it in smaller doses, that's all. I never imagined you'd take so much of it. I only put the vials out to encourage you to take it."

Ryder's eyes opened wider. "W-what day is...is it?"

"September first."

Ryder inhaled the foul scent of his urine. His gaze lowered to see his neighbor's stomach fat bulge from beneath his shirt. He recoiled.

Claude pulled his shirt down. "Due to the amount you ingested, I couldn't wake you up sooner. We should get you to an emergency room. You don't look so good."

"W-why...why did you wake me?" he choked; his throat full of dust. "I was h-happy asleep. So happy."

Claude repositioned himself, which exposed another fat roll. "I had to. If I didn't wake you, then you would've died. In fact, I thought you were dead at first." He reached for Ryder's arm. "Come on, let's get you to the hospital."

Ryder couldn't take being pitied like this any longer, and he sure as hell didn't like Claude touching him. He pulled away, rolled on his side, paused, and then rose to his feet with a groan. Perspiration broke out on his forehead and his eyes fluttered. The world was now a series of strange dream-like pictures within a kaleidoscope.

"Are you okay?" asked Claude.

Ryder's nerves were violin strings stretching tighter and tighter. His fingers and toes twitched and all the air in his chest squeezed out in one big push. Then he made eye contact again with his neighbor, which brought a cry of anger to his lips and he lurched toward the fireplace mantel. Tears and mucus poured from Ryder's face. Saggy, old pajamas hung on his frame. That crazy man had changed his clothes.

"You should go to the hospital," hummed Claude's voice.

"Stop." Ryder threw up a hand.

"Then come and lay down at my place. I have a spare guest room you could use."

Ryder shook his head. He tightened his grasp on the mantel and reached for the fire poker with his free hand. "I can't believe I live next door to such a...a l-lunatic." He turned to see Claude's confused expression.

"I've saved you. I don't understand why you'd be so angry at me."

"Angry? That's nothing compared to what I feel for you."

"But—"

"Get the hell out, you i-idiot." Ryder's voice approached a shriek as he swung the fire poker at Claude but bashed the floor instead.

"Just listen to me." Claude backed away. "Let me explain how to use Summoner of Sleep so this doesn't happen again... so you won't die. It's already changed your life, don't you see?"

"You don't know me. You don't know a goddamn thing about m-me."

"I know more than you think, Ryder. I know all about your struggles. I even know that Julie didn't believe you and that she left you."

The mention of her name crushed his soul like a thousand bricks. Anger boiled his blood, and he cracked the fire poker against the floor. "What's the matter with you? Why are you so involved with what's going on in my life? D-don't you have a life of your own?"

"I'm just trying to alleviate your suffering." Claude twisted his mustache at the side of his mouth into a sharp point.

"Alleviate my suffering?" cried Ryder. "If you want to do that, then g-give me more. Give me all the bottles you have of that stuff."

"I don't think it's a good idea to give you more."

"Give me more." Ryder raised the poker.

"But I, umm, I don't have any more. Besides, I'm not sure if there are any side effects yet, or how safe it is."

"You willingly gave me something u-unsafe?"

"Well, I wouldn't put it like that."

"You are c-crazy."

"Hey. You've tried a hundred other tonics without knowing the side effects, so how is Summoner of Sleep any different? Besides, I did research on how to stop the nightmares and learned of the plant from Marble Woods. It's said to numb the nightmares and it worked. That's what matters, right?"

Sweat beads dripped down his face. His fist clenched tighter. He blinked and raised the fire poker higher. "You're the reason for all of this. You drove me insane with those vials. Y-you exposed me to god knows what. You spied on me and broke into my house. You even dressed me. It's time to get the h-hell out of my house or I swear to God I'll kill you right here."

Claude scampered toward the front door like a scolded dog and stopped at the threshold. "Ryder, please, don't send me away. Just let me help you. I don't have anything going for me in my life either. I'm all alone over there too, so please let me do this one little thing for you. It would make me so happy to help you."

Ryder took two steps forward and stomped Claude's forgotten glasses beneath his shoe. "I'll kill you before I'd let that happen."

Chapter 4

Claude

Claude slammed the door.

Who did that stuffed shirt asshole think he was anyway? Ryder would wither and die without me.

He was drenched in sweat by the time he reached the far edge of the lawn, all the while, his mind flooded with what-ifs. He grasped the lamppost with one hand and ran over the chain of events. Whichever way he looked at it, the magnitude of the misfortune he had just encountered crushed his spirit into pieces.

Tears collected in his eyes.

"I've sacrificed everything for you, and you make it seem like I'm the insane one. Didn't you know those were my favorite pajamas? No wonder your wife left you. Why no friends ever visited." He panted. "You're an asshole. Selfish asshole, Mr. Ashling." He glowered at his neighbor's unkempt garden where the wisteria had claimed the entire west side of the house. There was no sound in the entire neighborhood, just his hoarse voice spewing hatred. "You have no idea what I had to do to obtain the tonic. No idea. We are both alone. Don't you get it? I'll get you for this."

His mind raced. The last person to see his brother was Ryder. Another reason to despise him. Claude recalled the parade of lights blinking from the yard several days ago. The police had come, but given Ryder's comatose state, it prevented him from answering the door, and with the foreclosure sign on the front door, the police must have assumed he left town, so no more questions were asked.

Claude couldn't help but imagine that beyond Ryder's innocent exterior wickedness puppeteered him. The psychiatrist had said he could be dangerous.

Was Ryder the reason for the disappearance of Vern and Belinda?

He now frowned at his own house ravaged by wild plants. Ragged weeds and bugs ran rampant—a further indication of how much he abandoned everything in his life for Ryder.

Unsure whether to return home, his gaze was drawn to a figure illuminated by the moon—black tentacles jerked and whipped around inside his neighbor's living room.

He rubbed his eyes and dabbed sweat from his forehead. He blinked, and the figure vanished. Ryder's house was black again—like his selfish soul.

Claude was glad it was gone, though the sight still sent a rush of adrenaline through his veins. A sharp pain pierced his hand and he realized he had swiped a bottle of Summoner of Sleep that dug into his palm.

How did you get here?

Claude couldn't recall picking it up or even touching it, but here it was, swirling with glittering emerald secrets. And even though it was still corked, his nose could detect its gingery, earthy scent from inside the bottle. The substance beckoned to be released. Guilt no longer hung over him for having given Ryder the tonic without knowing the side effects, or for the fact that he hadn't been brave enough to take the stuff himself.

"You get whatever is coming to you," he said with such violence that it spooked some creature in the bushes.

As his gaze plunged into the depths of the enigmatic liquid, a wave of anger washed over him. He cast the bottle into the ground with all his might.

"Ha." The liquid from the cracked bottle seeped into the ground.

Claude inhaled. The fragrant gingery scent came with a peppery kick. Just as he was getting ready to weep into the cold night air, a bright light shot through his mind and body and absolved all the dark, hopeless thoughts that plagued him. It was as if he had taken a shot of moonshine.

A jubilant, surprised cry escaped his crooked lips, and liquid trickled from his ear down his neck. Curious, he touched it and gazed upon blood.

"That's funny." Claude rubbed his thumb and index finger together. "That didn't happen to Ryder."

Claude smiled. Then a new sensation consumed his body— like the sun peeking through the clouds on a cool day. He was lucid, his body uplifted with magic—all smoke, stars, and fairy dust.

As he stared entranced at the crimson blood, a far-off call swept through the empty street and enraptured him in a tunnel of dead leaves and night magic. Claude's neck hair stood on end and he got a funny feeling that he was being watched.

"Brother?" He looked around. Without his glasses, everything was blurry shadows. "Is that you?"

The call echoed louder, and Claude turned toward the blackness of the woods at the end of the lane.

"Brother?" He stepped into the street.

Claude's aged muscles pulsed with hot invigorated blood as if awakened for the first time since he was a teenager. The limp that had plagued him since the war ceased its incessant throb, and he now stood tall with perfect posture. A peculiar warmth bloomed deep within his chest and his lungs felt free and clear. His heartbeat thundered and a euphoric cry erupted from his lips.

He rushed across the street—and the farther and faster he ran, the more the pain in his body dissolved.

Claude rubbed his spot-free, smooth hands and touched the taut cheeks with glee. He had reached the edge of the woods a changed man.

A sheet of torrential rain fell from the sky and thunder shook the whole town as Claude took a step onto a patch of pine needles. He smiled again and gazed at his new and stealthy body as it carried him deep into the forest despite the sky drenching him. Claude didn't realize he was laughing until hours later, but he didn't care—it was his last expulsion of an old, wretched body and life, and the beginning of a new chapter.

Chapter 5

Ryder

When the woods enveloped his neighbor, he smiled. "Good. Don't come back, you big fat looney."

Ryder kicked the Summoner of Sleep bottles as he staggered toward the kitchen. His stomach grumbled, but only a few expired cans of tomato soup remained in the bare cupboards. He pulled the pop-top and guzzled it cold as he gazed out the window at his neighbor's forgotten yard.

The little pond in front of the neighbor's house had become a swamp of putrid black water. Frogs and strange white fish lived there despite the clogged fountain spouts. He couldn't stand to see such a messy sight next to his home—then he remembered the eviction notice. He only had a few more days to remain in the house.

Ryder rubbed his hands across his eyes, dislodging the crustiness that had gathered at his tear ducts. A glimmer from his neighbor's downstairs window caught his gaze.

He squinted at the circular object that peeked through the

heavy drapes.

"A telescope? I don't believe this shit."

Ryder stormed out of the kitchen and through the back door, strode across the lawn, and entered through the front door of his neighbor's unlocked house.

The scent of must, shoe polish, and mature flesh wafted up to his nostrils. He stepped across the Aubusson carpet in the foyer and paused. He flicked on an old lamp and jolted at the black insects that scurried into their hiding places.

Disgusting slob.

He took another step and tripped on dozens of amber bottles scattered across the floor with illegible labels.

When he looked up his heart stopped.

The floral walls overflowed with photographs pinned alongside formulas, sketches of plants, and incoherent notes about lack of sleep. The photographs documented a variety of Ryder's facial expressions, but the majority were of him crying, illuminated by the faint lights in his upstairs bathroom.

"What the fuck?" He ripped a photo off the wall.

He glanced around the room full of junk—stacks of weathered notebooks, yellowed newspapers, piles of dirty clothes, shoeboxes full of medications. He marched over to a pile of notebooks and pulled a smallish one with scuffed corners and smeared markings from the top. He rifled the pages with one thumb. It smelled of tissue-thin paper and sweat.

There was a passage about the origin of Summoner of Sleep, another about how its creator vanished, and how Marble Woods couldn't be found on a map. Then there was a peculiar passage that offered extensive evidence about the magic of plants and provided a set of theories concerning their nature, origin, and function.

a) plants are intelligent masterminds and do not sit idly in the dirt. Matter and energy flow through them, and so does concentrated and innate magic as old as time.

b) this magic can be contained through a certain degree of

leakage, but if one drains too much magic, the plant will die. Genetic mutation and environmental factors result in evolution of plants and thus the evolution of their ever-changing magic.

c) plants are fragile and picky things. They have personalities and their adaptations are superbly inventive. Once their magic has been tapped into though, it cannot be closed by any means.

Claude's penmanship was shameful. Each sentence was a crude mix of capital letters and small letters all cramped together. His spelling was perfect though. Ryder heaved a breath of stale air and flung the notebook on the pile. For the next five minutes he thumbed through the remaining notebooks of more crowded letters accompanied by stippled drawings of plants in the margins.

He set it down and followed the muddy footprints upstairs to find a room packed with new horrors.

"Just when I thought you were already a psycho; I find that you collected the clocks I threw out from my nightmares and brought them back here." Ryder's hands went clammy. He slammed the door, tried to take a breath, but lost his balance. His head thumped against a table.

The world buzzed as he stared at the closed door from the ground as if the horrors inside it could still be seen. The exertion heightened his panic.

"You've got to relax," he said aloud and willed himself to stand. "They can't hurt you in reality."

He swallowed and slinked down the hallway. The air went stale. He was tired and wanted to go back to sleep, but another telescope positioned at the upstairs bedroom window sent him into a manic episode. Ryder marched up to it and peered through the lens of the telescope, which looked into his bathroom.

"That sick freak." Ryder kicked it over with a huff.

He turned, ready to punch something, and discovered daily journal recordings in a stack on the bureau. The journals detailed all his nightmare episodes with dates, times, and classifications of screams heard in the night. They had been graded on a scale of one to ten in terms of severity, and there was even a space provided for additional notes, some of which detailed specific words or sounds he made at his most vulnerable moments in the night.

Ryder's hands shook as he turned page after page of the disturbing and intrusive notes. There were details about the clocks he awoke with. Their size, shape, weight, and color. There were hundreds of scribbles, random patterns, and detailed drawings of his eyes—both opened and closed. The detail was photographic.

A weepy metallic voice distracted him.

He darted an inquisitive glance around the room. There was movement, he was sure, somewhere in the empty bed on the opposite side of the room. Sweat trickled down his forehead. He couldn't breathe. A hollowness echoed in his chest.

"Claude?"

Ryder stared at the bed—right through it.

Had the pillow just moved?

Something rustled behind him.

His fists tightened and he turned.

The house fell quiet.

"Hello?"

Quiet.

He relaxed and heaved a sigh of relief that the sound had stopped.

He continued to scour Claude's writings into the dark morning hours and stopped on a passage that read:

June 1, 10:15 p.m.

Astounding. Even the origin of his name is destined. After conducting more research, I've discovered that the etymology of the name "Ryder" means "summoner" or "messenger." It's derived from the Old English "ridire." Then, there's his surname "Ashling." Its etymology means "sleep" or "dream." Its origin refers to an "Aisling," a poetic genre developed in the 17th and 18th centuries. Although he appears stronger and in good spirits today, the dreams remain frequent. I'm still searching for a means to obtain the precious plant.

Conclusion: "Ryder" is the "Summoner of Sleep" himself. His name perfectly spells it out. That can't be a coincidence. I'm convinced it's intentional. I wonder what will happen once I find the plant.

~Claude Wick

Ryder recalled in his childhood that a stranger told him that his name had a powerful meaning, but he never thought twice about it until now. He pored over more entries.

August 24, 3:00 p.m.

The train of events that have plagued my neighbor would be enough to destroy the strongest man, yet he still stands. I watched as his wife left and now feel an inconsolable regret for not having stopped her had I known that he would've then lost his job as a result of taking the tonic and been faced with eviction shortly after. At first, I believed it was a series of bad luck, but upon closer inspection, I am now convinced it is the work of Summoner of Sleep. It wants him to seek solace in its arms. It all ties back to his name.

~Claude Wick

Another read:

August 28, 1:10 a.m.

I fear I have done great harm. Now that I have encountered it, it's all I can think about, but the expense is too great, especially since Ryder must have it to stop the nightmares. If only I could eliminate the middleman and have access to Summoner of Sleep whenever I desired. Then I would be happy. But the task at hand is much more difficult than expected. Marble Woods can't be found anywhere. All my connections haven't the slightest idea where this phantom town may even exist.

I've received one report that the town became a settled community by a vagrant or pirate of some sort, but I've never been able to verify this account. Another report said that Marble Woods was founded by a fanatical preacher who had created his own religion. He called it The Order of the Signature Saint Hood or something to that effect, but then all the people who followed it vanished. It could all be hogwash, but I'm intrigued about this strange and ancient place—that is, if it does indeed exist anymore or ever did, for that matter.

But one thing is clear to me now—selling my house isn't important to me anymore. What I've discovered in my naïve attempts to help Ryder is far too powerful and intriguing to shut the door on. I do not trust him, but I must rely on him. I am close. I can feel it.

~Claude Wick

The final entries were dated the previous day and seemed written by a different hand and person altogether:

August 31, 10:30 p.m.

I dare not sleep for fear of missing anything. I must remain awake always. The night is when the clues and answers like to find me like little mosquitos thirsting for my blood. Sweet blood.

~Claude Wick

His pulse ramped up. Ryder steadied the page to read his neighbor's final entry, the floor beneath him swelled and groaned as he read the unbelievable words his neighbor had written:

August 31, 11:47 p.m.

I tell you; I'll leave it all behind willingly. I will do it because I can. I'll leave all the black alleys of mortality and dank gloom of the cosmic doorways behind, the shallow pearls of filth, the starless metropolises of madness, and their septic arms. I'll leave behind the infinite cesspool of society to chase the imaginings I dream about. I can go, but he mustn't visit that place which leads to the origin of his nightmares. It will destroy us all if he does. But for me, I think I'll leave it all behind and go there. I think I'll go there and never look back. That would be quite nice.

~Claude Wick

Ryder dropped the notebook with a gasp.

He fixed his eyes on the hearth in front of him where gray embers smoldered in the ash. Whatever his neighbor had intended to destroy hadn't burned.

Ryder perked and snapped up the smoldering pages with his bare hands and blew out the remaining hot spots.

Despite the tremors of pain through his limbs and extreme fatigue, a smile lengthened across his cheeks at the realization that he now possessed a map to Marble Woods.

—

The enormous mass pulsed in his thigh, so swollen that the entire skin covered in black veins was ready to burst. The veins raised, spread, and pounded. Whatever pushed under his skin grew larger by the second. It ached and throbbed through every unbearable inch of dermis. Ryder's pants ripped open like confetti as he screamed in agony.

The mass grew bigger.

He tried to stand but fell.

"This is a dream. You're in a dream." He slithered across the floor and knocked over Claude's journals and furniture as something danced and tore its way through the tendons and muscles.

Ryder tobogganed on a quilt down the stairs and crawled into the kitchen. His pulse thundered in his ears as he grabbed one of the knives and gritted his teeth.

The first cut of flesh was the hardest. The warm sensation of blood ran down his legs, which made him think of urine. His jaw tightened.

Ryder peeled back the folds of skin to reveal a clock stuck inside. Its gears and splinters twisted deep.

Fire raced up his leg and Ryder screamed.

"Get outta—"

He threw down the knife and pulled the clock with his bare hands, but the exposed gears turned, mashed, and mutilated his delicate skin like meat sliding through a grinder. The clock hands spun out of control and caught a large chunk of groin skin. The sound of ripping echoed through the room. His voice strained from the screams. Through the blood and goo, he read the words Summoner of Sleep carved upon its wooden face.

Ryder stuck his long, thin fingers inside the folds of his leg and pulled hard. He reached so far down he passed out from the pain, and when we woke, he yanked again at the stubborn clock.

This is a dream. This is a dream.

The clock tore through his skin. His teeth chattered nonstop when it was halfway out of him. A chill passed down his skin and he pried the clock free from his body with a tremendous jerk, then bashed it against the wall.

Chapter 6

Claude

Despite having committed the map to Marble Woods to memory and destroying it so no one else would have access to Summoner of Sleep, Claude still encountered a devastating number of obstacles. In the three days he had left home there had been a dark tangle of woods, mud, steep mountains, hostile people, and night creatures that blurred together in a timeless warp.

By day four he learned to bear the disappointment when the people he asked claimed to have never heard of Marble Woods or Summoner of Sleep. One pale-faced man threw a rock at him and called him a *Fripterit*—whatever that meant. The angriest person was a dirty straw-haired woman who held up her rusty shotgun and threatened to "shoot that blasted face off," if he breathed another word about Marble Woods. Such annoyance from these people was surely a sign he was on the right track though.

Claude continued to travel north toward the Sierra

Mountains. He wandered from town to town like a vagrant. He loved the smell of fungi, rot, and pine, and slept on the ground each night, the stars pulsing in their blue glory as the cool wind tickled his cheeks. The earth cradled his spine like a hammock, and he was able to fall asleep pain-free within seconds like he could do when he was a child.

He lost track of time after day seven but knew he was on the right track when the terrain became more mountainous and the types of birds changed. The California Quail were his favorite with the stripe forming a question mark that flopped as it pecked about in search of food.

That night he made his camp on a pile of leaves and lowered to the ground to view the thick canopy of trees above. An owl hooted and flew from the branch as a light breeze sailed across his body.

"I missed nature so much." Claude sighed and stretched his arms and legs like a snow angel. "Ahhh." He eased deeper into the earth.

He went to take another stretch accompanied by a yawn and discovered a white chalky substance on his clothes.

He rolled onto his side and stood. He had been lying on some sort of pattern made of white powder, much of which now covered his backside. Its shapes were difficult to ascertain due to the disturbance from his body, but he was able to make out the shape of a figure and a strange arrow-like symbol.

"How wonderful," Claude squealed at the odd discovery.

Something crackled in the woods. When he looked up, a glittery kingdom of rainbows and coiled auroras whirled above him. He smiled, intrigued by this mysterious place where he had chosen to rest.

An iciness drifted from across the black treetops. Claude's mind relaxed as he realized that his eyes were closed, and he was physically unable to open them.

From out of nothing came a burst of inaudible foreign words, which echoed through the woods.

The tingle in his bones didn't lie. He wasn't alone.

"Brother?"

The words *you aren't dreaming* floated into his mind, then the words repeated and echoed far and distant, and the warm sensation of blood cascaded out his ear and down his cheek. It tickled his ear, but paralysis prevented him from scratching it.

The sound became Vern's voice.

He turned and opened his eyes, then gasped at his brother's profile on the other side of the thinned clearing.

Vern stood naked and covered in a slippery, gelatinous sheen. His face was noble, handsome, and no longer bore the marks of age. Vern's glasses were noticeably absent too. His brother's lean muscles and tendons pulsed as if no skin contained them, and something about the sight disturbed him as much as his brother's features intrigued him.

"Let's go, dear brother. I've been waiting for you," Vern said.

"W-what happened to you? How did you f-find me? Are you okay?"

"I've never been better, and I knew you'd come to find me." He stepped closer to Claude and into the rays of moonlight.

Claude gulped.

Vern's lips crooked. "It's okay." He gestured to his shiny skin, and at that moment the light caught him in an utterly different perspective—one that was wild and tormented. "Go on. Touch it."

Claude's hand inched closer to his brother's strange skin. He expected it to be cold and sticky, but instead, it was like warm velvet. His heartbeat echoed through the woods. On both sides of the clearing, trees leaned over them as if they watched in contemplation. A cool breeze passed over him. He shivered for a moment and blinked several times as if he were waking from a dream. "What are you? Is that really y-you?"

"I'm who I was meant to become," Vern said with a smile. "And you're on your way there too."

"I am?"

"Yes." A brown vial appeared in Vern's hand. He held it out. "I can see that your body is already reversing. That's the first step. Just imagine what will happen if you drink Summoner of Sleep and don't just inhale it."

Claude's mind flashed to the bottle he broke in front of Ryder's house. He remembered that unique, gingery scent. "How did you know about that?"

"Doesn't matter. You must drink it. Now."

"Drink it? But I don't—"

"Amazing things are in store for you and this is just the beginning." Vern pressed the vial to his brother's lips. "Trust me, brother."

Confused and overwhelmed, Claude stood silent in his tattered clothes and opened his mouth a moment later, and swallowed the contents. The liquid tingled in Claude's throat and he let out a phlegmy cough.

The world grew bigger. The forest was a point of wonder on which all things converged. Claude's eyelids fluttered, his gaze wandered to the stars and drifted into infinite, dreamy joy.

"Oh, my God."

"How do you feel?"

"I feel so...happy...clear."

"You see?" Vern said.

Claude nodded with a grin.

"Now let's go. There's so much more to discover in Marble Woods."

"Marble Woods? You know how to get there?"

"Yes. It's right up there. Our new home. Won't you come with me?"

"I want to. This is all happening so fast. I just can't believe—"

"Believe it. All your dreams will come true if you join me." Vern extended a hand.

Claude took Vern's velvety, shiny hand and rejoiced in the reunion with his older brother. This was all he ever wanted—a brother who loved him and wanted to be with him. Together they disappeared into the trees and feathery mist as their laughter sailed across the wind and through the entrance of the mysterious and sleepy town of Marble Woods.

Chapter 7

Ryder

The clock had ripped through Ryder's thigh over a week ago, but the wound hadn't closed and bled when he walked. Even as he drove, he tried to distract himself from the pain with the picturesque rolling hills speckled with cows, but his leg ached and pulsated so hard he couldn't breathe.

He cracked his neck side to side and ignored his eye twitch.

When was the last time I stopped? Was it six or seven hours ago? When was the last town?

Ryder's mind wandered to the worrisome discoveries he had found inside Claude's home. The room of clocks. The telescopes. Endless notebooks. It seemed like a century had passed since he broke in and discovered the truth, but one journal entry stuck with him. "He mustn't visit that place which leads to the origin of his nightmares," Ryder said. "Origin? What the hell were you trying to say, Claude?"

He cracked his neck again and sighed. He'd give anything to see his masseuse again.

A sign announced the town of Garden Grove–A Town for Leisure and Love.

"Thank God." He shifted his hip to take the pressure off his full bladder.

He exited to the small town, which consisted of nothing more than a run-down restaurant, a few old trailers, and a pile of tires. Craphole was an understatement. He pulled into the gravel lot and glanced to the left. Something rustled in the trees and slinked into the bushes. He swallowed and rubbed his eye with his knuckle. The rustling stopped.

"You need to get out of this damn car, Ryder," he muttered and exited the car.

The restaurant smelled like cleaner. Perhaps bleach. He wanted to smell the sweet scents of pie in the display case though. After he relieved himself, he settled in the back booth and stared at the outside world. Ryder slouched at the table; his sharp chin drooped to his chest. The menu lay across from him. He didn't want to touch the greasy thing. Julie would've never eaten in a place that had pictures of the food on the menu like this. He glanced at the clock above the door and exhaled. *Dammit.* He'd have to sit and listen to the ticking as he ate. Didn't people know that they didn't need a million clocks everywhere always announcing the time?

"What'll you have?" the horse-faced waiter asked.

"Beer."

"What kind?"

"Don't care."

The waiter grabbed the menu and said, "We make the best roast beef sandwiches in the state, and you look like you could use a good meal. I'll bring you one. I insist."

Ryder shrugged. "Sure."

As he sat in his booth, he was conscious the whole time of something outside. He eyeballed the spot in the bushes every few seconds. Something was there. He felt it.

When the waiter set his food down, Ryder devoured it. It

was the best roast beef he ever had, and he used all the free French bread to sop up the juice. He wished he had ordered two sandwiches.

The waiter came back with a huge grin. "Told ya you'd like it."

"You weren't kidding. Thanks for making me eat something. I really needed it."

He winked. "Anything else I can get ya, or do you wanna close out?"

"I'll go ahead and close out, but I was also hoping you could tell me how to get to Marble Woods."

The waiter's grin vanished. "Don't know."

Figured.

The waiter disappeared into the kitchen as Ryder grumbled and readied to leave.

A few moments later, the waiter plopped his check on the table and walked away. He'd only been charged for the beer, but he didn't know whether or not the waiter was being nice or had calculated incorrectly. Didn't matter. Ryder grabbed and check in one hand and reached for his wallet with the other when he noticed something was written on the back of his check. He flipped it over and read:

Keep going north toward Juniper City. Don't go there if you can help it.

Too excited to rest, Ryder left an exorbitant tip, hurried to his car, and locked the door behind him.

He followed signs to Juniper City, all the while, his gaze glued to the rearview mirror to see if he had been followed.

He stared at a questionable white van behind him, but his car began to cough. He lessened pressure from the pedal, then the gas light dinged.

"Are you fucking serious? There's nothing out here."

He drove past another little town if you could call old, dark, and abandoned buildings a town.

"Shit. Shit. Shit."

Where did the van go?

He later passed a sign for a gas station a mile ahead. Ryder exhaled and drove, then pulled off at the station a few minutes later. He killed the engine and sat there a moment in front of the deserted mechanic's garage.

Ryder took a shallow breath and looked over his shoulder. When he was positive he hadn't been followed, he left the confines of his car and fiddled with the filling station's dim buttons.

Come on, work.

The stupid thing didn't take his credit card the first two swipes, then it took a few moments of nervous playing around with the machine until gas rushed through the hose, and as it did, he locked the handle and went to have a quick look under the hood. He peered into the engine and regretted his lack of mechanical knowledge. He wiggled the oil dipstick loose and squinted at it in the moonlight.

Orange couldn't be good, could it?

Something crackled behind him.

Ryder jumped and swung around so fast that oil splattered his pants.

"Sorry to startle you," a man in a greasy jumpsuit said as he stared at Ryder's oil-stained crotch.

"I thought you were closed. I didn't see a light inside."

"Someone's always here," the man threw him a stained rag that hung from his belt. "So, what's the problem?"

"I think there's something wrong with my oil."

Without another word, the man snatched the dipstick, hunched over the car, and began working. He yanked on some hoses, examined the fluids, and sniffed the engine.

"Thank you for your help at an hour like this. I appreciate it."

"Notta problem."

"How long have you lived out here?"

"Whole life."

"Like it?"

The man shrugged. "It's fine I guess, if you don't like to do much."

"Have you ever heard of Marble Woods? Someone told me it's close by."

The mechanic grumbled and spat a wad of tobacco juice, which almost hit Ryder's shoe.

"Do you know how I can get there? To Marble Woods?"

The man's muscles tensed. "I heard you the first time."

"Oh."

"Anyone who wants to go to Marble Woods must be stupid or will soon be. Only evil lives there." The mechanic stopped what he was doing, turned on his heel, and lumbered toward the garage.

"Hey. Where are you going? What am I supposed to do about my car?" He kicked the dirt and faced the engine. A headache was coming on.

Footsteps crunched behind him. He spun around. "Why did you—?" A huge man clad in a mechanic's jumpsuit and faded bandana around his neck stood in front of him. "Oh, sorry, I thought you were the other guy."

"No. Sorry about that, sir. I hope my cousin wasn't too much trouble," he said. "Doesn't interact with people too much. He gets overwhelmed easily, but I was on the phone before." The mechanic grasped the top of the hood and leaned closer to the engine.

From the frightened look of the first mechanic's watchful eyes through the dusty window, Ryder's heart softened. "That's okay. He was helping me with my oil and then I asked him a question about something unrelated. I apologize if I scared him."

"Oh? Maybe I can help you, sir. Need directions or a recommendation of a place to eat?"

"No. I wanted to know how to get to Marble Woods."

"Ah, what's why," the man said with a sudden change in

expression.

"I didn't realize that talking about the town was such a touchy subject."

"It is and it isn't. It's because that strange plant was created there."

Ryder shot to life. "Yes. What else do you know?"

The mechanic now toyed around with something that looked like a big black snake. "I know everyone went mad when that funny plant leeched into the soil and tainted the water supply. Last I heard, there are a few people left. No one is right in the head there if you know what I mean. What business would you have in a place like that?"

"Well, I'm a...botanist. I'm writing a book about exotic plants. Summoner of Sleep, right?"

"You don't look like no botanist. Especially in a suit like that."

Ryder took out a wad of cash and smiled. "Yeah, I get that a lot. I like to look nice for the job, you know. Helps to be taken seriously."

The man chuckled and grabbed the cash. "Yes. Summoner of Sleep. I think that may be the only reason anyone would ever want to go up there."

"Up where?"

"Oh, you want to just climb the steep road here all the way to the top of Bald Mountain. There ain't no signs for it, but it's exactly sixty miles from here. No more. No less."

"That's great info. Thank you."

The mechanic slammed the hood shut and faced him. "She definitely needs some work. Can you leave 'er overnight so I can have a proper look in the light of day? I got a cot out back for drunkards if you need it for the night."

"No. I'm sorry. I'm on a very tight deadline and have to get there tonight."

The man wiped his greasy hands on an old towel that hung from his pocket but didn't break his gaze with Ryder. "I see."

"Can it make it to the top of the mountain at least?"

"Oh, I think so. I just wouldn't push 'er. Don't ride the gas. You should come on back as soon as you can to have 'er worked on though."

"I will. Thank you. You've been immensely helpful."

Ryder shook the man's hand and got in the car.

Just as he put the car in reverse, the mechanic tapped on his window.

Ryder jumped so high that he hit his head on the car ceiling.

With reluctance, Ryder rolled down the window. "Yes?"

"I really must tell ya something before you go on up that way. There's a story that there's a whole legion of demons who live up there in them woods—walking about and darting in and out of the trees. It's a desolate, cold place, and most people drive outta their way not to pass through Marble Woods. I wouldn't go there if I were you."

"Thank you for the warning, but it's imperative that I go there for my research," Ryder said.

The mechanic's stern expression didn't budge.

"Listen, why I have you here, I'd love to know why it's called Marble Woods...for my research."

The mechanic lowered his surly gaze.

"Their skin resembles marble."

"Whose skin?"

"That demon skin is dark and smooth with branching white veins. I saw 'em once when I was a kid. Never was the same."

Ryder swallowed hard as a line of goosebumps ran up his spine. "Well, um, I'm sorry to hear that."

"Don't say nobody warned you about going there. I offered you my cot and a warning and that's all I can do I suppose." The mechanic sighed and walked away from the car in silence.

Ryder pondered the warning. Something about the mechanic's story seemed so provocative and peculiar that he couldn't put it out of his mind as he rolled up the window and zoomed along the road following the mechanic's directions.

He grew nervous as he neared sixty miles on the odometer and there was no indication of an approaching town. He consulted the remnants of Claude's burned map a few times. The rough drawing didn't supply much detail and the scaling was off, so it wasn't much help.

He drove on a few more miles. The mountains turned barren. He traveled sixty-three miles, stopped, and turned back. Ryder counted and subtracted miles, looked for a road, sign, tire tracks, anything.

He turned around some ten or eleven times between the fifty-five- and sixty-five-mile markers.

Nothing.

His eyes were so tired he saw spots, so he pulled the car to the roadside and into a ditch at the sixty-mile marker.

"That guy is insane. There's nothing out here but trees."

Ryder got out of his car and stretched his legs. The cliff overlooked the town he had just come from. The streets below glittered like yellow jewels at the base of the mountain.

"Great. Just great. Should've never listened to that idiot. This was probably all a trick and now they're gonna come and rob and murder me out here."

He walked deeper into the thicket on the other side of the road. Branches clawed at him, and between the massive tangle of weeds sat aged metal parts from some car that had broken down long ago. Was his next? The air grew more leaden as he continued, and in the distance, a rotted wooden gate with a faded *No Trespassing* sign swayed in the wind. Behind the gate, far in the distance, an overgrown path wound around and disappeared into a thick forest that hadn't been visible from the road.

Oily goo coated the pale gray trees so that the leaves made a peculiar sound when the wind blew, similar to a rusty playground swing.

Being alone in nature was the only time Ryder ever felt safe, and on occasion, when he was young, he was inspired to write poetry about the beauty of it.

Ryder had started off writing poetry by scribbling his artful words in the dirt with a stick. His mother and stepfather were frugal and refused to provide him with anything that wasn't required by the school, arguing that "journals and notebooks were for homework and nothing more." He was resourceful and became more creative in his quest to obtain paper for his poetry, so he started saving discarded junk mail.

Ryder went to painstaking lengths to hide his poems. He shoved them into the tips of his shoes and sometimes down his pants until he could get home and secure them properly in his lockbox. Once he found a book of poetry in his mailbox with the works of Edgar Allan Poe, Virginia Woolf, Sylvia Plath, and other great poets. Ever since then he fantasized about becoming a published poet and imagined that he would use the pen name, Ashling Poe.

But that all changed when his stepfather found his poems. He read them aloud to his poker buddies, all of them laughed at Ryder's secret passion and called him terrible names that indicated his lack of masculinity. He ran from the laughter, shut and bolted his bedroom door, and cried. He never wrote poetry again.

The shiny trees and the cloudy sky made a beautiful contrast, and he fought the urge to write a poem. Although he was a grown man, his stepfather's sinister laughs still plagued him even though they hadn't spoken in well over a decade.

"It would be better to take a photograph instead," he said. "Maybe Julie left her Polaroid in the car."

Ryder marched back to the car and was delighted to find the camera nestled between old, crinkled maps and the car manual in the glove compartment.

"Yes," he cried.

The light dimmed in those few moments he took to fetch the camera, but the sky was more brilliant than ever with eggplant purples and yolk-colored meringue clouds.

He walked a few feet back to the path barred by the gate. A sudden chorus of laughter erupted in the distance.

Not having seen another soul, Ryder paused, scanned his surroundings, and listened.

Was this another dream?

He took a step to investigate, but the laughter stopped.

Ryder could not escape the sensation of wide, lidless demon eyes. The longer he stood in the woods alone, the more the story that the mechanic told him about the demons got to him, but he refused to let an old folktale scare him.

"I'm a grown man. I don't believe in demons or ghosts. Come on and take the damn picture."

Ryder pointed the Polaroid and pressed the button. He delighted in the distraction of the click the camera made followed by the pop of the photograph through the slot. He stepped around the dirt and gravel, waved the photograph between his fingertips, and smiled.

The last remnants of the orange sun popped through an alabaster cloud and shone on the winding path. He took a second shot and slid the first photograph into his pocket. He retrieved the second photograph from the camera and waved it.

"That's weird. Why is this one black and white? Maybe it's old film."

Snap.

Ryder whipped around.

"Hello? Who's there?"

There was nothing. No one.

He would take one more picture then get back in the car. He wasn't afraid, dammit. Ryder repositioned the camera to his eye and attempted to focus.

Fingers closed around his ankle. He screamed. The camera dropped and rolled to the side as he jumped. He went to grab the camera and realized a vine had gotten tangled around his ankle.

"Jesus, Ryder." He kicked off the vine. "You've gotta stop being such an idiot."

Ryder positioned the camera and took a final picture.

He studied the photograph as it developed. He loved how he had captured the charming path. Julie would've loved the photo and framed it for the mantel. But there was something gray and square-shaped in the middle of the path which disrupted the fluidity.

He squinted.

Had a speck of dust or something landed on the lens or the photograph?

He scratched at the photo, which formed into a clearer picture of a signpost.

His eyes strained harder. The sign read:

Welcome to Marble Woods

There was no such sign as in the photograph.

"Come on, this is crazy."

A church clock struck the hour, like a warden reminding his prisoner who was boss, and he was seized by one of those panic attacks where you feel transported out of your body and that you're dying at the same time.

He did one of his breathing exercises and willed himself to stare at the photograph. He asked himself in all seriousness if he was hallucinating. Nothing was there. Right?

He hopped the dilapidated gate. Again, he looked at the photo as he stood in the exact spot of the phantom signpost.

He waved his arms and tried to feel for the sign he couldn't see but knew was there. Ryder was so close to Marble Woods he could taste it. His heart overflowed as the damp air penetrated his face and lungs. He bent forward, touched the air, and blinked for a moment. What trickery was afoot?

Laughter erupted again. There was no doubt about it this time.

Chapter 8

Claude

A piece of half-eaten apple pie sat forgotten on a patio table; the fork covered in sticky cinnamon and buttery crust. A book lay open on a blanket in the field. Its pages turned as if a ghost read each passage. The wind rocked a bright red ball next to a tree. The black cottage doors were ridden in soot, broken windows covered in graffiti, and crumbled roofs that stank of decay depressed him. The worst part was the weed-choked gardens littered with mounds of garbage and liquor bottles. Perhaps the most miserable thing about Marble Woods though was the grim cherub statue at the park entrance. Its smile had faded away long ago, and its broken wing forever stranded it here. It was happy once. Everyone in Marble Woods was happy once too.

Claude pondered how there were signs of life at every glance but no one in sight. When he passed a shop window, he caught a glimpse of himself in the reflection and cried out.

"Is that me?"

"Pretty incredible, isn't it?" Vern said with a smile.

"I'll say." He touched his youthful face.

Where had the wisdom of his wrinkles gone? Or that scar above his eye from the war? Not even the pock marks from childhood chickenpox remained.

"Come on, brother. I want to show you something." Vern continued to lead Claude through town and stopped near a patch of trees.

The townspeople appeared all covered in a slimy substance. They moved with disturbing speed, picked up dark-colored shrubs and flowers, and placed them in baskets. They were so preoccupied that they didn't seem to notice them across the street.

"What are they doing?"

"Looking for ingredients to make Summoner of Sleep," Vern said.

"How do they know how to make it?"

"I'll explain that in time."

A short, red-haired man with a small pink mouth stopped what he was doing. He squinted his large, heavy-lidded eyes and raised his bulbous nose. Claude smiled and waved, but the man remained expressionless. The man blinked, a flash of a translucent brille over his wide, frozen eyes.

"What was that?" Claude clutched his brother's arm.

"Relax."

"What's happening here?"

A smile wiggled across Vern's face. "Don't worry. We're almost home. I've made one for us to share right up the road. Just a little bit farther and once we get there, I can get you more Summoner of Sleep and explain everything."

Claude swallowed. "At least tell me why you've changed and what's happening to me."

"Well," Vern said and scratched his head. "I guess the easiest way to explain it is that we've improved our genetic structure."

"But that man's eyes...they weren't natural. That man isn't

human."

"Do you think you're a human?"

"What? Of course, I do."

Vern cocked his head. "Some would argue differently upon seeing your skin and your transformation, wouldn't they?"

Claude gazed upon his dewy, shimmery hands. Not even the oil burn remained from the time he had made his wife an anniversary dinner when she was first diagnosed. "I don't think I like this, Vern. I sorta miss how I looked before. They say one possesses more character as they age." He rubbed the invisible scar on his hand and wished it back. It was one of the only things that remained of his wife's memory and now it was gone.

"But aren't you happy you don't have to wear those glasses anymore? That your limp is gone? That you don't have to take your heart medication? You're in better health now, which means you've improved your quality of life. Be grateful for these blessings."

"I am."

"Well, you don't seem like it. I thought that you wanted to be here with me, brother, but I guess I was wrong."

"I do."

"You're lying. Look at you. You're a grown man too afraid to continue, and just when the going gets good."

"I'm not afraid. I've been to war for crying out loud. I just don't believe that those people are human. I mean, look at how they move. It's like they're phantoms or something."

"There's nothing wrong with them. I'll prove it." Vern pointed to a white-haired skinny woman. "See there, that's Vera Belle, she runs the general store. Also makes the best apple pie you've ever tasted."

He pointed to a fair-haired man in a brown jacket. "Over there is Charles Piper, our town's carpenter, and handyman. Last week he fixed a plumbing leak for me."

Vern gestured to a small and beautiful woman with radiant hair that hung in long gold strands over her bare arms. Her dress, which clung to her like a ballerina's leotard, showed off her pink legs, and her blue eyes were as big as a cat's. She gave off a radiant light, which softened the world around her as she carried a bag of groceries. She was like a bright star among ugly black meteors in the galaxy. "And that is Mary Moon," he said with a heavy, sensuous breath. "She's the town's seamstress and innkeeper."

Claude stared at her. Her delicate veil of gold hair swayed as she maneuvered across the cobblestone street and disappeared into a ramshackle cottage. He turned his attention back to the man with weird eyes.

"And who's that?"

"That's Doctor Achilles."

"Achilles?" Claude gasped. "I think he was the one who supplied me with Summoner of Sleep."

"Wouldn't surprise me. There's not a whole lot of business in Marble Woods given the dwindling population. That's probably why he's watching you right now. He recognizes you. He wants to see how you've changed as a result of taking the tonic."

Claude scanned the townspeople once again. "Is my friend Belinda here?"

"Who?"

"My friend, who was helping me conduct research?"

"Why would you think she'd be in Marble Woods?"

"You and I were both exposed to Summoner of Sleep and found our way here. I found her laboratory covered in blood just like your apothecary shop. I thought she'd find her way here too. Isn't that how it works?"

Vern grasped his brother's shoulder. "I'm afraid not. Not everyone possesses the sight."

"The sight?"

"Yes, one must have an innate aptitude to navigate the world to find this place. Not everyone makes it, unfortunately."

"So, Belinda is lost somewhere between here and home?"

"Maybe. I'm sorry, but it would be impossible to locate her

at this stage, and besides, not everyone can survive such blood loss if they don't receive the appropriate amount of Summoner of Sleep as they begin to change. I got to you just in time."

"But Belinda wasn't exposed to any," Claude said.

"Then I'm sorry to say that the outcome is much worse," Vern said. "If she wasn't exposed to the actual herb but only the knowledge of it, there's no helping her."

Claude tried to lose himself in people watching to avoid his heartache. His weepy gaze swept the townspeople once again, their peculiarities, their strange and rapid movements, the unusual oily trees. That's when he caught sight of a wisp of high-piled coppery hair.

"Who's that?"

The figure darted behind a tree.

"Is that Belinda?"

"Who?"

A few people gathered in front of the tree, which obscured his view.

Claude pointed. "I s-saw Belinda behind that tree."

"Oh, dear brother, you're just tired, that's all." Vern tightened his grip on his brother's shoulder.

"No. I swear I saw her right there." His voice cracked. "No one has that hair color. No one." His mania drew more attention from the crowd, which caused him even greater unease—the people positioned themselves in front of the tree that he swore concealed Belinda as if intentionally hiding her. The thick and heavy air burned Claude's lungs.

Vern turned his brother away from the sight. "Don't you think I would've told you if your friend was here?"

"I do, but—"

As he started to crane his neck toward the tree, Vern placed a hand on Claude's cheek and eased his gaze back. "Look at me, brother."

"I don't know, Vern, I just think something is wrong about all this."

"You need to rest, Claude. When's the last time you slept?"

"Couple of days."

"We need to walk a little bit farther to get home." Vern directed Claude's gaze toward the house atop a jutting point of earth. Behind it there were acres of trees and plants—vines, bushes, and creepers curled around the gray trees.

Claude stared at the cottage with the decayed bricks, blackened shingles, and rotted planks. No one had taken care of the place for some time, and he still didn't know why his brother wanted to take him to the decrepit structure. He shook, not wanting to leave if who he had seen was indeed Belinda. The awful, fetid red flowers and roots hung in bunches from the trees above; their scent nauseated him so much so that he plugged his nose.

Vern's face turned darker as he stood tall above his brother. "Do you remember when we were young, and we would dare each other to walk through the dark sewer tunnels alone?"

Claude nodded.

"Remember that the one who could go the longest without turning back got to pick the candy of his choice from the stash in the attic that Mom didn't know about?"

He nodded again.

"Good. Then I dare you to continue. Your reward is an infinite supply of Summoner of Sleep."

Claude glanced at the world behind him and returned his gaze to Vern.

"I would never let anything bad happen to you, brother." Vern's voice was heavy with importance. "I wouldn't lie to you about your friend, and I promise you that what happens here will give you a new lease on life. A meaningful life—full of wonder, contentment, and serenity. Don't you want that? Don't you want to enjoy that with me?"

"Well, yes. I—I do."

"Then what's the problem?"

"Vern." Claude swallowed and looked at the ground. "Do

you think I'm a coward?"

"I think you're too afraid to enjoy life and this is the perfect example of it. You're afraid of what's the come."

"I've just been through so much. I feel like I keep making stupid mistakes. I don't want to make another one."

"I know, which is all the more reason to listen to your older, wiser brother."

"Everyone shuts me out. I don't want to be alone anymore, Vern." Claude reflected on all his frozen dinners consumed in front of the television set, all the times he'd go to the park and watch families together, and all the times he cried alone in the shower. He wanted kids when he was younger, but his wife was infertile, so he didn't pursue the issue. He was too old to be a father when she died, and he was never able to meet somebody new. Now he had no one to take care of him or keep him company.

"You can do it, I'm sure you can."

Vern had so much confidence in him that it shook Claude. "I'm s-so lonely. So lonely," Claude wept. Sometimes he had been so lonely he thought he might wither into ash and float away on the next cool breeze. Sometimes he felt that nobody would notice if he died. His brother's comfort was new and assuring, and the strange sensation made him sweat. Little droplets trickled down his sides into his fat rolls.

"I know we haven't always been close though we lived in the same town. I want that to change."

Tears poured down Claude's cheeks. "Really?" His face grew hot.

"We're together now and you don't have to worry about being alone ever again." Vern extended his arms and swaddled Claude. "I won't let that happen. Let me be here for you."

"Do you mean it?" Claude sobbed like a blubbering child.

"What are big brothers for?"

Claude lost all control, and for the first time in his life allowed himself to let go as he took refuge in his brother's welcoming arms.

Chapter 9

Ryder

Ryder's stomach grumbled as he stared at the derelict, Puritan town. That roast beef sandwich hadn't held him over and he'd give anything for another home-cooked meal. He walked towards Main Street, faced the cluster of lopsided houses, and wondered about the human beings lying asleep behind these closed shutters. To the right was a little jail behind a cluster of trees; and on the left, all along the cobblestone street were overgrown hedges. A few streetlamps shone in two straight lines that stretched into the depths of the neighboring woods. Further away, an orange luminous haze floated over the rooftops; all noise melted into a single melodic buzz. He took another step and yawned. He hated when he had to choose between sleep and food. At the end of the street swung a weathered sign that read: *Belle's General Store.*

He headed there first but then sighed at the closed sign. He cupped his hands around his eyes and peered through the dusty, aged window. Inside were shelves of canned food, an enormous cash register, and some wooden tables with chairs. A terrible stench of damp wood drifted through the cracks in the windows and the nearby trees groaned. The smell made him think of the old clocks from his dreams and his body twisted away.

"Dammit."

He wandered back to the path where he entered the mysterious town, amazed that no one seemed to live in this community.

Julie would've had a big laugh if she could see where Ryder ended up; the man she married never would have been caught dead in a derelict place like Marble Woods. From a clean and posh man in designer clothes, Ryder had changed into a man careless in appearance who wore the same crumpled and stained suit for days on end. He undid his tie and let it hang free.

Someone had carved S.O.S. into the thick trunk of a giant gray tree that grew against a cottage with the name Moon painted on the mailbox. Did the carving mean help was needed, or did it stand for Summoner of Sleep? Either scenario unnerved him.

The wind whipped through the trees, a rhythmless burst of air thrashed at his face and neck.

Crack.

He stiffened.

Two unblinking eyes peered from the bushes.

Devils?

The brush wiggled as he walked toward it. He imagined a red devil with pointy horns crouched beneath it, and hungry, black eyes behind the gnarled branches. Ryder poked the bush with a stick.

Not a sound.

He took a step closer and pushed some of the branches out of the way, holding his breath as he waited for the devil to grab him. But there was no devil. Only branches.

"What are you doing?" a sweet voice said.

Ryder spun around to find a shadow had appeared in the threshold of a nearby cottage. A gorgeous, petite woman with long blonde hair stepped into the light. Heavy necklaces adorned her neck, and the oil lamp she held projected long, ethereal shadows behind her. There was something special about her, like a brilliant radiance from within.

"Oh, hello there," he said. "I just thought I heard something in the bushes."

"Are you in need of a room for the night?"

Surprised that such an opportunity found him in his hour of need, Ryder smiled. Perhaps he had misjudged Marble Woods.

He glanced again at the still bushes and returned his attention to the woman. "Yes, I am, actually."

She stepped a little farther out of the doorway, which revealed a white nightgown trimmed with crimson embroidery and red stockings underneath. She was simple and hid nothing—not even the bareness of her naked skin.

"Then you may stay here. I promise it's much prettier inside," she said. "There's a spare room with a private bathroom in the back that's available."

"I'll take it, but I must tell you that I don't have much money left."

"Oh, that'll be fine. Now come in from the cold night air." She motioned him with her free hand.

The moment Ryder crossed the threshold, the woman came up to him and extended her hand with a firmness that surprised him. "I'm Mary. Mary Moon. Welcome to my home."

"Thank you. I'm Ryder." He eyed the foyer. Dolls and their houses ruled the table behind her. Strange yellow dolls with giant green eyes. Short, stubby ones in antique wedding dresses. Sleeping ones with a quivering eye. Victorian ones with long, curled hair. Each one stood or sat in front of their prospective house all decorated like a frosted pink and white cake. Amongst the cadre of this little doll world, Ryder's heart leaped at the picture of the golden horse oddly positioned in the middle of the table.

"Akhal-Teke," he said.

"Akhal-Teke to you," Mary replied with a cocked head.

He smiled. "No, it's the breed of horse in the picture behind you."

She glanced at it for a second, then smiled—a dimple puckered her flushed cheeks, which gave her a look of supreme innocence.

"It's one of the rarest and beautiful horses in the world."

"Oh?"

"Yes, I used to have one. Had an entire stable of them in the country before they re—" He cleared his throat. "I mean, they're just...stunning creatures. Absolutely stunning."

"Really?" she asked as she studied the picture. "I don't know anything about horses. To be honest, I sorta thought all horses were the same."

"Why do you have that picture, then?"

"I inherited it from my grandfather and liked the color of its pretty coat, so I kept it."

"You'd be surprised how many breeds of horse there are, but the Akhal-Teke holds a special place in my heart. My favorite horse's name is...I mean was *Alfrodul*. It means sun from *The Prose Edda*—one of my favorite books."

"Did you say Alfrodul?"

"Yes." He waited for the inevitable label of being called strange like so many people had called him, but instead, she smiled and gestured to the gilded cage in the corner which held a golden canary.

"My bird's name is Alfrodul. I named him for the sun as well. I wanted something unique."

His smile lengthened. "Well isn't that quite a coincidence."

"I'll say. I've never met anyone who has used that name or knows its meaning...or even what *The Prose Edda* is, for that matter."

"Maybe we were meant to meet, then," he chuckled.

"Maybe so. How are you enjoying your visit so far?"

"Well, it's like no place I've ever visited before."

"Is that good or bad?"

"It's very—" He paused to think of the right word. "Piquant."

She gave a slight nod. "Not many people come here, you know. I haven't had a guest in quite some time, which is why I run a few other businesses on the side. Did you travel here on foot?" She walked over to the window and looked through the crack in the lacy drapes that overlooked the street.

"I had a car." His thigh throbbed. It was time to change the bandage soon, but he had left them in the trunk.

"So, arrived on foot, then. My goodness. That must've been quite a trek. There aren't any neighboring towns, and that terrain is so rough. What happened to your car? Did it break down?"

He scratched his head. "Well, a mechanic gave me bizarre directions. I was driving along and saw this beautiful view and wanted to take a picture, then I stopped and saw a sign for Marble Woods, but it wasn't really there, but then again it was like a phantom sign. Then I started walking and ended up here." He studied her worried face. "So, I guess my car is somewhere on that road leading here. It's sort of a weird story and I'm afraid you think I'm crazy now for telling it."

A grin grew across her rosy face. "My family's story of ending up in Marble Woods is much weirder than that."

"Really?"

"Yes, my great ancestor, Cadartha Moon, was a pirate who fled from the Caribbean. The legend says that he came here since it was the highest and furthermost point from where he found his treasure. He buried it somewhere in these mountains."

"That's not so weird."

"It is because Cadartha never left these mountains and died here, yet he managed to start a family in complete isolation. My family has resided in Marble Woods ever since. I can trace every single person in my genealogical line to Marble Woods."

"Maybe he brought a bride back with him or someone from one of the neighboring towns found him."

She shook her head. "That's just it. Cadartha was so paranoid about his treasure being stolen that he built himself a bunker sixty feet beneath the ground, which he filled with rations to last ten years. The tunnel was filled with a dozen intricate booby traps and sealed with dirt, so he encapsulated himself in that bunker."

"Archaeologists found the tunnel about a decade ago, and when they went to excavate it, one person died from one of the traps, and three others were injured. After they were able to get past the traps and to the bunker, all they found inside was the treasure but no trace of Cadartha. No bones or anything. To this day, no one can explain how the bunker and traps were made from the inside out with no trace of escape or the legendary pirate. All that remains is the Moon family."

"You win," he grinned. "Your story is much stranger than mine."

As his gaze met hers, she looked down and moved the topic along. "You should eat and rest as much as possible. The altitude can make people goofy if they don't rest, and I'm afraid there isn't another town for a good sixty miles, so I should show you to your room." She placed the lamp upon a table, which illuminated old photographs. None of the folks smiled and seemed unlifelike judgmental relics, but they bore the same piercing blue eyes.

"That's very kind of you." Ryder smiled, despite the uncomfortableness of his height that dwarfed Mary's petite figure. "I've been traveling for a long time."

As they sauntered down the dim hallway, Ryder fantasized about returning home from his trip as a renewed and better man—he would start his own law firm, get a bigger house away from nosy neighbors, and a wife who stood quietly by his side at galas. He had once won the affection of his former colleagues and partners and could do it again.

They proceeded up a few carpeted stairs and went down a cold, narrow corridor lined with frozen-faced relatives. At the end, she threw open a heavy door to a room brimming with charm. A great fire roared in the hearth, a plate of bread and fruit sat on the nightstand, and quilts were piled at the foot of the bed.

"Not bad at all." He strode toward the platter of food. "It's like you were expecting me."

"Help yourself," she said.

Ryder picked up a fluffy piece of bread dusted with oats and took a ravenous bite. "Umm. Fantastic. Did you make it yourself?" He raised his bread toward Mary, and then back to his mouth.

"Yes. There's not a whole lot to do here in Marble Woods as you'll soon discover, so I pass the time baking, sewing, and gardening. Sometimes I make wine. I try to make everything from scratch."

"I bet you're never bored."

"No. I'm far too busy for that. It can get a little lonely sometimes, which is why I offer the room. It's nice to meet new people."

Ryder ate a fresh strawberry from the platter, though he liked the homemade bread more. "Have you ever left Marble Woods?"

"No. Not even to go to the next town."

"Really?" He recalled the dozens of stamps on his passport, which was probably sitting at the bottom of a garbage dump now. It never crossed his mind that people who never traveled existed.

"Oh, but I bet you've been everywhere, haven't you?"

"I have, but I've always envied people with strong hometown roots like you. That's something I never had because my family moved all the time when I was growing up."

"That's too bad."

Ryder shrugged. "I think people want what they don't have."

"Agreed." Mary lit a candle by the bedside and slid her hand along the bed to flatten it. Vanilla wafted into the air. "I hope you will find everything you need here."

He adjusted his collar, indulged in another piece of bread, and smiled at Mary. Her kindness and courteous welcome dissipated his fears of coming to Marble Woods, and although he planned to return home after he found some answers about Summoner of Sleep, he found himself wavering over whether to stay a little longer in this quiet town where no one knew him.

Ryder scanned the cozy room and froze at the grandfather clock perched in the shadowy corner. The heat drained from his face, toes, and fingers and he shivered.

"What's wrong? Is the room not to your liking?"

"No, it's not that."

"Well, I assure you that the bread and fruit are fresh. I made the bread this morning and picked the fruit a few hours ago."

There seemed a stillness over the room, and as he listened, he did not hear the dreaded ticking that haunted his soul.

"Oh, you're looking at the clock. You needn't worry. It stopped working a long time ago, so it won't wake you if that's your concern. It's just for decoration because it was a gift from my late grandfather—the same one who gave me the horse picture. It would be too expensive to fix, but I haven't the heart to get rid of it."

Ryder drew a shallow breath. It was the fatigue that lowered his guard, but he was tired of hiding who he was.

"The truth is...um, I'm afraid of clocks. I've had nightmares about them ever since I was little and now, they're following me back into this world. I'm glad that it's broken." He paused a moment. "There it is. My horrible and embarrassing secret."

"You mean you have *chronomentrophia*?"

Ryder's eyes bulged. Mary didn't laugh like the others he had told his shameful secret to, who included his wife when they had first met. Instead, she said, "That's okay. I'll tell you one of my stupid little fears to make you feel better. I'm afraid of... balloons."

"What?" He cocked his head. "You are?"

Her peach-colored lips curved into a smile. "Yes. I never told anyone. It's so embarrassing, but at least I can try to avoid contact with them. But you, you poor thing, how do you manage to avoid clocks when they're everywhere? It can't be done."

"You're right. It sucks, but that's okay. You've made me really happy right now."

Her brow arched. "Oh?"

"You're the first one to believe me about this."

"That's unfortunate. I don't know why someone would lie about a legitimate fear like that."

"That's what I've been saying this entire time."

"So, do you want it removed? I'm sure the two of us could manage it."

"Oh, no. I couldn't disrupt your beautiful room here, especially so late in the night. You've already done so much for me."

"Are you sure?"

"I'm sure."

They stared at each other for a moment. Her perfume drove him mad. All flowers, witchery, and beauty. How he missed the soft embrace of a woman.

"Well, let me leave you so you may rest now. I'm right down the hall if you need anything."

"Ms. Moon?"

"Please, call me Mary."

"Mary?"

"Yes?"

"Thank you for not laughing at me."

"Of course," she said with a wink and shut the door behind her.

As soon as she left him alone, Ryder covered the clock with one of the extra quilts. He hated that he had to spend the night in the same room as a clock, but at least some of its power had diminished given its broken state.

Ryder glanced out the window at the town, shut the butter-colored drapes, and poured himself a glass of cold water from the pitcher.

Ahhhh.

He breathed easy again, reclined on the soft bed, kicked off his shoes, and closed his eyes.

Chapter 10

Ryder

Sunlight streamed through the window, which sparkled in the morning light. Ryder sat up, yawned, and stretched his arms.

"What time is it, Julie?"

His eyes batted and he scanned his surroundings. Bars lined the tiny window opening above him and a floor-length barred door stood opposite of the cot. Petrified roots and pea-green moss covered the walls. The whole structure was ready to crumble like a cracker.

There was a great ocean of time between today and yesterday and for the life of him he had no recollection of how he had ended up in some sort of cell. He jumped off the cot, rushed to the door, and yanked on the metal bars.

Locked.

"Hello?" His voice echoed down the shadowy hallway. "Where am I? Is anyone there?"

Silence.

Ryder returned to the sad little cot and rubbed his head.

His thigh throbbed like a hangnail ripped down to the flesh—a sting that never stopped. He couldn't help but poke at it with his index finger.

Ryder remained alone in the jail cell for hours. A few times he pulled with desperation at the crisscrossed bars that covered the dilapidated window, which sent an avalanche of pebbles, small slabs of rock, and hard roots down the walls.

His gaze fell on a tiny handprint embedded in the concrete in the corner of the floor. From the size and shape, it was from a toddler but he couldn't fashion a story that would justify the imprisonment of a child nor how its handprint had become stamped in concrete. Then again, he never fathomed he'd be imprisoned.

He shuddered.

Ryder stood and peeked out at the street from his window. The town was empty. He paced in silence. He hated being alone. His torn heart made the scenario even more tortuous.

The cell became a coffin. He had a vision of himself lying dead on the cot—his rotted body wrapped in dreary tendrils of darkness, liquefying alone in the cell. His leg all green and yellow. No one would ever find him.

By the chilly evening, he talked himself. He walked across the cold floor in the quivering light from the window and repeated to himself a string of conjectures about his past. All the nonviolent criminals he convicted who received the max sentence must have had a tiny cell just as he did. He prosecuted them just because he could. Because he was good at arguing. Because if they ended up in his courtroom, they must have already been guilty. Today was the only time he thought twice about those people. But what if some of them went to solitary confinement like this? What if they cursed his name every night before they went to sleep, waiting for the day of their release to then torment him? If Ryder didn't know Claude put those vials of Summoner of Sleep in his house, it would have been one of the criminals he persecuted. Maybe his imprisonment right now was revenge from one of them? Whatever way he looked at it, he'd meet an awful end inside these unforgiving walls.

This thought cycle lasted hours. Every minute, the walls suffocated him a little more. Bizarre sounds plagued him. There was a low buzz deep in the ground. Rain falling on the roof. Then what sounded like guitar strumming. Something rattled. A chain. Was it real? How could he be sure? Was that ticking? And now it sounded like somebody whistling.

He rubbed his temples.

The cheerful whistling continued.

"Hello? Who's there?"

A tall, heavy figure lurked in the shadows. It took him a full minute to realize who it was.

His blood boiled.

Claude sauntered down the hallway, tooting a happy tune. He moved without a limp, and his face not only looked smaller without glasses, but his skin was also free of wrinkles. A slippery coat on his skin illuminated his new and defined features.

"Claude?" gasped Ryder. "What the hell are you doing here and what happened to you?"

"Ah. My dear neighbor. Funny to see you here too." He approached the cell and gripped the bars. "I didn't think you'd make it to Marble Woods for a long time, but it appears you figured out the way, which means you must've gone through my things."

"That doesn't matter. What matters is that you get me out of here."

Claude paused.

"I went to sleep in that girl's house. She put me in here, didn't she?"

"Oh, don't blame Mary. She's sweet as pie. It was the neighbors who saw you and got you in the night without her consent. If anything, she was trying to protect you by offering you a room out of sight."

"What?" He slapped his palms against the bars. "I didn't do

a damn thing. You know I'm a lawyer, right? You are holding me illegally. I haven't been read my Miranda Rights or anything. I have grounds to sue you and this entire town."

Unfazed, Claude got up on his tippy toes to peer out the vine-covered window in the corner of the cell behind Ryder. "I shouldn't be here, you know. They told me to leave you until they could figure out what to do with you, but I snuck in anyway, even though you never apologized for the way you treated me back home."

"There's no way in hell that you're getting an apology from me. You broke into my house, drugged me, spied on me, and documented everything about me. If anyone should be in this cell, it's you. You've broken at least a dozen laws."

Claude shrugged. "I feel sorry for you. I've always felt sorry for you. A man with everything yet nothing at all."

"Stop changing the subject. And you've no reason to have ever felt sorry for me," Ryder scoffed. "I always felt sorry for you living all alone in that giant house with no one to love you and nothing to do but spy on me."

"I'm referring to the torment of your dreams and how you lived a life of destruction," Claude said. "It amazed me that you were never aware of it or how your actions impacted others."

"Ridiculous. I've lived a good life, it's just that bad things happen to good people. That's the way of life, and life hasn't been kind to me." Ryder wiped his brow and continued, "Bad things happen to good people like me. I did nothing wrong as a child, and my father abandoned me, and in stepped a horrible replacement—a stepfather who hounded my every action, who shamed me for my hidden talents, who never showed me a shred of care. And Julie...I gave her a good life. I provided everything she ever wanted—vacations, jewelry, spending money—but I got the short end of the stick. She didn't even give me the courtesy of telling me to my face that she was leaving me."

Claude's eyebrow arched. "There you go again. You really are arrogant."

"How dare you. You don't know anything that I've been through, and if these bars weren't here, I'd—"

"You're forgetting I watched you and her," Claude interrupted. "I know everything. Do you want to know why she left?"

Ryder went silent, his temples pulsed.

"Julie left you because you were a jerk who cheated on her and you worked all the time."

"You're full of shit."

"I heard her conversations with her friends, Ryder. She knew. I heard her pleas for help. The nightmares were just the icing on the cake to her misery."

"None of that is true."

"Money doesn't buy love. Work doesn't replace the importance of family. Of a relationship."

"I know that. But when you grow up in an impoverished house, when you couldn't eat some days and would go to bed hungry, and when you didn't get something as simple as a blank journal to write poetry on, what's the harm in spending money when you have it...to please yourself...to please the people you care about? And how does one accomplish that? By working."

"I never told you how to spend your money. I'm just trying to get you to examine how you ended up like this. To look at the real reasons."

"I already told you, I'm a victim of circumstance. Of bad luck."

"You're claiming all your misfortune is due to bad luck?" Claude's laughter blasted the cell like a gunshot.

"Screw you. Do you even know why you lost your house? You lost it because you spent your money on extravagant toys, unnecessary objects, and getaways. You were someone who controlled people's futures. You had such vigor. Such power. Yet, you didn't even know how to balance your checkbook."

The vein in Ryder's forehead throbbed, which made his vision go red. He reached through the bars and yanked hard at his neighbor's collar.

Claude stumbled about, unable to maintain his footing as Ryder pulled him so close that his soft doughy flesh pushed through the cold steel bars like Play-doh.

"Stop—stop, you're choking me." He hacked and coughed.

A few seconds later, Ryder let go.

Claude fell to the floor with a gasp.

"I'm not an asshole, you know. I'm not my stepfather, who worked all the time and only cared for himself. I spent my life making it a point to be the opposite of him. So, what I want to know is why you came here to tell me all of this? To just watch me suffer more?"

Claude grabbed at his throat. "I came here to help you."

"If you've truly come here to help me, then let me out."

"I can't do that."

"Then tell me why I'm in jail because I committed no criminal act."

Claude crawled away from the jail cell and continued to cough. "There's something strange about you. That's why they put you here."

"That's absurd." Ryder kicked one of the bars. "You can't arrest someone because they're strange. I could say that about anyone in Marble Woods, including you. I mean, look at you. How is it possible that you turned back time since the last time I saw you? How is it possible that your limp is gone, and you no longer need glasses? Hell, the last time I saw you, you looked like you were ready to go to a convalescent home. And I'm the one who's strange?"

"That's part of it, Ryder. Things have changed for me. Things have changed for all of us here in Marble Woods, except you. Summoner of Sleep is supposed to change you...give you abilities...make you young and fit, and the higher the dose you ingest, the more change comes. When you can't take a dose, horrible things happen to you."

"What things?"

"It starts with tiny pinpricks, which well with blood, and then pulse with hot, unbearable pain. The body's age accelerates the more it's deprived of Summoner of Sleep."

"I don't understand what this has to do with me."

"You exhibit no symptoms. I gave you an astronomical dosage back home to stop the nightmares and nothing changed. Not your skin or features. Then you quit taking it altogether and nothing happened. No rash, hives, bumps, cuts, burning. Nothing."

"So, you're telling me that just because I'm not morphing into a younger version of myself or having withdrawals, that's why I've been imprisoned?"

"Yes. We've seen the way withdrawal goes. You should be covered in a bumpy rash by now. You should look different. Your organ temperature should be elevated."

"My organ temperature? What the hell are you talking about?"

Claude gestured to the luminous sheen upon his skin. "This is a protective coating. It's meant to cool our organs so they don't combust. It's necessary for Summoner of Sleep to work, as vital organs need to heat to an abnormal level. From there, it's transformed into an absorbent acid that's seeped into the bloodstream. You remained normal, despite you drinking the water with Summoner of Sleep in it last night."

"It was in the water?"

"Yep. That's how this whole thing started. The townspeople of Marble Woods were exposed to Summoner of Sleep some years ago due to water contamination from the local botanist's garden. The plant's roots had ripped through a planting box, tore into the hard clay-rich soil, and sought out the local water system. It didn't take long for the town to realize how incredible they looked and felt when they drank the water, and when they discovered what had happened, they traced where the contamination had occurred."

"What happened to the botanist?"

"Well, they all showed up at the botanist's house demanding to know what strangeness had tainted their water supply and how they could maintain the feeling of strength and happiness. But the botanist only divulged that in an attempt to create a sleeping aid, he had accidentally 'summoned dark spirits' into his concoction and the result would be ruin for anyone who consumed it."

Ryder swallowed.

"They didn't heed the warning though," Claude said. "They demanded that he make Summoner of Sleep available to buy. When the botanist refused, the town grew furious and desperate to make the withdrawal pains stop, so they broke into his home, seized the plant, and stole the recipe. Everything was burned and the botanist disappeared."

Ryder took a shallow breath. Everything Claude said was madness. Ryder was drowning, sinking in the confusion of it all.

"The townspeople will stop at nothing to find out about Summoner of Sleep and they want to study you."

"They're going to keep me here and study me like some sort of human science experiment?"

Claude nodded.

"And I bet you did nothing to stop them imprisoning me?"

His neighbor drew a breath and fell silent.

Ryder's stomach twisted. "You and everyone here are insane. I'm not staying here a second longer."

"I wish I could let you out, but I can't. My hands are tied."

"You're full of it, old man."

"Okay, fine." Claude smiled from the floor and pulled the collar of his shirt down. "I could let you out, but I don't want to." The old man's face flushed, and the sheen intensified on his fat red nose. Ryder would give anything to punch it.

"Well if you're not going to help me, I have no other choice." Ryder marched over to the tiny, barred window. His pale, slender fingers wrapped around the cold bars.

"Hey. Wait. What are you doing?"

"What the hell does it look like? I'm getting the fuck out, and when I do, I'm going to kill you."

Claude rose and lunged to the jail door. "No. Don't. You're about to make a dangerous mistake."

"What do you care?"

"Ryder, please. You don't know what you're dealing with."

"The hell I do." Ryder glanced back at Claude. If looks could kill, Claude would've dropped dead. Then he yanked the bars loose as hard as he could.

Chapter 11

Claude

Claude choked and hacked as he waved away dust plumes and bits of concrete. His knees wobbled even as he hugged the wall.

He glanced through the old jail walls, torn open by Ryder's stupidity. The townspeople glared at him; and once they realized Ryder was helpless and could do nothing more, they descended upon him. With frozen horror he watched Ryder pull himself to his bloody knees in the middle of a mob of townspeople and swing his battered fists with a drunken aim.

How had Ryder survived and managed to crawl from the wreckage?

Then through the golden speckled twilight, a slender figure approached. His brother could pass for a young man of thirty without question. But the pallor in Ryder's face and emaciated limbs revealed nothing but decrepitude. Why hadn't he changed along with everyone else?

Claude's mouth went dry.

The air went out.

Ryder froze, a look of awe plastered on his face.

"Well? What do you think?" Vern asked.

"You're a—alive ."

"Indeed I am."

"And you've changed t-too?"

"Yes, we've all changed." Vern smiled. "And it's all thanks to you, Ryder."

"Me?"

Claude inched forward to listen better, concealed by a pillar.

"Yes. If you never had those strange dreams of yours, you never would've piqued my brother's interest in seeking out Summoner of Sleep to quiet you, and then you would've never exposed me to the plant all those weeks ago." Vern strutted into the center of the circle of townspeople. "I mean, look at me. I've never felt or looked better, and it's all thanks to you."

"You've quite a way of showing your thanks." Ryder rubbed the side of his bloody head.

"Oh, that?" Vern glanced at the collapsed jail. "I'm sorry about that. We just needed you to stay put, and we were afraid you'd leave Mary's cottage in the morning. We're old friends though so I hope it'll be water under the bridge. All I want is to study you a bit since you seem immune to Summoner of Sleep, yet it stopped your nightmares. I want to know why. I want to know so many things that you hold the key to, and I promise that if you'll oblige me, I won't lock you up again. You'll be free to explore the town—I just ask that you don't leave it." Vern paused. "You will soon have magic powers too once I unlock this riddle. So, what do you say?" He bent forward and extended a hand.

Ryder spit at Vern and took a swing.

Claude's heart jumped to his throat as the mob descended upon his neighbor, and in a matter of seconds, Claude lost sight of both his brother and Ryder in the tangle of faces, elbows, teeth, and legs.

Claude plucked a large patch of hair from his mustache and wondered what he should do. He had never been in a fight, then again, he could think of nothing better than punching Ryder in his stupid face. There would be hell to pay though if Vern found out he had gone to see Ryder in jail. Then it occurred to Claude that this was the first time he had been alone since he arrived in Marble Woods. He was anxious to continue his research of the botanist who invented Summoner of Sleep, so he slipped out of the jail to visit the burned homestead for clues.

As he speed-walked across town, he zipped up his jacket and admired the sky. It had turned the color of pumpkin, and the trees in the distance faded into rich purples and grays. A few gas lamps flickered in front of the more maintained cottages, and the air smelled like wood rot and cedar.

Claude arrived on the other side of town full of energy.

He scanned the terrain scorched beyond recognition. There were remnants of a collapsed chimney, a heavy doorknob and knocker in the shape of a face, and an old iron gate.

Claude wandered around the wreckage and past a birdbath blackened with soot. He sat on a heap of old bricks and kicked at the stones and dirt. A moment later he spotted something that was not part of it all: several of the bricks had letters.

He hunched over, picked one up for closer inspection, and read the letter *N* imprinted on the surface. He picked up another toppled brick with the letter *S*. Ecstatic, Claude rummaged through all the bricks and gathered each one that bore a letter. He then placed them with care in a dirt clearing he had made.

He began the laborious task of positioning the bricks with letters to spell different words, but nothing worked well. One passage read *S.O.S. illuminates the devil in man.* Several *I*s and *E*s in a different font remained unused. There was a *have* and a *you* in the passage, but Claude couldn't make sense of the other letters.

Something crackled in the thicket and he paused.

A drop of sweat beaded and fell down his forehead.

A full minute of silence passed before he rearranged another set of letters: *Residing within you, you have summoned the devil.* Something didn't seem quite right about the statement though.

He continued his work.

Then he tried: *You're the devilish summoning*, which didn't make sense at all. There were also letters leftover, which he matched in various word patterns and continued to come up with nothing of use. Claude turned over a random brick. He sat there for a long time deep in thought.

"You're useless," Vern said.

Claude lurched back, fell onto his rear, and toppled over a pile of rubble. A glimpse of Vern's crestfallen face sent his heart into a frenzy. He was going to have another heart attack. He opened his mouth to say something, but Vern gave him a blow with the back of his hand that brought out tears and snot.

"Ow," Claude wailed and cowered on the ground. "What did you do that for?"

"I told you never to come up here without me."

Claude's teary gaze shot to the ground. Direct eye contact would only spark Vern's fury. Shame burned within Claude's breast that he was still susceptible to feeling fearful as a grown man.

"What are you even doing here?"

"I was just curious." Claude sniffled, then wiped his nose on his sleeve. "Curious if we could learn more about the plant."

"I hate it when you don't listen to me. Why do you always do things like that?" Vern asked.

"I'm sorry. I was trying to learn...to discover another way to ingest Summoner of Sleep and benefit from it because something still bothers me. I want to know what's happening here. That's all. I saw these letters on the bricks and thought I was on to something."

"Well, you were off. The answer is 'You have summoned the devil residing within you.'"

Had the botanist carved this into the bricks as a warning,
or was there some other piece of the puzzle he was missing?

Vern walked to the dilapidated gate. The rusty hinges creaked as he knocked it over with one swift kick.

Shivers scurried down Claude's spine and the reek of the burned and sulfuric pineapple lily burst through the cold air. The ground was slimy. A mist descended on Marble Woods, and he felt the moist darkness would suffocate him.

"You shouldn't run off like that." Vern stood by the downed gate with a frown. "You're acting just how you did as a child. Remember how I used to call you *Big Baby*? I called you that up until college. Always running off and getting yourself into trouble—never listening to me—filling your head with a bunch of crap. I think I'm gonna call you that from now on, *Big Baby*."

Claude rose to his feet, not bothering to dust himself off. He was remorseful, but since he could never win a battle with his older brother, there wasn't much to say, and the threat of the returning nickname made his breath stop.

"You're wasting valuable time when you could be making more Summoner of Sleep. You lost an hour's worth of work coming up here. And since Ryder broke out of jail and that whole ordeal happened, no one was there to watch the cauldrons and a bunch of the batches burned." Vern sauntered over and kicked at the bricks and sent them scooting along in a mix of incoherent letters. "Well, what do you have to say for yourself?"

"I'm...I'm s—sorry."

Vern scoffed. "Remember, I told you to trust me and you'd be okay? Remember I told you to stick to your job and everything would be fine? Well, this doesn't look like trust."

"I do trust you, Vern, and I'm sorry about the ruined batches. I'll make up my hours, okay? Whatever it takes. Just please help me understand more about all of this."

Vern grimaced.

"I came here with you and I've seen amazing things. I feel good. I feel like my body chemistry has altered for the best, but I want to know why. I also want to know why we have the withdrawals. What if there's a way to adjust the potion? To make it better? To eliminate the withdrawal rash ?"

Vern shook his head. "That's why I captured Ryder in the first place, you idiot. To run experiments on him to find a better Summoner of Sleep, but now he's escaped."

Claude raised an eyebrow.

"We can't find him anywhere. Some people saw blood at the bottom of the cliff, so they think he jumped off. I'm gonna be so pissed if he's dead now."

Claude's head throbbed from where Vern had hit him. His mouth tasted metallic. "I'm sorry. I thought maybe I could find something of use up here."

"You thought wrong. Don't you think I've been up here a thousand times already and done the same exact thing?"

"I guess it didn't occur to me."

"Well, you guessed right, *Big Baby*."

"But Vern, please listen to me for a second."

His brother turned on his heel and approached Claude. "I'm listening."

Claude swallowed and said, "The fact that the message is S.O.S. illuminates the devil in man, you have summoned the devil residing within you is concerning. Maybe Summoner of Sleep isn't as good as we thought. What if this town awakened something dark? Something evil?"

"My dear brother, when will you learn to mind your own damn business?" Vern said and struck Claude unconscious.

Chapter 12

Ryder

Ryder pressed his achy back into the tree trunk and squinted. The wind picked up, so he tucked his chin into his jacket. It whipped so hard that the smaller branches popped off and scattered the forest floor like a great ocean of barbs. Something dark and greasy rained down from the dead leaves.

How did I get here?

The boggy moonlight illuminated an odd structure of mismatched logs in the shape of a tiny house. His eyes wandered to a figure draped in heavy woolen robes on the porch, its head angled at a book.

Then, without warning, he was overcome by a coughing attack that shook the leaves loose from the trees.

The figure set down the book and stood.

The memory of Vern wanting to experiment on him rushed back. What horrible fate awaited him?

Ryder couldn't breathe, each intake of air strangled him like a noose. The wind screeched again and burst through the trees as if to prevent him from rising to his feet.

"Please—" Ryder grasped the tree behind him.

The figure shuffled closer.

A deep silence possessed the air, and the tar-like substance from the trees added a dark haze that diffused the brightness from the lantern light that flickered from the porch.

Ryder was flush against the tree. His thigh pulsed. "Please don't hurt me."

The figure stopped and drew back the hood.

A gasp erupted from Ryder's throat.

The stranger had prominent cheekbones, an extraordinary pallor in his face, and deep-set black eyes—as black as coal.

Ryder had seen a few photographs of his father and was aware that he left his mother when Ryder was a child. She spoke spitefully of him. Ryder was so hurt over his father's abandonment that he didn't ask questions or concern himself with his father's genealogy. When grade school reports had required him to map his family tree, his mom filled out her lineage and Ryder seized the opportunity to create an impressive imaginary story about the father he always wanted.

Ryder's chest tightened as the man stepped forward and extended a wrinkled hand.

The man was too old to be Ryder's father though, so who was he?

Ryder peered at the interior of the cottage behind the man, which looked like a rustic log cabin he had stayed in once while visiting Tahoe. A roaring fire inside caught his eye.

He shivered.

The old man inched his hand closer; his huge black cloak filled the entire woods, and from his hand there drifted a scent of ginger; an unmistakable scent of fresh earth. What had he been digging?

Calluses knotted the man's palm. When Ryder got to his feet he sighed.

The man let go, turned, and headed toward the cottage as

Ryder limped behind him.

In the center of the warm, cozy kitchen sat a long wooden table with a little shag carpet underneath. Stained-glass cabinets covered with vines and flowers lined the room. The low wooden ceiling reflected a sleepy orange light. Next to the hearth was a cluster of potted plants, their multi-colored leaves hung over the sides. The only sound was the crackle of the fire. The cottage was so much better than expected that Ryder was sorry he had even hesitated to enter.

The old man brought him a bowl of soup that smelled like cardamom and was garnished with some green herb. Ryder sucked it down without even tasting it and broke a piece of bread between his fingers.

From time to time, the man got up to poke the fire but never said a word as Ryder finished every morsel of food.

When Ryder had satiated himself, they stared at each other from across the table. It took another fifteen minutes before warmth returned to his body and he could sit without swaying, but the longer he gazed at the old man, the more conscious he became of a great bond between them.

Well into the hazy embrace of night, the old man rose from the table and hobbled over to a bookshelf next to the dying hearth. He selected the largest volume bound in leather. Ryder feared the old man would tip forward from the weight.

He thumbed through it with one hand, paused, and grinned. He made his way toward Ryder with the open book in tow.

"Everything you want to know is right here. Read," he said in a foreign accent.

The book smelled like secrets and smoke, and something about the gentleness of how he handled the book made Ryder less cautious about him.

"Good night." The man headed toward the doorway.

"Wait. Sir, please don't leave. What if they come back?"

He paused. "You're safe here. This house is protected."

"Please don't go. I don't even know your name."

The old man turned. "I'm Botanē. It's Greek for botanist."

"You're him," Ryder half fell out of his chair. "You're the botanist who created Summoner of Sleep, aren't you?"

"My parents knew my destiny of becoming a botanist and named me as such," he said. "Yours did the same. Your name, Ryder, means messenger of dreams, which is why you are here. To deliver dreams."

"But how could you know that? I haven't said a word to you. Not even my name."

Botanē chuckled, his face full of deep wrinkles. "What kind of grandfather would I be not to recognize my own grandson? Now, if you'll excuse me. I must rest."

He disappeared into the depths of the shadowy cottage as Ryder sat there speechless staring at the book of secrets.

Chapter 13

Claude

Claude huffed as he leaned forward and perched his chin in his palm. The pretty garden view from the parlor window hadn't distracted him from his conniving brother. Not even the hypnotic, blue-chinned hummingbirds that chirped and zoomed through the larkspur helped.

The cure for Claude's curiosity was a calm, structured environment, so his room was stripped of everything comforting or colorful. Vern destroyed all Claude's notebooks of research. The bookshelves were cleared. The art exchanged for white walls. Visitors were forbidden. Then there were the supervised meals, bathroom time, and outings in town. In the past few days alone, Vern removed the bureau from his room and only a thin, uncomfortable cot remained. Twice a day Vern checked under the mattress and the loose floorboard near the door. Vern had even forced Claude to shave his mustache of twenty years because "it wasn't becoming to the Wick name."

Fear and tension occupied the house. Vern's judgmental gaze

wafted through the hypnotic air scented with jasmine from the garden, it danced in the soft moonlight of the bedroom window, rose in the steaming morning oatmeal, and his scrutiny lurked in every shadowy secret of the cottage.

Once Claude got up in the middle of the night for a midnight stroll but found his brother in the corner facing the wall as if possessed, or, perhaps a secret invisible threshold lived there that he just returned from.

"Brother?" Claude asked and slid onto his elbow. "What are you doing?"

"Nothing."

"Why are you staring at the wall like that? You're scaring me."

"It's nothing. Go back to bed."

That bone-chilling episode was nothing compared to the warning he had received at the botanist's burned-down home some weeks ago. It was so embarrassing that Claude couldn't help but repeat the chain of events in his head and question why he allowed his brother to treat him that way. He still couldn't get the smell of blood out of his nostrils. No matter what he ate he tasted copper like his mouth was full of pennies.

If only he could muster the strength to stand up to him once and for all, but his bravery had died long ago—along with his wife, whom Vern had never approved of.

Claude's mind jumped to Ryder. The escape from jail. The fight against the townspeople. A sick sense of guilt engrossed him for a moment, but now it made him grin. Claude always liked justice—no matter how brutal. He reveled in the idea that Ryder was dead at the bottom of the ravine.

Claude sighed. Something moved in the house. He paused. The thud came from down the hall, followed by a horrible gurgle. Was it coming from the same spot Vern had been staring at in the middle of the night?

Claude rose, crept across the floorboards, and lingered his gaze on the light from the bathroom spilling onto the floor of

the hallway. Scratches followed and a moment later the thuds
started up again. He listened, swearing he heard a creepy laugh
in all of it.

"Come in here now," Vern shouted so loud that the
knickknacks rattled.

He shuddered.

"Claude," screeched Vern a second time from the bathroom.

Claude gulped. The icy doorknob prickled his palm. He
eased open the aged door with a squeal.

"Well, it's about time." Vern sat up in the clawfoot bathtub,
which shattered his reflection in the water. "Don't let the heat
out. Hurry and close the door and come over here."

As Claude scooted inside and drudged toward his brother,
he tried not to look at the bathroom's nauseating shades of
yellow and ruby that clashed all around him—from the floral
shower curtain, the shell-shaped bathmats, to the askew shelf
of tacky beach knickknacks next to the vanity mirror. All of it
made him think of pineapple upside down cake he once got food
poisoning from.

"Check this out."

Claude's eyes widened at the scales that wrapped around his
brother's thighs and black horizontal lines that ran down the
length of his neck.

Any alarm Claude felt dulled his adrenaline, and the sharp
scent of vanilla bubble bath distracted him, but he couldn't help
himself from blurting out, "What the hell is all that?"

"I'll show you in a minute. I got you a little something and I
want you to open it first." Vern gestured to a wrapped package
on the sink counter. "Go on and open it."

"You got me a present?"

"Yep."

He tore through the delicate gold wrapping paper like
a kid on his birthday to find a picture of him and his brother
set in an intricate silver frame inside. He smiled. They were
standing in front of the lake sticking out their tongues at the

camera, the water looming behind them like a swamp monster. The precious memories of that day flooded his mind and he delighted in the fanciful feeling of recalling something he had once cherished but forgotten. The memory never left—it had just been hibernating—and now he was re-experiencing the sights, sounds, and hypnotic smells all over again.

They had taken a long swim across the cold black lake and returned to their camp to sunbathe like lizards all afternoon. Their skin was the color of rust—half bronzed and burned. Then they gorged on soda and chips and poked each other in the stomach to see who would vomit first. Their mother scolded them for doing something so revolting, and she insisted they take a picture as punishment, but at the last second, they stuck out their tongues.

"Remember that day?"

"Ah, very much so," Claude said, high on nostalgia.

"I've kept that photo of us in my wallet all these years. It's the only possession I have left since I came to Marble Woods. I know you've been having a hard time here and I wanted to give you something that reminded you of home. Of the good old days. And I thought it'd be a nice thing to put in our new home to enjoy together."

Emotion welled up inside Claude. He loved and hated his brother in equal measure, but it was these little crumbs of affection that allowed him to withstand all his mean-spirited actions and words.

"I'll cherish it forever," he said. "Thank you."

"I'm glad you like it. I have something else to show you. Come and look."

Claude's brow arched. "Oh?"

"Watch this." Vern took a deep breath and plunged himself under the soapy water.

At first, Claude was confused, but something magical happened as the minutes ticked by. Vern remained underwater without struggle and the gills opened and closed.

Claude's gaze darted between the tiny clock on the shelf and Vern, counting the time and looking for signs of distress. Every now and then bubbles erupted and popped, but Vern remained under the water for a full ten minutes before surfacing. Even when he surfaced, he didn't appear out of breath.

"That was incredible."

"I know." Vern gestured for a towel on the rack. "I noticed it a few days ago but wanted to be sure about it before showing you." When he stretched his torso to one side, a large fleshy bump jutted from his ribs. "It's a new lung. It's been getting bigger every day. The time I can hold my breath increases every time I see it enlarge." He poked it and it moved.

Claude's eyes bulged.

"Don't' worry, it doesn't hurt."

"But I thought Summoner of Sleep was supposed to make you young and beautiful. I don't understand why something like an extra lung would grow. If I could just get back my research I could—"

"Stop." Vern held up a hand and got out of the tub. "I told you there would be consequences if you mentioned that again."

"I just want to understand what I'm seeing."

"You're witnessing a gift, brother. An incredible gift." Vern stepped closer. "Are you still taking your prescribed doses? You haven't missed any?"

"I've taken all of them."

A flicker of anger flushed Vern's face despite his grin. His teeth lengthened and a growl emitted from deep within his belly.

"Come on, Vern." Claude's rear bumped into the door handle. "I'm not lying. You've been with me every second of every day. Why would I lie to you?"

"Then why don't I smell Summoner of Sleep on your breath? I thought we had a deal that we were in this together. That we both wanted this new life. It's all or nothing, remember?"

"I just had coffee." Despite trying to remain calm to avoid further suspicion, Claude's breath quickened. "Haven't I done enough to please you?"

"Enough? You'd be nothing without me." Vern wrapped the towel around his waist. "Had it not been for me, you wouldn't know what to do with S.O.S." Vern leaned forward. "I've given you an incredible reward."

"I—"

He lunged forward. Vern's teeth hovered above Claude's jugular. A loud, sinister growl emitted from Vern's parted lips. "Maybe I should have just left you alone that day I found you in the woods—covered in mud and blood."

"Don't be silly, Vern."

Vern raised his head and steadied his gaze on Claude. "I think you are only saying that because you have nothing to go back to. You have nothing to live for because you ruined your life. When you enlisted you left your friends behind and then they moved away. You left me alone to take care of Mom and Dad, who died in your absence...just like your piggy little wife shortly after. All you had going for you was spying on your insane neighbor. I'm all you have left, and don't you forget it."

"I know. You're right." Claude pulled a vial of Summoner of Sleep from his pocket. "Look, I'll increase my dosage right now." He held it to his lips. "Will that make you happy?"

"No." Vern knocked it out of his hand. It smashed against the yellow tile in a vomit-colored puddle.

"But I thought you wanted me to take more?"

"You still don't get it." Vern sauntered over to the shelf and grabbed a vial of orange, fizzy liquid hidden behind the clock. "You'll take this instead. This is much better. It's something new that I've been working on in secret. It's what's allowed me to grow the extra lung, not Summoner of Sleep."

"What's it?"

"It's still S.O.S., but cold-pressed and unfiltered, making it a much higher concentration. I also added a few more ingredients to help with the taste and potency. The bubbles are a natural chemical reaction. That's another trick. I heat it by moonlight."

A wave of disgust hit Claude—like the feeling he had when he first arrived at Marble Woods and thought he spotted Belinda.

"I want you to take it right now. Prove to me that you're in this, brother."

Claude cowered against the door, but Vern grabbed his arm hard and pulled Claude toward him. Claude yelled as his knees buckled beneath him. Vern raised his hand and Claude extended his arms to block the incoming blow.

"I'm not going to hit you, brother," Vern laughed. "Just take this little miracle and everything will be better. I call it Summoner of Chaos as it offers endless possibilities. You could develop multiple unique physicalities and abilities all at once, and with instantaneous results. It's like a potent, magical wild card."

"You mean you have other attributes besides the lung and gills?"

"Of course. So many you couldn't even begin to comprehend the treasures bestowed on me." Vern propped Claude up and shoved the vial into his palm. "Join me."

"I'm not sure I—"

Vern leaned closer. "What's wrong? Don't you want to change for the better?"

"Well, yes, but—"

"This was your idea, to begin with, Claude. You wanted to improve Summoner of Sleep, remember? You said so at the botanist's old house. And I did. This is it."

Claude bit his lip. "I just—"

"Brother, if you don't want to drink it you don't have to. I've told you a million times that you can leave at any time. No one is forcing you, but you do understand that I'm the last bit of family you have remaining though, right?"

Claude swallowed.

"What do you want to do?"

Claude took a deep breath, pushed down his sadness, then poured the entire orange contents into his mouth, which sent a dazzling euphoric glow through his insides. Was this what a firefly felt like?

Unease and confusion replaced the moment. Within seconds his scalp ached, and his hair pulled as if someone yanked at it, and then there was a tremendous pressure on his forehead and skull. Something popped and split. His head burned like fire. He stood with his mouth open and eyes closed as two unstoppable streams of tears flowed down his cheeks.

"Ahhh. I feel weird," Claude cried in a panic. The sensation was ten times worse than a migraine. The pain intensified every excruciating second. "What's happening to me? Am I dying? Ahhh." Claude screeched as colors swirled behind his eyes, too afraid to touch his head. "What's happening?"

"Amazing," Vern said with a strangled laugh.

"What?"

"It's glorious. A masterpiece. I couldn't have imagined it better."

Vern touched him on the shoulder, and Claude panned to his brother's face agleam with mischief and triumph; in the midst two stupid, muddy eyes. Claude tried to scream, but nothing came out. His shoulders shrugged so high they disappeared into his ears as he gritted his teeth, and he tasted blood. The sound of cracking—like sandals stomping sun-soaked seashells on a beach—was the last thing he heard in the steamy, pineapple bathroom from hell.

Chapter 14

Mary

She sighed and set her purse on the bureau. She had dreaded another meeting at the Ladies Exchange Group, and now that it was over, she cursed herself for attending. Mary walked to the kitchen and poured herself a much-deserved glass of wine. She took a generous sip.

Just once she would've liked to skip out on the meeting, but those old biddies would've never let her live it down. Besides, they were desperate to trade items and offer odd household jobs in exchange for something they wanted, and it didn't help that her mother led the charge. It started innocently with her offering Mary's sewing and baking skills in exchange for an exotic spice or new kitchen utensil she wanted. But when her mother started to offer more of Mary's services than she could handle, it became so difficult to maintain the demand without any financial return that she started to produce shoddy work. It began with the lopsided quilt she gave to Mrs. Jasper. Once word spread that Mary would only produce her best craftsmanship in exchange for money, her orders decreased.

She took another sip of wine. Her mind wandered to Sarah Tart, a lazy, flaxen-haired girl with whom Mary had played dolls when they were kids, and how Sarah had inherited a hefty sum from a distant relative and moved to Paris.

Not fair.

Then there was pudgy Elton Marks who sold his pecan pies in the closest town and was offered an exorbitant amount of money by a big company to sell the recipe. He sold his possessions and bought a yacht to sail around the world.

Not fair.

"When I'm rich and I have no family left, I'm leaving," Mary said and gulped more wine.

She entered the parlor, glanced out the window, and recollected the scene of Ryder breaking free from jail and then vanishing before everyone's bewildered eyes. She'd never forget how much blood gushed from Ryder's forehead, or the ache in her stomach. Why hadn't she told him not to look out the window? Everyone had searched for Ryder for days, but they only found a trail of dried blood that stopped at the edge of the jagged mountain. Beyond the sinister peaks and rocky crevices, there was nothing. The townspeople didn't search for him anymore after that. Vern convinced everyone that Ryder was dead or would be soon given the injuries he would've sustained and Ryder's lack of resources to survive alone in the woods. Not wanting to end up like the mysterious visitor, not a soul scaled the cliffs to the barren terrain below.

She sniffled. Hasn't she done a good thing by offering him shelter in her home, and this was the payback she got?

Mary sighed. She hated how Vern had arrived in Marble Woods with an air of supreme confidence. She hated how he came around to each house every day with his sniveling brother to inquire if the prescribed dose of Summoner of Sleep had been taken and ask for a report of any new characteristics. She hated his immense knowledge of herbs and chemistry which rivaled the botanist's. But most of all she hated the gifts and letters he left on her doorstep. Candies. Chocolates. Flowers. All of it went straight into the trash, except maybe a few chocolates. Those butterscotch squares were too irresistible to her.

Several times she caught Vern spying on her through her windows, so she took to having her drapes drawn day and night, peeking out if she sensed someone's presence.

She disliked this new ability she had developed. Whenever she felt a person's presence, she experienced a distinct warm tingle on her right wrist, and within seconds she felt the color of someone's personality.

When it first happened, she convinced herself the sensation was caused by the hot candle wax she had spilled on herself and the color was from an ocular migraine, but when the wax washed off, the sensation remained, and so did the color.

It had been bright, lilac, and felt sleepy. She panicked that she had developed synesthesia, but a few moments later she discovered that her mother had come over and was sitting in the other room radiating a lilac glow around her.

Mary didn't tell anyone about her ability—not even her mother. Nor did she divulge that she sensed Ryder's presence, which was forest green and felt like cotton, or that another presence accompanied it, which was dark brown and felt like rust.

She lost herself dreaming of his enigmatic black eyes and hair that fell over his pale face, which somehow had a balanced mixture of worldliness and ruggedness.

Ryder's presence radiated from the east side where the gray trees flourished, which didn't explain why the trail of blood led to the west side of town—unless it was a diversion. Even if it was a diversion, Mary couldn't wrap her head around how he had vanished from the middle of the mob. She wouldn't have believed the story if she hadn't witnessed the disappearance with her own eyes.

Hope remained alive within her heart that she could escape

Marble Woods, so she worked to devise a plan where she could sneak away from the town and find him.

A few times she had ventured into the gray woods alone and tried to follow the presence and colors she felt, but each time got lost and despair wrapped itself around her like a vice. And when the wind blew through the weak trees, the branches snickered— like little laughs—and she became paralyzed. Perhaps the legend about the demons with the marble skin in the woods was true? She'd return covered in scratches from the branches and a chill in her bones that only a hot bath and a scorching cup of tea could cure.

She wanted to go back, but Vern convinced everyone to observe a curfew so that their bodies could rest and absorb the tonic. To her surprise, everyone complied without hesitation. It was impossible to get away without being seen.

The town was under the spell of something sinister and Mary knew lying about her characteristics and faking the physical ones was the only way to remain normal. Of course, there were physical side effects from not taking doses, but a little makeup took care of the visual issues. And there was a tremendous pain she endured daily. Various pills and teas didn't do much to help. Mary had to remind herself that this was the price of her humanity. She knew Summoner of Sleep was a numbing agent that would transform her body and mind in a way that would make her lose everything. She didn't want to be anyone or anything other than herself.

Mary took another gulp of wine.

She closed the drapes, turned, and gazed at her adored canary in his gilded cage. "I love you, Alfrodul." She sniffled and wiped away a tear. "The day I need you most is coming. Please don't let me down."

Chapter 15

Ryder

Ryder sneered at the scent of lavender that assaulted his nostrils. Dozens of herbalists had prescribed it for sleeping, touting its calming properties, but now the scent just made him nauseous. It wasn't the only aroma in the botanist's greenhouse that made his toes curl though. Some of the botanist's extraordinary plants had buttery leaves but reeked like a sewer. Others had big, flat red petals with tints of blue that smelled of death. Some were tall and leafless with waxy white stems and wooly umbels of pinkish star-like flowers on branches that smelled of halitosis.

His favorite was a small plant the size of a kitten with tiny purple blossoms. It grew sideways out of a hanging pot and perfumed the air with sugary sweetness, and with each whiff, a fragrant new scent wafted from its dewy petals—waffle cones, vanilla ice cream, and gumdrops.

The purple plant was called Mimir—named after the Norse god to whom Odin had sacrificed his eye. His grandfather claimed that if consumed in high enough quantities one would gain all the secrets of the universe. Botanē refused to consume it. "I already know too much that I wish I didn't," he said.

Ryder sniffed Mimir so much that a purple dot stained the tip of his nose. No matter how much he scrubbed it, the dot didn't fade. He wasn't brave enough to consume it but took a quiet delight in the temptation. Just as he went in for another whiff, Botanē burst into the greenhouse.

His arms erupted with roots and soil that spilled on the floor as he hobbled toward Ryder. "I've got it," he said.

"Got what?"

His grandfather's eye widened. "What we've needed this whole time."

"At least let me help you with that." Ryder moved away from Mimir, but his grandfather swatted him away like a fly.

"Once I stop doing things for myself, everything else will follow, and then I'll be dependent and miserable. I'll become withered and decrepit. Do you wish this upon your grandfather? You wish your grandfather decrepitude?"

"Of course not," Ryder said with a grin. "I was just trying to help."

"I know you were. That's all you've been trying to do since you arrived and it's driving me *trelós*...crazy." Botanē plopped the pile upon his workbench and dove his filthy fingers into it, sorting, moving, and picking through every bit. "Ah. Here it is." He held up part of a blackened root to the light, then cracked it in half. Red liquid oozed from the root and dripped onto the workbench. "The townspeople harvested most of it, but they haven't ventured much past the old homestead toward the creek. That's where there are some last remnants of the plant used to create Summoner of Sleep. Of the original plant. Ah, such beautiful *aíma*."

"Aíma?"

"Blood. That is my next duty, my boy. To teach you Greek."

"Why would you want a plant's blood? I didn't know plants

even had blood."

"Didn't you read the book I gave you?"

"Some of it."

Botanē groaned. "Well, if you had read it, then you'd know what special plants like this do, for it is these plants with blood that resemble humans. They hear and listen just like us. They have their preferences just like us. They know things." Botanē's eyes widened, and in the light, he looked eerily like Ryder's father.

"To make the antidote to Summoner of Sleep we must use the blood from my original batch. Then I can cure the townspeople of the mutation."

"Why would you want to help those monsters? They tried to kill you. And me. They burned down your house, forced you to live in the woods all alone. They're out of their minds."

"It's not them. It's what's inside them that makes them behave as such. You wouldn't scorn a lion for killing an antelope, would you? It's their nature."

"All I hear are excuses. They are terrible, selfish people hell-bent on becoming more powerful and ageless. They deserve what's coming to them."

"You don't understand, my boy. It has to stop here...it has to stop before—" Botanē quivered and set the bloody root upon the workbench. "Before it infects more."

The words shot him dead. "Infects?"

"I'm ashamed of myself, Ryder." The old man's gaze turned toward the floor. "I've unlocked terrible secrets, and now there's not much more I can do but try to stop it in those infected, but even then," he gulped, "there's no telling what will come of it. The consequences—dear God—the consequences. They could be cataclysmic. The formula—it just takes over people like nothing I've ever seen. Even a sniff of it will infect them forever."

"But I consumed it too. Lots of it." Ryder's throat tightened. "What's going to happen to me? Will I change? Am I going to die?"

"You only need to worry about them."

"I don't understand. Tell me what's going to happen to me. To them. It seems everyone who has taken it ends up bleeding from the ear and then runs off as if they lost their sanity."

"Oh, that. What happens is something like an autoimmune disorder called Anti-NMDA receptor encephalitis. It's when your immune system attacks the body."

"Attacks the body? Like a virus?"

"That's the general idea. Summoner of Sleep causes inflammation in the brain, then the immune system attacks the brain. This process can cause temporary neurological systems such as hallucinations, bleeding, and loss of muscle-movement control."

"That's awful." Ryder paused and visualized Vern and Claude's trails of blood. "How do you know all this?"

"I read a superhuman amount, my dear boy. Plus, you come from a long line of intelligent men. Where do you think you and your father get your smarts from? He was a successful neurosurgeon after all. Performed the most advanced surgeries in the world."

"He was? I thought he was a deadbeat who couldn't hold a job."

"And my father was a scientist, and let's see...his father before him was a brilliant inventor and he published complicated mathematical books that are still in print to this day. You see, it's in our blood."

Ryder rubbed his head.

"There is good news in the business about Summoner of Sleep though. I believe Ashlings are immune to the ill effects of Summoner of Sleep, which explains how we were both able to consume it and cease taking it without repercussions. We benefitted from its positive qualities. None of the bad ones. From what you've told me, it stopped your nightmares about clocks, which was your intention. That is a good quality, no?"

"It's true," Ryder said as he grinned. "The dreams weren't

as intense after the initial exposure and the clocks stopped
attaching themselves. I haven't had one since I arrived in Marble
Woods. It's a strange sensation to be so used to something
and then have it disappear overnight. And now—" he froze.
He became conscious of a clock ticking as if the gears of the
clocks whispered a dark story among themselves. Ryder always
had this dreadful agony of feeling eyes watching him, ready to
morph into clocks. He never grew callous. On the contrary. He
grew more sensitive with the daily torture. He tried to anchor
his thoughts, but the sound grew louder.

Tick, tick, tick.

The room went cold.

Ryder scanned his surroundings, but there was no sign of a
clock.

The huge greenhouse morphed into an empty space that
was no longer comfortable. He didn't feel safe. It was different.
Smelled different—like wood polish. It even looked different.

"Do you hear that?" Ryder asked, unable to control the pitch
of his voice.

Tick, tick, tick.

"Hear what?"

"Ticking."

"No, I don't."

"Where the hell is it coming from?"

"Just calm down."

"I am calm. Don't I seem like I'm calm?" He touched his
thigh to make sure a clock wasn't about to burst through his
skin again. Oh God, what if it happened again in his other leg?

The sound grew louder. The clocks were bound to him—
their torturous grasp eternally embedded in his psyche. His
heart palpitated. If what Claude said about him was true, then
maybe he didn't deserve to be free from them. Whatever the
reason, the clocks weren't gone yet. They would always be there
stealing a bit more of his sanity with each grinding of the gear.

The same terror from his nightmares overtook Ryder at that

moment, that same desire to curl up and die like that night when he downed all the vials alone in his empty house. He closed his eyes and keeled over.

His grandfather's voice cut through his madness.

"There's no ticking."

Ryder glanced up and Botanē was holding the back of a rickety chair.

"Come." Botanē motioned to Ryder. "Sit. Recover your senses."

Ryder staggered and plopped in the chair.

A second later his grandfather gasped. "My word. It's like you've regressed all your progress from Summoner of Sleep recovery. Your bottom eyelids have drooped. And your face, it's so gaunt and lean that your cheekbones look like tent poles stretching thin, translucent skin."

"Really?"

"I understand your struggles still haunt you and affect you. I'm so sorry for you."

Ryder nodded. "Me too. I just don't understand all of what's happening."

"Let me tell you more about what happened," Botanē said, and placed a hand on Ryder's shoulder. "So, you can understand better."

Ryder didn't budge.

"I took a lot in the beginning. A vial or two a day because I liked the taste, believe it or not. But then the plant started to grow so fast that I couldn't contain it despite the trimming and pruning of it each day. That's why it grew into the water supply. I knew plants were powerful and quite cunning to get what they want, but they grew so strong and fast. One night it tore through meters of earth, concrete, and pipes before I could get to it."

"It's like it knew what it was doing," murmured Ryder.

"Perhaps. The point is that I didn't have the clock dreams like you, my boy, but oddly enough, Summoner of Sleep affected my dreams too."

"They did?"

"I had normal dreams like everyone else, but I wanted more. I wanted to invoke desired dreams. I wanted to make something that allowed me to have specific good dreams." His face blackened as if a shadow had crossed it. "But as I said before, I'm ashamed of myself for opening that gate. It wasn't worth the brief, sweet serenity I experienced."

Ryder swallowed.

"Call me a hopeless romantic," the old man said, "but I loved your grandmother so very much. I still love her so much it hurts. I wish you could've met her. With my ailing mind and body, the only way I was able to remember her was in my dreams. There was one time when I dreamed so vividly of her. Oh, I had held her in my arms and awoke with the scent of her perfume and skin in my nostrils." His eyes went glassy as his wrinkled lips formed a smile. "Oh Ryder, it was the happiest I felt since she was alive back in Greece. She was a saint, that woman. I'd do anything to be with her again."

Ryder closed his eyes and tried not to let jealousy overcome him. Julie had been his longest relationship, but there was an element of coldness to her—like she always had one foot out the door.

"The way to visit her, to relive my time with her, was through my dreams. But Summoner of Sleep was never meant for anyone else. And since it was concocted just for me, the characteristics developed by the townspeople—their feelings of youth, their abilities—they're all side effects. It's very powerful and one can be exposed to it via inhalation or ingestion. But I also suspect that knowing too much about Summoner of Sleep can push someone over the edge too. You're the exception, my boy because you're an Ashling. We have the same blood, you and I, and Ashlings have a level of control over it."

"Control over it? You make it sound like it's a living, breathing thing."

The botanist stopped his wheezing for a moment.

"Wait. Is it a living, breathing thing?"

The old man evaded Ryder's eyes, now fingering the roots. "'The world is a looking glass and gives back to every man the reflection of his own face.' That's from one of my favorite books. *Vanity Fair*—the first book I ever read in English."

Dreadful scenarios danced in Ryder's head. "What does that mean?"

"Summoner of Sleep is the reflection."

Ryder was going to tear his hair straight out of his scalp if his grandfather didn't speak more directly. "I don't understand anything you're saying."

"My boy, all I can tell you is that the answer you seek is one that will displease you, therefore I don't think I have the stomach in my old age to tell it."

Tick, tick, tick.

"There. Did you hear that?" asked Ryder.

"Yes. I heard it that time."

"See I'm not crazy. Where's it coming from?"

A bright flash zipped across the far end of the greenhouse.

The botanist tottered toward a menacing black plant he referred to as The Tower, but which emitted the scent of cinnamon. Ryder followed him and they found a cheery butter-colored canary atop The Tower's thorny branch.

"Well I'll be," the botanist said. "How peculiar it is to find a canary high up in the mountains when they originate in the Macaronesian Islands. Such a delicate bird would die on the journey or from the harsh climate of Marble Woods."

Ryder stuck out his index finger. "No. This is Mary's pet. Alfrodul." The bird perched upon it and nestled its tiny head against him. "She'd never let it out."

"Oh?"

"Yes, she loves him." He stroked the bird. "Look, there's a note." Ryder grabbed its tiny leg and unwound the note.

They both leaned in and hovered over the words that were so few yet so heavy with importance.

I'm not one of them.

It's getting worse.

Please help me.

-M. Moon

Chapter 16

Claude

Claude stood there speechless as the rays of light shone on the heavy spiraled horns that had just sprouted from his fragmented skull. His stomach ached—a deep, penetrating burn he never experienced before. He screeched and fingered the sharp end of one of the heavy twisted horns. They were smooth like ivory and stank of dirty vegetables. A cry escaped his lips and sent him fumbling forward. Then came the devastating smash of glass across the bathroom sink. His forehead split open and his legs gave out as he fell to the sparkling floor.

Blood pooled around Claude's body; it poured like thick oil escaping a drum and flowed under the claw-footed bathtub and to Vern's feet who glared at him.

"I'm a blasphemous abnormality from the depths of hell," he screamed. "A demon."

Vern scoffed and yanked Claude from the floor. "Stop throwing a fit. You're a grown man."

"I should've never taken your stupid Summoner of Chaos."

"You'll be fine," urged Vern, dusting shards from his brother. "Don't be frightened."

Claude's gaze widened with tears. "But I am frightened. I'm not a man. I'm a—creature. I was already ugly to begin with and now this."

"Remember, this is all part of it."

The world lowered to a low pitch. Then there was an unmistakable ticking. Claude's chest constricted.

"What is it?" Vern asked.

"Oh, my God. I hear them too."

"Hear what?"

"The clocks. They've come for me now."

—

Claude awoke to find his brother's coffee-bean eyes slicing through the haze of the old oil lamp. He wouldn't have been surprised if Vern had sat there all night.

"Are you feeling any better?"

Claude yawned and sat up. "I think so."

"Good. I gave you a sleep aid. I'm glad to see you're looking refreshed this morning."

Claude's hand ventured to one of the horns, then it snapped away.

"I have an idea," Vern said. "Let's go to town and share this gift you've been given. Let's share Summoner of Chaos. A great unveiling if you will." He stood and threw Claude a pair of trousers and a clean shirt. "Come on and get ready."

He hesitated a moment but didn't have the energy to fight his brother. He swung his feet off the bed and dressed without a word, Vern's gaze on him the whole time. Claude ignored the dozens of cuts from the glass. He ignored the black hole of sorrow in his stomach. And he avoided thinking about the strange ticking he heard yesterday. Whichever way he looked at it, Vern had him in his grasp.

Claude trailed behind his brother into town, but to his

surprise, people in the general store stopped what they were doing and whispered that Vern had gone too far. That Claude's neck would collapse from the weight of the horns.

Claude smiled for a moment. Was the town on his side for once?

"Come and listen, my friends," Vern said. "Let me explain how you too can have such extraordinary gifts."

One of the ladies who gathered shouted, "Why would you do that? The horns don't serve any purpose."

"*Au contraire.* The horns protect his skull, and my brother is able to adapt to a variety of environments. He is now a natural fighter and can defend himself. There's no limit to the characteristics he may develop along with these horns. Perhaps he can also scale steep cliffs, or his eyesight has improved."

Claude swallowed hard and lowered his head.

"I want to share this with you. I've improved your favorite concoction, dear friends." Vern held up vials of the bubbling orange liquid he retrieved from his pocket. "The effects are immediate, the characteristics far greater, and the withdrawal symptoms non-existent. And it's all right here in this little bottle."

"But how do you know it works?" Charles the carpenter asked.

"My brother and I are proof. Who knows how long it would've taken to develop those horns on the old formula? The horns grew right after he ingested it. And I, I can hold my breath longer than anyone thanks to an extra lung and my gills." Vern grinned. "But there's so much more I can do."

Vern went on to reveal all his powers as a result of taking Summoner of Chaos and the townspeople nodded as if hypnotized by his spiel.

"Sheep," Claude whispered under his breath.

"I don't have much of this batch left...just these bottles, but together we can make more. Lots more. For everyone to share and enjoy."

"Are you sure it's safe?" Doctor Achilles asked Vern.

"Indeed, and I'll prove it."

Claude's throat constricted when Vern started to administer the liquid to Doctor Achilles.

Claude clenched his fists and pictured the hole he'd puncture in Vern's chest with his horns. A big, bloody hole.

The ground vibrated. The world melted away in ribbons of red.

A low, encouraging voice full of fear and anger filled the bowels of the earth below.

Claude's brain pressed tight against his skull. His limbs pumped with blood like a bird's wings, filling with potency. His fingers tapped the air as they gained strength.

With an inflamed face, he found himself racing toward his brother, a kaleidoscope of colors and fury before him—and accelerated so fast into him headfirst that Vern flew some twenty feet through the air. His brother's body slammed into the ground with a tremendous crunch.

On the ground lay Vern's deformed figure with a grotesque grin. Blood drenched him like a blanket, and the townspeople's screams buzzed in Claude's ears, but triumph energized him despite the vibrations of his hazy surroundings.

"He just tried to kill Vern. Get him," someone yelled.

Claude launched into a sprint. His feet pounded the pavement, but everything was in slow motion.

In an instant the townspeople tackled him. His back and elbows smashed into the concrete. Everyone's voices were shrill and hysterical, the noise deafening.

Claude found himself unable to move and a cluster of shadows and colors clouded his vision. The cosmos swirled and gnawed at him amid the mad cries of the vile townspeople, and his heart sank knowing that whatever they would do to him would be awful.

He couldn't move from under their hands, though he didn't stop struggling.

A chorus of ticking rang in his head, clicking, chiming, reverberating. Was he trapped in one of Ryder's dreams?

Their hands tightened on his body. There was pressure everywhere.

"Yes, that is what we should do," a woman's voice said, but he hadn't heard what her comment was in response to.

"The glory of Marble Woods has fallen with this condemnable man," someone else said.

Claude's heart pulsed in his ears. He was sightless and full of fear, now hearing fuzzy, shadowy words.

"Please let me go," he cried.

Vern's voice cut through the nightmare of blurred senses. Claude listened, concentrating on his brother's words.

"You see," Vern said from somewhere. "That's the other thing about Summoner of Chaos. We can't die with it. It's too powerful."

Everything blackened inside Claude's mind like spilled ink, and when he came to, he was still on the ground; the townspeople had tied him up. He opened his mouth to scream, but no sound came.

A distant voice cried out, "This'll show him."

A blurry object disappeared above his head and then someone stuffed a smelly handkerchief in his mouth. Blood was on his face. Flesh ripped like cheap fabric. There was a weird grating humming noise. Pounding in his head. Then a dry unpleasant smell like attic dust. The sound was so loud that Claude tried to cover his ears but couldn't budge—not even an inch. Blood ran down Claude's head from his scalp. The pain exploded into the rest of his body, and he tasted metal.

His legs thrashed uselessly. Their faces were without features—all bare ovals with hair. Their demonic eyes stared, consuming him with their darkness.

His chest rose and fell in quick jerks.

Death loomed.

Claude's scalp tore under the pressure of the townspeople's

hands and one of his horns cracked and they wiggled it back and forth like a stubborn loose tooth. There was a horrible snap. He flinched. He would never forget that sound of his horn breaking off.

Claude's gaze stared at his brother's contorted face.

Someone steadied his head and the grating consumed him again. They were going to cut off the other horn. The ground was a sea of blood. Claude opened his mouth, ready to plead and beg, but Vern's face zoomed away right then and disappeared into a long dark tunnel.

—

Claude's sore, bruised eyes popped open and scanned his surroundings. For a moment he was convinced it was a cold storage room. Black blood caked the concrete floor. There were shackles too and no windows. His head throbbed. There was the scent of sour milk in the air. His fingers reached toward his horns and touched raw, exposed flesh.

"Oww." He retracted his fingers, sniffed his hand, and gagged. "It's your infected head that reeks, you dummy."

Confused and lightheaded, he looked for anything familiar to identify his whereabouts. He glanced side to side to make sure he was indeed alone.

There were debris and scraps of frayed carpet that covered parts of the concrete floor, boarded windows, and rotted furniture in an enormous pile just out of reach. In the corner sat a battered wine rack covered in dust. There was a dark, cobwebbed archway that led upstairs to a cellar door. He stared at it in disbelief.

Claude had been in Vern's basement once but under much cheerier circumstances—to retrieve a bottle of blackberry wine to celebrate his first night in Marble Woods.

The house was a prison. The scenario deadly. His brother meant him real harm now. The realization choked him, as did his claustrophobia. His teeth chattered. He sobbed nonstop, calling out Vern's name. Calling for help. Calling for someone to save him. Calling for God to forgive his sins, but only his sad, desperate voice echoed through the cold cellar.

Something crinkled on his chest. He looked down at the piece of paper pinned to his bloodstained shirt. He wiped away a tear and steadied his gaze.

As of today, your Summoner of Sleep and Chaos have been revoked and assistance with withdrawals will not be granted.

As of today, your horns have been singed and will never regrow.

As of today, this will be your new home.

As of today, you are without family.

As of today, you will pay dearly for what you did.

~V.

Chapter 17

Mary

With every whistle of the wind, every rustle of the leaves, and every yowl from the town's feral cats, Mary's soul flooded with both excitement and dread.

Was that Ryder coming? Did someone know she wasn't taking her dosages? Was that Vern with another gift? Had Vern found the note? Would Alfrodul remember his training and return home as planned?

She couldn't take another second of her rambling mind, so she poured herself a shot of whiskey and threw it back in one gulp.

Mary strode into the living room, delighted by the warmth spreading through her chest, and settled herself in a cozy chair. She clicked on her lamp and tried to read a book. For a while, she couldn't retain the words she read. Mary was too disturbed by the wind sweeping over her chimney. When the whistle of the furnace turned on, she tried not to listen to its incessant noise. The rain beat on the window next to her. The walls closed in. The same noises repeated, only louder. All sounds combined into one monstrous roar.

"Quiet." She slammed down her book.

The back door lock clacked.

Her heart paused.

It squeaked open.

"Who's there?"

A petite figure entered the parlor on a breeze of lavender and fresh rain. Her shiny blue gaze landed on Mary, and one short glance communicated all her frustrations. "Where have you been, Mary? I've been calling you for days and knocking on the door. Is everything okay?"

Mary eyed the phone she had taken off the receiver, sighed, then raised her book. "I'm fine and just want to be left alone."

Mother scoffed and crossed the floor. She grabbed Mary's book from her hands and set it on the table. "Look at me when I'm talking to you."

Mary got up. "I'm fine, and I told you not to use the key unless it's an emergency."

"Well, when you don't respond to your own mother, it is an emergency," she said. Mother approached the mantel and ran her pointy index finger across it. "I see you haven't been cleaning much either."

"Please, Mother—"

"You're so rude for missing the town functions, Mary, especially the distribution of Vern's new tonic, Summoner of Chaos."

"What? He made another tonic?"

"Yep, and everyone's worried about you. It's very unladylike to behave like this. You've caused me tremendous embarrassment in the Ladies Exchange Group. Your shoddy work already distressed me, but then you go on and miss the last two meetings with no explanation."

Mary stood and stared at the floor like a daydreaming child. All she could think about was Ryder. She couldn't wait to climb into the guest bed tonight and inhale his musk left on the sheets.

"Mary. Are you even listening to me?" Her mother shouted and flung her arms out. "What's the matter with you? You look paler than usual. Are you sick?"

"No."

"Then what's wrong with you?"

"Please just leave me alone," Mary whispered.

"But why? What happened? Are you still thinking about that odd man who stayed here and then disappeared?"

"Look, I just want to be alone. I want some privacy. I'm asking you nicely. Please leave."

"No." Her mother's nostrils flared like a rabbit's. "Not until you talk to me and help me make sense of your behavior."

"Fine," Mary said. "You want to talk, then let's talk. Tell me why we never left Marble Woods when we had a chance? Why didn't you take that job all those years ago? My life could've been different. Better."

"Is that what this is about? You want to leave Marble Woods again?"

"Of course. I hate it here and always have. You know that I hate it here, but you won't let me leave."

"We've been over this a million times. Our family roots are here, Mary. And who would take care of me if you left? You know that Doctor Achilles said the cancer came back much worse this time."

"I know. I just wish I at least had a choice in the matter. I think I could've had a wonderful, exciting life if I had the opportunity."

"Where would you even go? You have no money or contacts outside Marble Woods. Where would you sleep? How would you get food? I'm telling you. It's best just to stay."

"That's my point. I'm trapped."

Tears came to her mother's eyes. "I don't know what's going on with you lately, Mary. You've changed since that outsider came here. Have you even been taking your doses?"

"Yes, Mother," Mary fibbed.

"Well, it's all such a pity and quite embarrassing, but what can I do?"

"You can leave and put your key on the table on your way out."

The moment her mother turned away from her, the sharp pain of regret stabbed Mary's chest.

The back door slammed and rattled Mary's dollhouses and the golden horse picture.

Her muscles ached. Dealing with the townspeople weighed on her chest and exhausted her. She turned. In the slant of light reflected from the reading lamp, Alfrodul's empty gilded cage glistened. God, she missed him.

Mary sighed and picked up a blanket from the back of the chair and wrapped it around her shoulders, then walked to the window. She peeked through the curtains and saw Emelda and Charles in the street. They were huddled under a cheap polka dot umbrella. Emelda wore a long floral dress and her hair was swept into a tight bun. Charles was still in his brown jumpsuit, with his hair disarranged. Their complexions glistened with a fishy gelatinous sheen.

Mary's gaze swept across the little houses that lined the cobblestone street and directed her to stare at the sky. She wished she could drift away like a storm cloud. Light, free, endless. It was there in the high gray clouds that a yellow dot zipped across the sky.

Her heart stopped.

"No, no, no. Why are you traveling in the opposite direction I trained you to fly?"

Mary burst into tears right as a tingling sensation enveloped her, then the colors beige, black, maroon. She frowned. Who was it? Which direction were they heading?

Knocks erupted from the front door. She jumped and knocked over an antique vase full of tulips on the table next to her.

Shit.

She skirted around the mess, hurried to the door, undid the metal latch, and pressed her face to the opening.

"Hello, Mary," Vern said with an enormous grin, a giant bouquet of roses covering his face. "Is everything all right? I saw your mother rush away and just now I thought I heard a scream."

"I'm fine," she answered. "Busy."

"You are so beautiful."

Mary remained still. "What do you want, Vern?"

"These are for you." He held out the bouquet, but she didn't open the door further or make any movement to receive them.

"Thank you, Vern, but I already told you I'm not interested and don't wish to receive any more gifts. My house looks like a funeral parlor."

"Then I give them to you as a friend. They are too beautiful to go to waste. Please at least look at them."

She examined the black roses with delicate crimson borders. "What unique flowers."

"They're from Turkey. They bloom dark red during the spring and change to black during the summer. Do you like them?"

"The roses are very pretty, but I beg you to stop wasting your money on expensive gifts for me."

"It's not a waste if they bring you joy. Will you please take them and enjoy them?"

"This is the last time." Despite his rugged handsomeness and the closeness of their perceived ages now, she still despised him. "Vern, I've told you before that you're much too old for me. You're my grandfather's age whether you look it or not. I'm accepting them as a friend, so after this, no more flowers, okay?"

"No more flowers."

"And no more gifts."

He smiled. "I promise."

She opened the door just enough to grab the bouquet. "Thank

you," she muttered in a most unappreciative tone, despite the intoxicating scent.

Vern continued standing there with his stupid sure-of-himself grin.

"Anything else?"

"As a matter of fact, yes. I want to show you something incredible, my dear, sweet Mary."

"Vern, I told you not to call me that. And it's not a good time. Can you please just show me later?" She started to inch the door closed.

"No. It can't." Vern slid his foot onto the threshold. "I promise I won't be but a moment and it will be worth it."

Mary caught Charles' concerned gaze across the street. Her gaze darted to a shadow on his roof. Another raccoon.

"Where's your brother?" she asked.

"Don't worry about him."

"Fine. You can come in just for a second." She opened the door and Vern sauntered in like he owned the place.

His gaze zipped to the broken vase. "What happened?"

She flung the fresh batch of roses on the table and said, "Oh, I was clumsy."

"Let me help you clean up the mess. I would hate for you to cut yourself." He strode toward the broom closet, passing Alfrodul's empty cage. "Where's your bird? The one with the weird name."

Mary swallowed. "Uh...he died."

"That's funny. I thought I saw a little yellow bird just outside. I swore it was him. I was going to offer to help you catch him."

She cursed herself for not lying that he had just escaped. She shrugged as sweat beaded on her forehead.

"I missed you at the distribution meeting earlier. I've been dying for you to try Summoner of Chaos. Are you still taking your S.O.S. doses?"

"Yes. I'm small so I don't need such a high dosage as others do. I had some extra, so I didn't need to come out."

As Vern started to clean up the mess, he stared a moment at the antique desk against the wall. She had forgotten to put the stationery and ink away. Was there evidence of her note to Ryder left behind?

"Writing some correspondence, I see."

The sweat trickled down her forehead and she pulled her braid in front of her face. "Vern, please, I have things to do. Will you please just show me what you wanted to show me?"

"Very well. I have a new characteristic that I thought you'd like to witness."

She leaned against the wall and rolled her eyes. "Okay. Show me."

"Well, there's my extra lung and the fact that I can hold my breath longer than anyone in existence." He gestured to the fresh wet slits that curved down the side of his thin neck. They were so cavernous they split his neck as they opened.

She gasped.

"It's all thanks to my new concoction, but that's not why I came here. I came to show you something even more remarkable. It's not so much a trait I can show, though. More like it's something I can smell."

"Good for you, Vern."

"Mary, I can smell everything, like all the ingredients in a cake, for example. Each ingredient is distinct. Vanilla. Sugar. Baking powder. I was able to figure out the secret ingredient in Emelda Berry's famous cookies that she makes once a year for Halloween. It's butterscotch, by the way. I can smell so many other things too, like which part of town someone just came from." He sniffed her. "I can smell what you ate for lunch even. Personally, I don't like turkey."

"Now please, I have work to do."

"Wait a minute. I'm not through. I can smell things in people too, like if someone is sleeping. If they are scared. Excited. Happy." He gestured to his nose. "I can smell everything."

The blood rushed to her heart as Vern towered above her. If

she screamed loud enough, would Charles hear her from across the street?

"I can even smell when people are telling the truth and when they're lying."

She was frozen, trapped. This was the moment she had dreaded for so long, and she cursed herself for putting herself in this precarious position.

"Vern, look, I—"

"Mary, I know you don't have work to do, and I know that your bird didn't die and that you don't have any extra vials. I'm having a hard time understanding why you would lie about all these things though. I thought we were friends."

Mary gulped.

Vern was flush against her—his hands on her—his hot breath on her neck—teeth barred.

"Please leave," she said and pushed him back.

"I don't like it when people lie to me, Mary."

"Yeah, and I don't like you coming into my home and talking to me like this."

His eyes flashed red and before she could blink his fingers were tight around her neck, gripping, choking. She groped for any object within her grasp. Nothing was there. His hands dug deeper. She couldn't breathe. Her body flailed like a fish out of water.

"I thought we agreed we were in this together and were to help each other change for the best. I thought better of you. That you were different, but you're not." He inhaled and exhaled in her ear.

She kicked his legs as hard as she could, but it was like kicking a bag of concrete.

Her heartbeat pounded in her ears.

"You're just like my brother who's getting everything he deserves now."

Everything was turning crimson.

He released her without warning, which sent her into a

painful coughing fit. She slapped him across the cheek and backed away.

"How dare you touch me," she choked. "You've no right to waltz in here and accuse me of lying or put your hands on me."

"But, Mary, you pushed me to this, don't you see? You led me on and then rejected me. I can't help myself."

"You've got the wrong idea about me. I'm not interested and never will be. You need to leave now."

"I'll gladly leave, Mary," Vern said with a look of contempt. "Right after you tell me about the new characteristic you've been keeping from me." He took a step forward.

She bolted for the door. Vern lunged for her, his fingers raked the back of her dress and he grabbed at the hem. The fabric ripped like paper and she lunged to grab a shard of glass from the dustpan.

Mary spun around, the shard in front of her chest. "I said leave."

His mouth stretched wide open. "You think you're so clever, don't you? I could've made you so happy, Mary."

"Leave," she screamed.

"You make me so—" Vern roared and punched a hole in the parlor wall, burying his arm in the wood and drywall up to his shoulder.

Mary shrieked and held the shard so tight that her palms dripped with blood.

Vern retracted his bloodied arm from the wall with a grunt. His pinky finger hung from a single blue vein. Everything else dangled from the bones in wet masses, blood and yellow-orange tissue dripping on the floor like a runny eye yolk.

She dry-heaved. "Oh, my God," her cries echoed into the icy walls of her cottage.

The gleam of joy in Vern's eyes made her shudder.

The bright red blood on his hand and arm began to sizzle. His bones clicked together, and bit by bit, the translucent tissue slithered across their whiteness, and the skin reconnected itself, then sprouted a tuft of fur on the knuckle that had been broken a moment ago. The nails transformed into sharp, black talons that could slice metal in two.

Dizzied by the inconceivable sight, Mary stumbled backward as she babbled curses and prayers before her legs gave out.

Chapter 18

Ryder

Administering the antidote to a large group of people at the same time would not be an easy task. At first, Ryder and his grandfather conceived that it made the most sense to dose the water supply, which was the initial cause of the Summoner of Sleep contamination. When they observed that not many people drank water as a result of consuming too much of the draught, they decided against it.

The next viable option was to add the antidote to the food served in the only restaurant in town, but this presented more problems than the water supply plan. Not everyone ate there every day, and it would take an enormous amount of the antidote spread across many dishes and drinks for it to be effective.

They decided to study the townspeople's daily routines in search of clues. His grandfather took to spying on people on the outskirts of Marble Woods, and Ryder was assigned to the main parts of town.

Vera was quite boring and stood at her general store counter each day reading the newspaper while tapping her foot. Charles whittled wood all day and was a little more interesting, but Ryder could care less about carpentry. Then there was Mary. Her home remained under heavy watch by Vern, so the closest he could get was from the top of Charles' roof across the street. Each time her pale, forlorn face peeked through the window, his muscles stiffened, and her note flashed in his mind. Once she nearly caught him and he almost fell off the roof when he ducked.

Ryder also spied on a woman named Emelda through her kitchen window as she prepared the sweetest cookies he ever smelled. She was a stout, red-faced brunette with no eyebrows in an old polyester dress covered with stains. A Baker's Academy Gold Award hung on the wall next to the stove. This surprised Ryder, not just due to her meager appearance, but because her kitchen was filthy. Battered pots and pans were stacked in teetering towers on the countertops, thick sheets of reddish-beige grease coated the stove, her dishes were chipped and faded, and the apron strung across her heavy hips was threadbare and covered in crusted batter splatters.

Emelda stood at her kitchen counter stirring chocolate chips and cinnamon into the batter in a large mixing bowl and smiled.

Ryder swallowed the pooling saliva in his mouth and continued to watch her stir. She left the room twice while mixing ingredients—and when the cookies had been baked and were cooling on the countertop, she left the room a third time.

Unable to help himself, Ryder edged up to the glass, squinted through the flapping drapes, and hoped to inch open the window a bit farther and reach inside for a taste, but Emelda burst through the door with her daughter in tow.

Emelda rushed over to the window, smooshed her chubby face against the glass as her daughter wailed on her hip.

Ryder ran as fast as he could and cowered behind the big gray tree with the tire swing attached, unable to inhale. An abrupt window slam followed.

After that, he went back to his grandfather's cottage and ravaged the cupboards.

"Why are you so hungry, my boy?"

"This woman was making cookies. I can't get that smell out of my nose."

"Ah, yes. Emelda's cookies." Botané smacked his fists against the table. "That's it. We will put the antidote in her cookies."

"You want to put an antidote to a transformative concoction in a batch of chocolate chip cookies?" Ryder asked. "That might be the worst plan yet."

"Oh, but you don't understand. Emelda bakes those cookies for the townspeople once a year for Halloween. Everyone eats them. Even the diabetics. People look forward to those cookies all year, and there is never any left." He scratched his stubble in contemplation. "She must be making the test batch before the holiday, which is in three days."

"Test batch?"

"Yes, every great baker makes a test batch."

Ryder stuffed half a chocolate bar into his mouth. "I wouldn't know. I've never cooked a day in my life. Neither did Julie. Seems like making a test batch is a big waste of time if you ask me."

"It's anything but. Emelda is ensuring that her ingredients are fresh, and the oven is working. With the added complication of the high altitude here, which can be tricky, that's also something to consider." Botané drooled and gestured with a gnarled finger. "It's rumored that she will eat one cookie from the test batch and destroy the rest by bathing them in soap and vinegar and then flushing them down the drain. Not even her family can taste the test batch."

"How cruel."

"We will never get another opportunity like this, so we need to take advantage of it."

"How would we even administer it though? That woman is going to great lengths to prevent anyone from seeing or even smelling her cookies. She nearly took my hand off earlier."

"I'm afraid we don't have a choice and getting caught is a risk we must be willing to take, even if we may lose a hand in the process." Botanē's eyes widened, but Ryder couldn't tell if the old man was joking.

"You're telling me I might lose my hand for this?"

"My boy, I don't think you understand the severity." He flung open the cupboard door and removed a large plastic bag containing caramels wrapped in wax paper. He opened the bag and fished one out. "If people continue to consume it at the rate they're going, their bodies will mutate and never stop. But the worst will come if someone ceases taking the potion altogether." Botanē grabbed Ryder's arm. "There's an element of Summoner of Sleep that causes the body to reverse its age."

"I know. My neighbor, Claude, transformed into a younger man. It was like he was a new person."

"That's the problem, my boy. The more one consumes the potion, the more the body changes and clings to its newfound youth, but if Summoner of Sleep is removed, well then...then the body *exegérseis*."

"*Exegérseis?*"

"Revolts. If you give the body something it loves for so long and then remove it, hell will follow like any drug detoxification. But in the case of Summoner of Sleep, well, the body revolts by reversing the aging process again and then accelerating it."

"So, if my neighbor, Claude, consumed lots of the potion and turned young, but then stopped taking it, he wouldn't only turn back to his previous age, but his age would continue to be accelerated until—"

"Death," his grandfather interrupted. "The body doesn't handle old age well, and with the sudden flush of age reversal, it will not be long until the body catches up with itself."

"That's terrible," Ryder said with a shudder. "Claude would then be forced to take Summoner of Sleep forever or stop taking it and suffer a horrible, rapidly aging death?"

Botanē nodded. "Maybe you see why it's of utmost importance to get ahold of those cookies."

"But we're not even close to perfecting the antidote to distribute in the cookies. How can we manage to do this with Halloween approaching?"

"I suggest we get to work." Botanē furrowed his heavy white brows. "I fear that the heat of baking might destroy the strength of the antidote though, so it will need to be sprinkled over the final product. I can add an ingredient to mask the taste and odor, but we run into the problem of Emelda guarding those cookies. Did I mention that she is so fanatical about them that she doesn't allow anyone to take them home either?" he scoffed. "Everyone must consume the cookies in front of her."

"Under normal circumstances, I'd say this lady is crazy to go to such lengths to preserve a cookie recipe," Ryder said, "but after having just caught a whiff, I understand."

"Come, we must get to work."

Ryder followed his grandfather to the living room, where he placed an enormous pot on a hook over the hearth. He motioned for Ryder to hand him a satchel of colorful herbs on the table, which he then poured into the pot.

His grandfather reached into his cloak, which draped and folded around him in a lavish swooping pattern as if he wore a parachute draped around his body. He retrieved a bottle from some hidden pocket and poured the contents into the pot.

"What's that?"

"The original Summoner of Sleep blood from the burned root." He handed Ryder a ladle. "Here, you stir while I gather the rest of the ingredients I have in mind. Don't stop until I tell you."

Ryder stirred the pot for several minutes as Botanē added more and more peculiar ingredients.

"Don't stop or you'll ruin it," Botanē reminded him every few minutes.

Ryder had no idea he would be required to stir the pot for

two exhausting nights. He had lost all feeling in his arm and the right side of his neck formed a kink he feared would never relent.

Botanē reached out and stopped Ryder's arm from stirring on the third day and said, "The batch is almost ready, but I need you to fetch more root blood from the original plant. One of us needs to stay here and stir and I think you could use a break."

Half-awake, yet relieved to have a different job, Ryder stumbled out of his grandfather's homestead and into the woods. The large orange moon illuminated the trees like a creepy children's fairy tale. There was a chill in the wind that made him regret not bringing a jacket. As he walked, he forced himself to look straight and not think of the mechanic's warning about the devils living in the woods.

He reached the ruins a few minutes later and gathered some charred roots from high up on the mountain. The hillside was thick with vegetation and felled logs, and the wind beat him without mercy.

He tried to make as little noise as possible, but twigs crunched under his feet, and the branches clawed at him. The trees grew so close together he could only see a few feet in front of him. Voices sailed toward him from below. He stopped and listened.

Trees rustled then stopped.

Ryder crept to the edge of the hill.

Shadowy figures stood in front of a strange new building that reared above the town—bleak and cold like a cavern but resembling an ancient temple. The back of the black building hung off the cliff, with the front-facing Main Street. An oversized pyramid-like staircase led up to its enormous doors. Ghoulish stone statues hung from hidden crevices. The structure made a peculiar crying noise when the wind blew. The air was pure decay.

Had the temple been there the entire time, or did the townspeople somehow erect the monstrosity in two days? How had they gotten the supplies all the way up here and built it without a sound?

Nervous, anxious, scared, Ryder abandoned his hiding spot behind the tree and continued to creep along the vines toward the colossal, insidious creation to get a better view of the figures in front of the heavy gilded doors.

He went down on his haunches. Sap coated his pants, but he didn't care.

One of the figures turned in his direction and he ducked behind the trunk.

A few seconds later, he peered again. It wasn't a human being who stood there.

Ryder gazed upon a sight that no person could imagine without panic, fear, and confusion. The thing surged and bubbled with serpent slime. It moved and stewed its septic poison along the concrete. Glistening saliva collected around its open mouth as it drooled. It lurched forward, dragging its spongy, tentacle-like legs, expelling grunts and loathsome gurgles. The smell of rotten flesh tinged the air.

There was a familiarity in the creature though. It was once human or had been.

The creature's eyes shifted and bulged. It was none other than Emelda, the cookie master. But her body appeared to be torn apart and sewn wrongly together again with some parts missing. Her vertebrae were stripped of all muscle and replaced with wet sacks of yellow fat. And a few remnants of charred bone hung there. Such a thing must not live, but it did. The creature's lidless eyes, despite the blood that pooled in them, were rooted and alert, scanning its surroundings.

Ryder lost his balance. His fingernails clawed at the tree trunk to keep his balance to no avail and he fell into a pile of sticky leaves and sticks. The bark sliced through the skin on his fingertips. He forced himself not to shriek.

A moment later he dragged himself up and peered through the veil of moonlight, grateful he hadn't been caught.

His gaze fell on another shadow.

The second figure moved into the misty light from the street and he was able to recognize Vera. The flesh on the side of her face was now black and scorched. Two holes were all that remained where her nose had been. The foot she tapped at the general store looked like it had been boiled and drug across broken glass. Her eyes were black and glassy, and her foul livestock odor wafted all the way up on the hill. Despite the dark ooze coming from her ears, Vera smiled as she spoke to another figure. She appeared to laugh right before a bolt of fire flew straight from her disfigured finger and ignited a bush on impact.

"What the—" Ryder fell back.

His heart drummed against his ribs so hard he thought they would break. Another figure shifted its weight and turned, and Ryder was both relieved and horrified to see who it was.

Charles' face resembled that of a bird, complete with a symmetrical and pointed beak. Blood caked on parts of his half-human skin, half-feathered face. A portion of his skull was exposed; little maggots wiggled and fell from its crevices. His eyes glowed snow-white.

Ryder tightened his grip over the tree trunk. He couldn't look away.

When Charles moved, loose, wet translucent skin attached to his arms shook like a feather in the wind.

Wings?

The three creatures continued to converse, then removed vials of orange liquid from their pockets and downed them in one gulp.

Out of their rotten and diseased flesh, new appendages bubbled and lapped, and in a matter of seconds, their deformed bodies birthed a plethora of fresh parts—slimy hooves stuck out where necks should've been, blinking eyes on their backs and faces, tails darted from their arms and ears, semi-putrid congealed jelly oozed from their orifices. There were stains of disease on their melting, transforming skin.

In their empty transformative screams, Ryder heard the pain of monsters who had sold their soul for heaven but instead found hell in their rancid, decayed skin.

All sanity left Ryder.

A demonic, rat-like growl floated up to him. Then someone responded with the phlegmy gurgle of a death rattle. Ryder stood without blinking as they communicated in an alien language until they spoke actual human words.

"Hail Vern for the new potion—Summoner of Chaos," they croaked.

Behind them, similar creatures appeared out of the darkness, and shuffled about in front of the enormous temple—masses of tangled limbs and clicking mandibles towering above the trees.

He lifted his head in confusion. "Christ Almighty."

The creatures paused. Their faces turned to him and he jumped out of his skin.

The panic in his chest scrambled and beat its claws in frenzied terror. He wanted to scream. He wanted to vomit. Before he knew it, his feet hammered across the damp ground, and as he ran, he hoped that he'd fall into some other, better world.

Chapter 19

Claude

Claude's hands encountered a concrete pillar of stone, which he used to extend himself for a better look at his brother. The chains attached to his ankles allowed him an extra inch, but the rash burned with his every movement.

"How long has it been?" Claude asked.

The glow from the ember of Vern's cigarette stung Claude's eyes. "A few days."

"Can you let me go now?"

"No. I need to know why you would attack me like that. I just can't wrap my brain around it," Vern said.

Claude hung his head. He had bled so much from withdrawals of the different tonics that he fought with all his strength to maintain consciousness. "I'm sorry," he said, his voice strained with grief. I just can't believe you'd send me down here as punishment though."

"This is your doing. You're a traitor to your blood." Vern shook his head and took another drag. He shifted into the light, which revealed shaky red slits that ran up his exposed arms and quaked like bubbling hot springs. The bulge of his extra lung stuck out of his torso from under his shirt, and the skin on the back of his hands peeled in fleshy, bloody bacon-like strips. Vern's nails had even changed to claws, rising from the ends of his fingers, and curving down and forward. "I've come to tell you that I'm leaving Marble Woods soon, but I also wanted to give you something before I leave." Vern flicked the butt onto the ground and strode through the thick, musty air and toward the basement staircase.

"No. Wait. I'm sorry I did what I did, but please don't leave me down here," Claude screeched. "I couldn't watch you destroy those people's lives any longer. When I saw you giving them Summoner of Chaos, I just lost it. Forgive me. Please, forgive me."

Vern turned. His eyes glistened with tears as three different eyelids slipped over his eyeballs. One yellow, one black, one flesh-colored.

Claude shuddered.

"Destroy? You accuse me of destruction?" Vern shouted. "How could I destroy their lives?"

"Because you transformed all of those poor people into something horrible. Hideous."

"Are you kidding?" Vern marched across the room and snarled, "I should smack you right now for such an accusation."

"No, please," Claude begged and covered his face. "Let me explain."

"I'm listening."

"I think that you—" Claude said, but the words leaped from his mind.

"I what?"

Claude waited for the right words. His face grew hot. The sour milk scent was about to make him puke right then. "I just think you didn't have to poison them the way you did."

"What poison?"

"Summoner of Sleep. Summoner of Chaos. We both know they're poison, brother, and you gave it to them...forcibly."

"You're awful to me—hateful," Vern said.

"I'm trying to reason with you. There's no need for this. For any of this. Let's get things back to normal. Please, Vern, let's talk this out like two adults. Just let me go."

Vern's lips parted. The wet gums were bathed in blood as the needle-sharp teeth emerged from them like a cat's claw. There was a single row on the top that caught the light. "You think I made them do things they didn't want to do? You couldn't be more wrong." His eyes widened to an impossible level. "They are the ones who ingested Summoner of Sleep long before I even came to Marble Woods. They are the ones who wanted more of it, who requested a better version of it. Hell, even you did. Where they could go and take it together. And the tonics aren't poison. They're gifts. The greatest gifts which allowed humans to improve. To develop an unconscionable, magnificent existence. So, pray tell, how did I destroy what people wanted? How did I destroy what was already destroyed? And how the hell am I responsible for their paths of obsession?"

"That's true of the townspeople, but I can't say the same for me. I didn't want this." Tears welled. Claude wanted to collapse. "Why would anyone want horns? I told you so many times I didn't want this, that something was wrong with all of it, but you have this crazy power over me, and you know it."

"There you go again, *Big Baby*. Let me remind you that you came to Marble Woods of your own accord. You had plenty of opportunities to leave. To not consume S.O.S., but you chose to do so willingly from the beginning. You chose to take Summoner of Chaos after watching me hold my breath and seeing my new lung. It's unbelievable that you're now blaming me."

Claude sobbed like a confused child. Was he really a monster who had overreacted in a violent rage, almost killing his brother for no valid reason? Was it his fault for ending up in this precarious position?

"All I've ever tried to do is help you, brother. Ever since we were boys. Remember when that annoying neighbor kid got a BB gun for Christmas one year and I stepped in front of you? I saved you from the bullet when he forgot to put the safety on, and it lodged in my arm." Vern yanked his collar over his shoulder to show him the starburst-shaped scar. "Remember?"

Claude nodded.

"And what about the time I stopped those bullies from beating you up after school? What about all those times I gave those snot-nosed kids a beating for you and told them if they touched you again, I'd destroy them. Or what about all the times you cried on my shoulder when Mom and Dad died? Do you remember any of that?"

He nodded again.

"Well, this time is no different. I was trying to help you. To give you a healthier, better life with this miraculous elixir, and I thought we could experience this new wave of our lives together. Just you and me against the world, you know?" Vern had shuffled to the stairway and ran his hand along the banister. "But I was wrong. I was so completely wrong to trust you."

"I'm sorry," Claude muttered, unable to move in the unforgiving chains. "Nothing is going right, and I don't know what to do anymore. I was trying to help that damned Ryder Ashling stop his nightmares. I should've never interfered, should've never researched Summoner of Sleep. I realize that now. Never in my wildest dreams did I think people could be affected by smelling the stuff. Never did I think it would transform people in such a grotesque manner. And I can't understand why Ryder wasn't affected at all, yet his dreams stopped. All of it is driving me mad, and if you just let me go, we could figure it all out together."

"If you had asked me before you meddled around with that insane man, maybe I could've warned you."

"But I did. I asked you countless times about the plant, and you refused to tell me anything. That's why I contacted my old college friend, Belinda. It's why I started my own research."

Vern's lips curled back from the teeth; the white razor-sharp teeth shimmered in the basement light. He placed one foot upon the step. "I tried to protect you again because I knew the power of this plant, but you didn't heed my warning."

"So, you do know more about it?"

"Of course. I learned about it a long time ago when I first started studying plants and herbs. I heard the reports about S.O.S. Many said it was pure fiction, but I listened. There was something to their stories. It didn't take me long to piece together that the botanist was Ryder's grandfather. That he was the one who created Summoner of Sleep."

Claude shook his head, on the verge of understanding it all. "Ryder's grandfather is the mad botanist?"

"Yes. It was rumored he moved to Marble Woods for solitude so he could meddle in the dark arts—his greatest passion. That's how the stuff was created, you know. He invoked something evil."

"This is terrible."

"Oh, I wouldn't say that it's terrible."

Every time Claude steadied his eyes and concluded there was a hoof or a large tentacle attached to his brother, it moved and changed into something else altogether.

"Quite the contrary," continued Vern. "You see, the botanist has given us a great gift. I've experienced life in a whole new way. I'm younger. More powerful. Superior. And for that, I'm grateful. I'm better in every sense of the word. Genetically superior to regular humans. I feel great. I am great."

"But something invoked by evil must be evil."

Vern laughed.

"Please don't hurt me," Claude said.

"Well, the townspeople want to charge you with attempted murder, but the truth is they've got better things to deal with, and I'm tired of being embarrassed by you. I'm tired of how unappreciative you are of the gifts that were bestowed upon you. That said, I think the best punishment is to leave you here to think about what you've done and blame no one but yourself." He took a step, slid his clawed hand upon the wooden rail, then paused.

"Please, don't do this," Claude cried.

"I'm sorry, but I've given you countless chances and I can see no other option."

"Wait. You're going to leave me down here all alone to rot? You promised me I'd never be alone again."

"You're right. I did. Remember I said I have something for you?"

Vern disappeared into the house above. There was a noise. A jingling at first, followed by the commotion of footsteps. It was getter louder. Claude's stomach turned as he imagined the worst.

A moment later Mary appeared at the threshold, bound from neck to toe in rope. Claude gazed at the fringes of her hair; the spiky, jagged ends of which now caressed her jawbone. All her beautiful hair—gone. Her terrified blue eyes peeked out above the rope like an alligator over still water. She bent forward as if to try to speak.

"See, you won't be alone now. You've got company."

Claude couldn't tear his eyes away from Mary, and he steeped his soul in her frail beauty, yet he did not dare raise his eyes to look at Vern.

Vern shuffled her down the stairs and directed her to another set of chains on the wall opposite Claude. Her muffled protests didn't prevent Vern from locking her up.

Once finished, Vern dusted his hands on his pants with a look of satisfaction. "Although it hurts me to leave you two here—the two people I've cared about the most—you're both one and the same, you two. You don't see the ultimate vision and you've both conspired against me. You're both liars and deserve each other, so I can think of no better punishment." Vern sauntered under the fluorescent light bulb. There was no nose on his face, just eyes—feral yellow eyes agleam with secrets. In a matter of seconds, Vern resembled something brand new and uncontrollable.

Claude gasped, but couldn't inhale.

To Claude's mounting horror Vern said, "Now I must finish my new batch before I embark. Ah, just imagine, I'm going to be the richest man in the world once I introduce my newest concoction to the rest of the world."

"Newest concoction?" Claude asked.

"Oh, yes, I thought I told you. It's my favorite so far. It's called Summoner of Youth."

"Youth?"

"Yes, it's all the splendor and radiance of youth and beauty in a bottle. It'll make everyone beautiful and young again. Every human has a little bit of narcissism in them and this takes care of that desire. That urge in just a bottle. No plastic surgery. No needles. No diets or exercise ever again. It's no wonder I was able to sell my formula so fast. It was an all-out bidding war in the beauty market," Vern laughed. "But I won't tell you which company gave me top dollar. Let's just say that once they saw the results, I had dozens of seven-figure offers. I've already pre-sold a hundred thousand bottles. The entire basement in the temple is full of boxes as we speak."

Temple?

"But that's not all. Then there's my Summoner of Chaos which you've seen firsthand where anything goes. You could grow a tail, tunnel into the earth, run as fast as a cheetah, grow wings. It's so exciting and my marketers are gearing the formula toward risk-takers. To those who don't know what will be in store once they drink it and delight in the feeling of not knowing. It's brilliant." Vern took a few steps closer to Claude, which sent a sickening echo of grinding bones through the air. "That one was a bit trickier to sell, but I found a travel company willing to put up top dollar for the formula. They plan to market high-end excursions to exotic areas and offer Summoner of Chaos to the clientele to experience and adapt to that area."

"How do you mean?"

"Well, one might choose an African safari and develop an attribute indicative to that area like become part lion and experience what it's like to be that animal. They could hunt and kill. Experience the taste of blood in their mouth. Get out their aggression. Climb trees and roar like a mother fucker."

"But what happens after their vacation? Do they change back?"

"Does it matter?"

"Of course it does."

"Hey, the people are getting what they want. It's like those crazy people who pay for a one-way ticket to Mars. There's no way of coming back, but it's the experience they're paying for, and that desire is going to make me so very rich."

Sweat trickled down Claude's back.

The air grew thick like cake batter.

"Vern, no one is going to want to turn into a monster. And there's no guarantee that your potions will do what you say like turn someone into a lion. Look at everyone in town. It's like a bunch of random parts messily sewn onto people. Then there are the weird slits and orifices and things that are bleeding and oozing all over the place. It's disgusting. Have you looked in the mirror lately? You're a terrifying example of what could go wrong when customers take your potions."

"Oh, I wouldn't worry about it." Vern removed a little bottle of glittery pink liquid. He downed the entire thing in one gulp.

In the blink of an eye, Vern's nose reappeared, his slits vanished, the fangs retracted, and his whole body and face transformed into the most exquisite man Claude had ever seen, yet it disturbed Claude as much as his brother's features awed him. His face was too perfect, and he was still convinced that underneath the blanket of shadows his lower half continued to move on its own.

The warm sensation of urine ran down Claude's legs and he tried with every fiber of his being not to scream.

Chapter 20

Claude

"No," he screeched. "Please no, Vern. Don't you do this to me."

Vern climbed the cellar stairs, turned out the light, and slammed the door.

The noise of the lock deafened Claude. He dragged gulps of stale air and grasped the cold wall behind him. He wept, which sent his stomach fat folds into a violent quiver. His legs shook so badly under his weight that he fell through a cloud of dust and hit his tailbone on the concrete. Was he just as useless as a bag of garbage on the side of the road?

Mary stared at him in the dismal green rays of light cast through one of the broken windows. He stared at her with caution. Had she changed too? Was she put there to kill him? Would she morph into some wretched cannibalistic creature?

He lay on his stiff side. "Mary?"

She shimmed the loosening ropes from her bottom of her mouth. In the softest voice possible she said, "Yes, Claude?"

"Are you human or one of *them*?"

"I'm me," she said, then burst into tears.

"Please don't cry, Mary. I believe you. I shouldn't have asked you that. You look normal. I just needed to be sure. You saw how Vern was a monster one second and then normal the next."

"No, it's not that."

"Well, I'm sorry I let things get this far. All this madness. It's my fault."

"You did nothing wrong. Vern is the one at fault," she whispered. "I heard what he said to you. About how it was everyone's choice to consume Summoner of Sleep. That he shouldn't be blamed for the town's decisions." She sniffled and stopped her tears for a moment. "He's full of it. I never wanted any of this either. No one did and everyone's insanity has trapped us here now."

"What do you mean they didn't want it?"

"Summoner of Sleep made its way into the water supply by accident. People wanted more of it at first, but they also knew something was amiss about it like it was a toxin or drug. But then Vern came to Marble Woods and encouraged everyone to consume it. He egged them on. He edged the bottles to their lips. Whispered encouragement in their vulnerable ears. Everyone in town got addicted to the feeling of youth, power, and change and couldn't stand the terrible withdrawals. I've watched everyone I love change because of him."

Claude's stomach lurched.

"The worst part is I've had to lie to everyone I care about. I was exposed to Summoner of Sleep once at the time of the initial water contamination. I haven't taken any Summoner of Chaos yet, thankfully. I covered my body with makeup to hide the withdrawals. Although I don't think there are any with Summoner of Chaos. I don't know anymore."

Bewildered, Claude examined the little bit of her bare skin for evidence.

"I knew from the beginning that we had been exposed to

something sinister. It wasn't normal." She went quiet for a moment. "I'm the only one who questioned Summoner of Sleep. I felt like I was the only one who knew it was evil until you came along. You're my saving grace, Claude, because you know it's evil too."

"It is evil. I feel terrible for what you had to go through, Mary." He hung his head. "For seeing what you saw. I can't imagine watching everyone you know change like that."

"But I feel terrible for you. Hearing such dreadful things from your own brother's lips. Having him lock you down here like an animal."

"It's what I deserve, I think. I never should've attacked him. I have no other family or even friends. I'm a lonesome, sad old man who masqueraded as something I'm not nor ever could be."

"No. You don't deserve any of this. I know you're a good and kind person. I know you've always meant well and that you were swept away in Vern's lies like everyone else. You don't need him if that's how he treats you. And it's not true that you don't have anything in your life. You have me. I'm your friend."

Her words cut through the deep despair.

"There," she smiled. "Don't you feel a little better knowing you have a friend?"

He nodded and said, "I do, but I'm still filled with regret. The exposure of this new potion, it's my fault. It started with me."

"How?"

"Vern's exposure—it's all because of my actions. Had I never interfered with my neighbor's nightmares about clocks and inadvertently exposed my brother to Summoner of Sleep when Ryder took the substance to his apothecary to learn what it was, it never would've infected him, and we wouldn't be in this predicament right now."

"Wait a second. You know Ryder?"

"Yes."

"And you both found your way to Marble Woods?"

Claude nodded.

"Wow. That's incredible."

"It doesn't matter. What matters is that it was my fault for infecting everyone."

"No," she refuted. "It was an accident from the beginning. Long before you came here."

"Then the botanist is to blame."

"No. The botanist was a nice man who didn't want harm to befall anyone. He tried to warn everyone."

"Even so, what was the botanist doing in the first place creating such a thing? Wasn't the botanist an evil man himself? I'm sure you heard what Vern said about him."

Mary shook her head. "While it's true that no one can be sure what anyone does behind closed doors, I can tell you that the botanist kept to himself and I never saw him act wicked toward anyone. When the townspeople went to his house that day, I went along too."

Claude shifted in his chains. A fire burned within his stomach. He eyed the deep cuts across the veins in his arms which still bled and acted as a reminder of his many unsuccessful attempts to escape.

"I saw the look on the botanist's poor face. He didn't have the sheen on his skin. He didn't look any younger. And I know he didn't want any of it to happen. I feel sick over what occurred to his house and to him." Tears welled in her big turquoise eyes again, and Claude tensed. "I feel sorry that the people here were so desperate to fix themselves. I hate what they've become, and I refuse to have that happen to me."

The room went cold and silent.

"You said you had the initial exposure to Summoner of Sleep, which I can't imagine did much. Do you have any characteristics or deformities?"

"It's stupid." Her eyes rolled. "I hate it."

"You can tell me, Mary. Maybe it's something that can even help us get out of here."

She tried to reposition her rope-covered body, which was forced to stand erect and shackled to the wall without any slack. Her lips were pale and bloodless and fluttered without words or sounds. "I'm telling you. It's stupid," she whispered as strands of blonde hair fell across her bony cheeks. "I can sense the presence of others like I can see their colors. Yours is crimson by the way."

"Mary, if you sense someone coming, then perhaps we can call for help and they can save us."

"I tried something like that once and it didn't work."

"You did?"

"I signaled to Ryder. He's still alive."

"What? How is that possible?"

"I don't know, but I think he's somewhere in the woods and that there's someone else there with him too."

Claude gasped.

"I trained my bird to fly to Ryder with a message to help me escape and nothing happened. Ryder never came. My bird never did either. That was a while ago."

"I hope he doesn't think—" Claude cut himself off.

"Think what?"

"Well, he said he suspected it was you who betrayed him by poisoning the water with Summoner of Sleep that first night in your house."

"What?"

"Don't worry, I set him straight while he was in jail."

"You saw him in jail?"

"I did. Right before he busted out, but I don't know if he believed me though since he hates me so much. We have a tumultuous past."

She huffed.

"I could be wrong, and he did take my word for it. Maybe he got the message and is working on a plan to help you."

"I doubt it."

"Well, at the very least, there's got to be someone in town

who knows we're both missing and will start investigating. What about your mother?"

"She's lost like the rest of them. Once she saw her wrinkleless face and body, she consumed Summoner of Youth around the clock. Said it was the best she ever looked and felt. Her whole personality changed overnight. All she cares about now is her mirror and once she started getting attention from that bastard Vern, it overtook her. It was like trying to talk to an addict."

"There could still be hope," Claude said.

"Unlikely. It was her idea to sell the potions so that she and Vern could be rich together. I overheard her and Vern today. She said how much she loved him and wanted to be with him. How she wanted to leave Marble Woods, but when I wanted to leave this place, she refused and kept me here to rot. She threw away her daughter for her vanity. She's bottling and packaging the stuff as we speak. Everyone follows your brother like a god. I was astonished they built a temple for a plant."

"Vern mentioned a temple. I don't understand. Why would they build one?"

"The idea is that once they share their tonics with the world, people will come here as a sort of pilgrimage. To pay homage to its gifts and partake in the tonics together. Although I haven't seen it yet, I know that the temple is disingenuous; it's a disguised marketing scheme. And soon it'll be in the hands of millions of people." Her face twisted and she swallowed a sob.

Claude sank in his chains, a searing, gut-wrenching pain tore through his insides as he stared at the locked door at the top of the stairs. Would he ever be saved from his own stupidity that shackled him?

Chapter 21

Ryder

The sky pressed on Ryder's head as he stumbled through soggy leaves. There was a smell in the air—like burned hair combined with sage. His thigh bandage was already wet and sopping with blood, but he didn't stop running or scanning the gray trees with tear-filled eyes.

Had an entire town of people turned into repulsive fiends with greasy tentacles and unpleasant trumpet-like appendages? Had those things erected a temple in praise of a plant? Had they made something that altered human DNA? If it was all indeed true, just thinking it was deranged. The more Ryder analyzed the situation, the less he believed.

He was almost to his grandfather's home, two, maybe three minutes away. His feet ached. His heart knocked against his ribs. Screeches echoed in the distance behind the veil of fog. The voices changed direction.

They're coming.

Ryder sprinted across the icy forest floor, but branches

attacked him like little daggers, which slowed him down.

If I make it to the cottage, I'll be safe.

—

"Where have you been? I was worried sick."

Ryder's jawbone clenched as the incessant ticking chimed in his ears. The gears were inside him. They would chew through his skin again. Ryder stopped breathing, stuck in the madness of his insanity.

"Ryder. It's me."

He lowered his eyes from the minaret that peeked through the tree line and met his grandfather's milky black orbs.

"You were gone so long that I thought something dreadful happened to you." Botanē shook his shoulder. "Hey. What's the matter with you?" his thick Greek accent even stronger in his worry. "No. I can't believe it. Where are the Summoner of Sleep roots I asked you to get? I need them to finish the antidote. Can't you do one simple thing for your poor old grandfather?"

Ryder fell to his knees.

"Did you forget it, my boy?"

Ryder nodded.

"Well, I suppose there's still time to gather the roots. I can get it if you stay here to stir the pot, but it'll take me longer since I move slower. I am hopeful that when I return, I'll be able to prepare the blood in an hour. Then we can go to Emelda's home tonight to add to the cookies before Halloween tomorrow. She gives them out at eleven o'clock sharp in front of Belle's General Store. Emelda is militant. She counts each cookie, so there's no possible way that we'll be able to sneak one or two for ourselves. I sure will miss not being able to have one. What I wouldn't give—"

"It doesn't matter," whispered Ryder.

"What? About getting a cookie. Oh, I think you'd be whistling a different tune if you tried one yourself. They are like the Summoner of Sleep of baked goods."

"The antidote. It's pointless."

Botanē cocked his head. "What's the matter with you? You're wasting valuable time and we must get to work. Come on."

"No."

"Why?"

"Our work is pointless because they've modified Summoner of Sleep. It's made everyone turn into something different than what they were before."

"Different? How do you mean?"

Ryder swallowed. He refused to vomit at the thought of that hideous skin that bubbled and stewed like rubber and puss and gnawed at the moon with ravenous hunger.

"How, Ryder?"

"I s-saw."

"What, my boy? What did you see?"

"Enormous, monstrous fat. An explosion of flesh—sagging and oozing...contorting and whirling like a dervish. Their flesh rippled and folded, which birthed to new appendages. Hooves. Tentacles. Wings. Eyes. Heads. Everything you can imagine." He squinted his eyes shut. "And they were communicating in some repulsive alien tongue. They made these wretched clicking noises, ear-piercing chirps, and what can be described as the sound of dying whimpering animals. Then everything changed, and they were speaking actual words. I could hear the monsters speaking like humans. Humans. But they looked so far from it."

A great blanket of fog crept into the woods right then. It glided across the dead branches and darkened the clearing. The ground became damp and soaked the front of Ryder's pants where he knelt, but the unpleasant sensation didn't justify him moving from his spot on the dirt mound.

"They were horrible. Horrible. I'll never be the same. And they've even built a temple to praise it. I'm so afraid, Grandfather."

There was no sound from the botanist for some time. Then he said, "You know that we Ashlings have powerful dreams.

You know what I did just to be reunited with my love. And you know the ill effects of your nightmares and how you've woken in unexplainable places."

"Yes. Why?"

Botanē drew in a raspy breath. "I don't doubt you, please understand, but I must ask if you are certain that you were not asleep. That what you saw wasn't from a nightmare."

"You don't believe me?" Ryder rose to his feet. "I know the difference between reality and my dreams."

"How can you prove it?"

"You're asking me to prove that what I saw wasn't from a dream? If you don't believe me, then have a look yourself. You can see the temple there through the clearing." He pointed to a speck of the temple through the branches.

"I meant no insult—" started the botanist, but Ryder cut him off.

"Don't you get it? Everything we've worked for is useless. There's a new version of Summoner of Sleep that changes people on the spot—I saw them take it—and the antidote we've been making was created for the old potion. This new stuff...it's so much more powerful. What we made will be ineffective. We won't be able to stop their transformation."

The botanist fell to his knees. "Then we're too late. Oh God, forgive me for what I have done to these people for my own selfish desires."

Ryder walked over to his grandfather. He started to rub his grandfather's back in awkward silence, though it still didn't feel like it was enough.

"No. Don't," he shouted. "I don't deserve comfort. Only darkness for my sins. I deserve the wrath of hellfire."

"For creating a plant that would allow you to visit your dead wife because you missed her so much? It wasn't your fault that it got out of hand."

The botanist quivered. "I've been trying to tell you something, my boy, but it's so difficult to confess my sins of foolishness. But

I know I must. Despite the consequences. And what I tell you this night will be a secret between you and me. No one else may ever know."

"Tell me what?"

"I'm not just a botanist. You see, I'm a magician too, and I conjured something."

"What?"

"The demon of dreams, *Trem Autem Somno*—the Summoner of Sleep. And I asked the demon to help me create a plant that I could use to reunite with my love in my dreams anytime I wanted. That's how I did it."

Ryder's head throbbed. "I don't understand."

"The demon warned me that if it granted me such a magical plant of the same name, that any substance I created from it would be for my consumption," the botanist continued. "He warned me that if the plant made its way to an unintended soul, the effects would be disastrous. But I never imagined I would be unable to tame the plant or that it would ever reach anyone's lips besides my own. But that's not the worst part. For such a great gift I had to offer an exchange."

Over the roar of his blood, Ryder asked, "What?"

"A soul."

A wave of heat rushed to Ryder's face. He stepped back and said, "A soul? Who's soul?"

The botanist paused and then whispered, "Your father's."

The news tolled in Ryder's ears, shook his bones, and struck him in the head like an ax plunged into wood.

"So, my father is...dead?"

"Yes."

Ryder fell forward and wrapped his arms across his chest.

"I was offered a choice—either his soul or the soul of someone in my immediate bloodline—and I made the difficult decision to offer your father in exchange."

Ryder staggered. Hatred seeped into his bones. "You vile, wretched, selfish old man. "I could've had a different life if it weren't for you. I had the stepfather from hell. I never had a real family. I can't believe that it's all because of you."

"I deserve that. I deserve all your hatred for what I did."

"And you did it all just for a dream? A dream. It's not even real."

"I know. I couldn't handle my loss, and I made the rest of my family suffer for it."

"You chose to sacrifice your son for something not even real," Ryder screamed at the top of his voice. "For a thought. For a feeble memory. You're insane for doing something so selfish. Insane. I shouldn't have trusted you."

"My boy, I'm sorry for my actions, but I must ask—have you ever loved somebody so much that you would do anything to spend just five minutes with them again? Have you missed them so dearly that you would do anything to smell their scent again? Just to touch them and tell them that you love and miss them? To know they're okay?" He wiped a flood of tears from his wrinkled cheek.

"No. Nobody has ever loved me like that or ever will. Not even my wife. And even if I did love somebody that much, I would never kill someone for a dream."

Botanē grasped Ryder's shirt, but he shook him off and ripped his own shirt in the process.

"I was so desperate, my boy. So very desperate. So alone. She was all I ever had in this life. Those dreams gave me purpose again. Made me whole. My love for her blinded me like the sun," he said. "And your father and I were never close. We didn't get along, and I made a bad decision. Please understand that I didn't know he even had a son for the longest time. Not until he was already gone, and the deal was done. He kept me from you."

"If you summoned a demon, why didn't you just summon one who could resurrect your dead wife?"

"Resurrection spells don't work like that."

"Do you think your wife would have wanted it this way? For you to sacrifice your son just to see her again?"

Botanē lowered his head.

"I never should've come here."

"No, my boy. You came here for a reason. Your nightmares brought you here. Ashling blood is thick with magic, and our senses are more heightened than an average person's."

"So?"

"Your nightmares were part of a larger plan. They brought you here to help me because you sensed something was wrong."

"What plan?"

"The dreams were telling you I would need you. That's what the clocks meant, Ryder."

"The clocks weren't telling me shit. All they did was attack me and terrorize me."

"No. They were helping you."

"Helping me," he repeated with a scoff. "You're not making a lick of sense. You're just answering one riddle with another." Ryder turned away with a huff.

"No. Let me tell you how." His voice went weak.

"You've got five seconds."

"They were ticking down the time for you to arrive in Marble Woods. They were sending you messages. Flashing letters and numbers. Giving you directions. Geographic coordinates. Your body was working toward it too with the sleepwalking."

Again, Ryder scoffed. "Even if that's true, then you knew something bad would happen. You shouldn't have conjured a demon from the very beginning, but you did anyway."

"As much as I want to, I don't deny it." He reached out to touch Ryder's shoulder with his thin wrinkled hand.

Ryder jeered away.

"Your dreams led you here for a purpose. You must listen. I even left clues along the way for you to find. The bricks from my old homestead had a message, but you never found it."

"I don't believe anything you say anymore."

"Believe what you will, but I beseech you to listen to me, for I speak the truth. Your dreams brought you to Marble Woods."

"I've always had those dreams." He spun around with wild eyes. "For as long as I can remember. That would mean you did all this decades ago. That you knew you would need my help all these years later, and for what purpose, God only knows. What are you a fucking psychic too?"

"I did know what the future would hold, but it's more complicated than that. To a degree. Didn't your dreams start after your father disappeared? When you were a boy, no? Your dreams were sending you the signals to come here all along. Whether you realize it or not, how you came here was a conscious act. You navigated the signs you saw while you were sleeping."

Ryder was so confused and now second-guessed when his dreams had started. Although his father disappeared when he was six, he remembered having the dreams before that, but now he wasn't so sure. Hadn't he had the dreams the night of his fifth birthday? He remembered his birthday cake and the spinning clocks that made him vomit vanilla cake and miss his school's play of The Nutcracker. But was that really his fifth birthday?

Had there indeed been letters and numbers on the clocks, giving geographic coordinates? Did the clock hands change as if counting down the time to the exact moment he came to Marble Woods? Ryder then contemplated how someone like Claude found the map to Marble Woods without the clock dreams. Was it by pure coincidence or something more?

Whatever the truth of the matter was, his head spun, and it was all due to his grandfather's selfish actions that had cursed him with nightmares of clocks—a plague of pain and torture had followed him his entire life and left a permanent scar.

"I was cursed with nightmares my entire life because of you. Everyone I ever loved has left me as a result. My father was robbed from me. You killed your son. How the hell do you live with yourself?"

Botanē's face creased as he stood with an awkward hunch.

"It's not easy to be me, and I'm sorry," he whispered. "Please tell me how I can make it up to you. I'll do anything for your forgiveness."

It took all of Ryder's strength to not strike the old man down right there for asking such a stupid question.

"Make it up to me?" His face was numb as if someone had plunged him into ice water. "By doing what? Summoning another demon? Apologizing a thousand times? None of it will bring my father back. None of it will give me back the life I could have had," he murmured through gritted teeth, "and who knows what you'd do to me if given the chance."

"Please—"

"No. This is your mess," Ryder cut off his grandfather. The vile smell of the creatures wafted across the woods and he gagged a little. "I'm leaving this godforsaken place. And when those monsters you created come for you, I won't be here to help."

Ryder turned on his heel and headed toward the forest, but his grandfather's strained pleas pelted him like stones. For a moment, just a moment, his heart ached, and his gaze darted behind him.

His grandfather's eyes brightened, but Ryder's anger boiled and swept over any remaining empathy he had, and then he continued on his way.

Chapter 22

Claude

Claude awoke to heavy panting. The moon shone in little lines of light through the crisscrossed boards, which revealed Mary's pale face. She stared around the basement and little by little, her panting grew louder.

"What is it?" he sat up. "Are you all right?"

Mary grimaced. "Shhh. I think someone is coming."

"Who? Dear God, is it Vern? I can't see him again. I can't. He's coming to finish us off." He shook so bad his chains rattled against the ground. He took a breath to calm himself and gripped the chains to stop the sound.

"No, I don't think it's Vern."

"Well, then we should call for help."

"Shhh. I need to be sure it's someone safe first."

The seconds passed like hours as he waited for her response.

"It's someone else."

"Who?"

Her eyes widened, then squinted. "I think it's...Ryder."

"Thank God." Claude laughed, his heart beat faster under the burden of his hopes. "We're saved. I thought we'd never get out of here."

She cocked her head. "But he's...yes...Ryder is walking away from the house. We need to get his attention fast."

Cries of help and screams erupted from their lungs. Claude beat his chains against the concrete floor, while Mary screamed and kicked the wall. After a few seconds, he was ready to collapse from exhaustion.

When was the last time I ate?

"Well? Can you sense if he's still nearby? How far away is he?"

"I don't know. It's fuzzy to me. I can't tell where he is. Everything is gray. This has never happened before."

"It's okay. Just concentrate. Let's try to yell louder. Come on." He launched into high-pitched yells and beat his chains even louder against one of the concrete columns, which filled the air with great metal clashes.

Silence.

Claude slumped against the wall, broken. He thought of the misery of his life, the futility of everything. The idea of escape seemed ludicrous. His teeth chattered; half asleep and choked with tears he said, "It's no use. He has to be gone by now."

"Well I guess we tried," sobbed Mary.

The weight of his head pulled him forward, and he imagined his corpse. He'd never be laid to rest with his beloved now. Panic seized him just as white light burst from the top of the staircase.

Claude lost his breath.

Against the blinding light, a silhouette stood still for a moment, then descended the stairs.

"What the hell happened down here?" asked Ryder.

"Oh, thank goodness," screeched Mary. "Please, help us."

"We thought we were going to die," croaked Claude, his throat never dryer. "Please help free us. The key is over there." He gestured to the metal hook hidden in the shadows.

Ryder flicked on another light at the bottom of the stairs, which illuminated the entire basement. He gasped.

"Why are you coiled in rope from neck to toe?" His head swiveled to Claude. "And why are you chained up and covered in blood?"

"Please just free us and we'll explain," Claude said as he held out the chains like some pathetic beggar on the street.

Ryder sneered. "Why should I trust that you aren't monsters like the rest of them? The last time I saw you, Mary, I was drugged in your home and woke up in jail. And the last time I saw you, Claude, you wouldn't free me from jail and then stood there and watched as your insane brother and the town beat the shit out of me."

"I know the circumstances are bad, but I assure you that we're not like the rest of the townspeople. I mean look at me." Claude inched toward the light. "If I had superhuman strength or abilities would I look like this or be chained up down here in this hellhole?"

"We're human. Normal," added Mary.

"You've got to free us before Vern comes back, or the others find us. You're our only hope, Ryder," Claude said.

Ryder didn't reply or give any sign of what he would do. He just shifted a cautious gaze between each of them and then stepped back.

Claude's heart was going to explode if he had to stay shackled another second. "Don't leave us down here. We'll do anything. Please."

Seconds ticked by. Then minutes.

Ryder sighed, then made his way over to the key hook near the wine rack. He bent down and freed Mary from the shackles first, then worked at the knots. A moment later, he began the tedious task of unraveling the coarse wiry rope embedded in her flesh. Bit by bit, the harsh basement light exposed her scratched and swollen red-purple skin. She wore the sweaty remnants of a dress, and Claude recoiled each time another layer of rope was undone. Mary's face remained like stone despite the pain.

Ryder finished untying her, took her hands, and rubbed them in his own. "You're safe now," he said, and took off his jacket to swaddle her. He helped her to a chair.

He made his way over to Claude next.

"The last time we met I was the one imprisoned and you refused to help me, and now here we are. My, how the tables have turned. Tell me, then, even if you're not one of them, why should I release you when you refused to help me?"

Claude's blood boiled. He wanted to howl and scream. To strangle Ryder's thin little neck with his bare hands and watch his face turn purple, but that wouldn't help him at this moment. He had to play this game to win his freedom. "I couldn't help you before because Vern would've killed us both. You now have the power to help both of us. To help countless others."

Ryder jangled the keys, then his face softened.

Claude fought the urge to attack him once freed and rose to his feet. "Thank you. You won't regret this."

Ryder cocked his head and studied Claude's face. "You know you're missing a tooth and your entire body is covered in cuts. And what the hell happened to your head?" he said, restraining a gag.

"Vern," said Claude.

"Vern? I can't believe anybody could stoop so low as to tie up his brother like this. That's horrible. And why would he do such a thing to you, Mary?"

Claude rubbed his frozen flesh. It was the color of slate, while Mary's skin was bright and pink. He moved toward Ryder, but he was so fatigued that he strained just to stand. He stretched his arm to the wall and hunched into the rays of moonlight that scudded through the wooden boards.

"Mary didn't love him. My brother doesn't like rejection." With his remaining physical strength, he continued, "And as for me, he didn't think I'd attack him when he tried to force someone to ingest his new potion. I had big horns, like one's you'd see on a ram, which I used to plow him down out of protest. But then the townspeople captured me and sawed them off. Now my brother thinks I'm a traitor. Greed has gone to his head. His priorities have changed."

"Yes, I saw a new potion and its effect on people," Ryder said. "I'm still processing what I saw. They were all monsters."

"What if that shipment gets out? It'll take over everything," murmured Mary.

"Shipment?" Ryder said.

"Yes. My brother created two more versions of Summoner of Sleep and sold them to major companies. They're packaged and boxed and ready to go in the temple basement."

"Wait. You know about the temple too?" asked Ryder.

Claude nodded.

Mary's face was weary even though some of the color had returned to her cheeks, but the dark brown shades remained under her eyes. "You must help us, Ryder."

"I don't know what to tell you about any of this, so I'll tell you what I told my grandfather," started Ryder. "I'm not getting involved. I'm leaving this awful place."

Claude's heart skipped a beat. "Your grandfather, the botanist who created Summoner of Sleep, is still alive?"

"Wait. How did you know that my grandfather is the botanist?"

"That's the other presence," chimed Mary. "Your grandfather."

Ryder took a step back, brows furrowed.

"We wondered what had happened to you that day you broke out of the jail. You disappeared right before everyone's eyes," Claude said.

"It's true, Ryder," Mary said. "We thought you were dead, but I thought I sensed your presence. That's the only characteristic I developed from Summoner of Sleep. I knew you were alive, and you were with someone else. I just didn't know who. Now I know it was your grandfather who saved you."

Ryder straightened. "So you *are* one of them."

"No. That's why I sent you the note. I haven't changed much at all and I haven't taken anything since," Mary said. "Did you ever get my note?"

He nodded. "I did, but there was not much I could do since it was under such heavy watch."

"Where's your grandfather now? Is he safe?"

"I never want to speak about him or see that man again as long as I live. As I said before, I'm leaving this place. Alone."

"I don't understand," whimpered Claude. "How can you leave at such a critical time like this? What if those shipments go out?"

"I have every right to leave. If you knew what my grandfather did, then I think you'd understand and just let me go in peace."

"What did he tell you? Did he tell you why or how the plant was acquired?"

"Yes."

"Tell us," Claude said.

"No. I told you I'm not getting involved."

"But you're already involved," Mary said. "We need your help, Ryder, since you know so much. We need to figure out a way to stop Vern from infecting anyone else. We don't even know what the long-term effects are. Please you've got to—"

"I saw blood on Vern's lips," interrupted Ryder.

The room went silent and cold.

Claude's head swiveled. "Blood?"

"Yes. Before when I was watching the town, I noticed Vern developed certain predatory attributes like fangs. He was so strong and fast. Then there were the growls like a wolf." He swallowed hard. "Blood was smeared across his jaw and his gums were black with blood. I heard dreadful sounds one night in the woods. I thought I heard him chase after something or someone in the woods." Ryder's face twitched, recounting the incident. "Then…a screech, cries, tearing, chewing. Dear God, I don't know if it was human."

"You see? If Vern has become predatory, that means others have too," Mary said. "They're more dangerous than ever. This is why we need to work together to stop it here before it gets out of Marble Woods."

Ryder took a step toward the stairs and rested his hand upon the banister. "The longer I stay in this godforsaken place," he began, "the more I find out things I wish I didn't know." He placed a foot on the bottom stair. "I just want to go back to my old life."

Claude shot a lethal stare at Ryder. His head ached as he studied his neighbor's shiny skin. Had Summoner of Sleep affected him? Was Ryder turning into one of those creatures? Was this another trap set up by his brother? Would Ryder tear him limb from limb? He backed away and blinked, the shimmer vanished.

Then all he could think about was bringing Ryder down, hurting him, humiliating him just as he had done. Everything turned red. The world shrieked. The air went thick and hot like an Everglades swamp.

"I think the real reason you want to leave is that you're one of them," shouted Claude.

Ryder spun around.

Claude pointed to the cellar door. "Why else would you want to leave."

"I already told you."

"You're running away from your problems again. Just like you did back home. Sounds pretty cowardly to me."

"I'm not in the mood for this shit, old man."

Claude's control slipped away. "You're either one of them, or you're being a selfish asshole again."

"What did you call me?"

"You heard me. You've always been an asshole."

Claude delighted in the anger that flushed his neighbor's face.

"You've got some nerve saying that to me," said Ryder.

"Especially after everything you did. Do you want me to tell Mary here all the sick and twisted files you gathered on me?"

A twinge of embarrassment hit him, but he didn't care. He had enough in his arsenal to fire back. "Doesn't change the fact that's why your wife left you."

Ryder's nostrils flared.

"Doesn't change the fact why you lost everything you cared about. You've treated everyone like garbage who didn't contribute to your personal gain, including me. You came here to try and escape from your self-loathing, and now you're leaving again. You're going to leave when others need you. You're running from yourself. Typical asshole behavior."

Ryder was on top of him in less than two seconds.

Claude's nails raked across his neighbor's face, just missing his eyes. Ryder dug his fingers deep into Claude's scabbing horn stumps, and he shrieked as blood rained across his face. The rest happened with tremendous speed.

Something shattered in between them.

"Stop it," Mary screamed, her wild eyes with specks of gray were full of determination and sensuality and lit up the pale complexion of her thin face. "No one is leaving until we contain this madness starting with you two."

Ryder drew back, his face expressionless.

Claude released his grip from Ryder's shirt. As he stood in the darkness trying to catch his breath, he stared with disdain at the man whom he despised. The man who was the cause of this turmoil and suffering. He would do whatever it took to exact revenge on his neighbor. Whatever it took.

Chapter 23

Mary

Mary shivered underneath the dusty flannel blanket Ryder had placed around her as she stared at the limp flowers in the cracked vase on the kitchen table.

"Are you sure you're okay, Mary?" he asked.

She hated that he had to see her like this. So ugly and vulnerable. She nodded. "I just need to rest. And if there's any hot water left when Claude is finished, I'd like a soak too."

"You could've taken a bath first, you know. Ladies should always go first."

"The withdrawals affected him much worse though and his horns look infected. I couldn't stand for Claude to sit a moment more covered in filth and blood. Not to mention that we found his old college friend stuffed in the pantry."

"Yeah, that was rough. What a way to spend Halloween."

"I'll say. That's the first dead body I've seen, you know." She stared off into space for a moment and recounted her extreme dislike of horror movies because they rattled her to her core and she couldn't go to bed without a light on for a month after she watched one.

"Me too. I still can't get over the fact that Vern killed her like that. Those puncture wounds. Jesus. He's an animal."

"I know."

"I'm sorry you saw it first. If I had come up before you, I might've been able to prevent you from seeing it," Ryder said.

"It's fine. I was bound to see a dead body at some point, so I might as well get it over with, right?"

Ryder shrugged. "You've got an interesting way of looking at things." He smirked. She couldn't help but giggle.

"What's so funny?"

Mary gestured. "Why is your nose purple?"

"Oh, that." He rubbed the spot. "It's from one of my grandfather's flowers. I can't get rid of the stain from when I sniffed it."

"So, I guess you're someone who likes to stop and smell the roses...*literally*."

"Yeah, I guess so."

Mary scooted out of her chair, went to the cupboard, and rummaged around. She returned with a bottle of rubbing alcohol and a rag and wiped off Ryder's nose.

"There. All gone."

He flushed. "Thanks."

"I just don't understand something," she said and returned to her seat. "Why would someone *like you* come to Marble Woods?"

"Someone like me?"

"You know...*important*."

Ryder laughed. "And what makes you say that? You don't know anything about me."

"I guess I can tell by looking at you."

"Is that so? Is that another one of your magical abilities thanks to Summoner of Sleep?"

"No, I've always possessed this skill."

"Oh, so you admit to judging a book by its cover, then?"

"Yes," she beamed. "People have told me I'm a good judge of character."

He leaned forward and rested his elbows on the table. "Oh really? Then please tell me. Who am I?"

"Well—" She wavered on whether to be honest with him.

"Go on. I can take it. Who am I?"

"Well, I get the sense that you were a very valued man with an important job."

"Fair enough. What else?"

"I think people looked to you for advice and trusted you. I think that you were wealthy and had everything your heart desired." Her gaze zigzagged across his body, then she frowned. "But I don't think any of it made you happy. And I think you somehow lost it all."

"I hope you don't believe that garbage Claude spewed about me. I wasn't running from anything."

Mary shrugged. The lime wallpaper added cheery brightness to the defunct, empty kitchen.

Ryder reclined in the chair. "I'm curious how you came to assume all that about me. I've told you very little about myself. Just the bit about the horse. Plus, I look like hell, so how did you come to make such a harsh judgment about me?"

"Don't know," she said, distracted by the running water from the bathroom down the hall. "I don't think there's a single defining thing you said or did, I guess I just feel it."

"You've got me pegged. Congratulations. But I want to set the record straight that I wasn't running from anything back home like Claude accused. I came to Marble Woods for other reasons."

"Then why are you leaving Marble Woods so soon? Seems like you're pretty close to figuring it all out, don't you think?"

"I know you're right." He paused. "Hey, remember how I told you I was afraid of clocks?"

She nodded.

"Yes, well, I'm afraid of clocks because I've had nightmares about them for as long as I can remember. They attack me. They attach themselves to me from their dream world, and when I wake up, they are in the bed with me. Once, one shot out of my leg like a freakin' newborn baby. My thigh still hurts from it."

Her heart sank. "You poor man. Claude mentioned how you were neighbors and that you had nightmares about clocks, which explains why you didn't like my clock in your room."

Ryder's eyes fluttered. "I just can't get over that you believe me. Nobody does."

"Why wouldn't I? You seem like someone who doesn't play games."

"You're right, I don't."

"So then tell me where the clocks come from," Mary asked. "How could something from a dream come back with you?"

"I don't know. The most bizarre thing about all this is that my grandfather is the reason I've had these dreams."

"But I thought you never met him until coming here."

Ryder's black brows clenched together, which formed a perfect vertical line down the middle of his forehead. "That's true. He was trying to get me to come here."

"I don't understand."

"You see, taking Summoner of Sleep, which Claude gave me, somehow stopped my dreams. Before that, I had tried everything to stop them, but nothing worked. I was good friends with Vern and went to his apothecary all the time in search of a cure. My w—" He cut himself off. "But um, coming to Marble Woods stopped my dreams because I had followed the path my grandfather provided. So, I guess in a nutshell I came here to get answers about something unexplainable."

They exchanged an electric glance.

"Then you need to stay."

"Maybe."

Her heart skipped a beat. She wanted to tell him she was glad to have met him despite the peculiar circumstances, then he added, "But if I could do it over again, I wouldn't have come here at all."

"Oh?" she questioned. "Why?"

"I would've done things differently. Been a better person if I could." He repositioned his long legs and continued, "I'm going to make it right though once I get back home. I still have some money saved and could find a new job. I was a damn good lawyer if I do say so myself. I've already been thinking of the gala I'll hold and who I'll invite. I think some of my old friends will come if I just apologize for my behavior of just disappearing like that. I miss my old life and loved so many things about it."

Mary remained silent, her gaze cast down as she listened to him drone on about his former life and all the wonderful things that awaited him there. Why had she ever entertained the idea that she could cross into that glorious world? He was just like her old friends who had come back to Marble Woods to reveal their incredible lives only to leave again. Even after she successfully guessed the details about his former life, she didn't understand why he would even consider going back if none of it made him happy.

Claude entered the kitchen clean and refreshed, and Mary jumped to her feet and hurried to the bathroom to cry.

—

Mary gathered lighters, rags, a box cutter, and a few bottles of old liquor from the basement and loaded up the leather knapsack she had found near the door. She swung it over her shoulder at the same time Ryder did with his knapsack.

She followed Ryder and Claude through the gray woods, still trying to think of a better solution to stop the potion distribution, but her mind blanked.

As she walked, she envisioned the temple Ryder and Claude had talked about. Perhaps it looked like a traditional Catholic Church—a moderate-sized brick building with colorful stained-glass windows and some religious symbols affixed to the roof.

But when she made it to the clearing, she squinted. The temple soared above the small black town of Marble Woods and looked like a monument erected for Satan himself.

Everything about the structure screamed malevolence with impossible angles and height, and the closer she got to it in the dead of night, the more her bruised skin crawled. The black structure swelled to the purple heavens and dark smoke rose in coils from its steeple roof—all sulfur and decay. Thin, round towers protruded around the monstrosity, connected by fortified, solid walls made of black stone.

"No, it's impossible," Ryder said.

She turned. "What is it?"

"The t-temple," he stuttered. "It's different than the last time I saw it. Look. It's changing right now."

Mary glanced at the temple again. Her eyes widened as it surged and grew on its own, and its minarets stretched like the claws of ghosts into the clouds. Taller and taller. New sections grew at unusual angles, and each time they did, a strange hammering boomed through the town.

Mary took a few steps closer to the edge of the mountain.

"The back of the temple stands flush against the cliff, which is unscalable," Ryder said. "Looks like there are no windows, so the only way into the temple is to climb the staircase and enter through the front doors."

"But we'll be seen," Mary said. "Are you sure this is such a good plan?"

"That's a risk we have to be willing to take. It's like you said, we need to stop this, and the only way is to get inside that temple."

"I think it'll be fine," Claude said. "It's the middle of the night so no one should see us."

"But what if the temple changes while we're inside it?" Mary asked with a tremble. "I think this is a bad idea. What if we can't get out?"

"We just need to remain calm," Claude added. "We all must

remain calm."

"As much as I hate to agree, Claude is right," Ryder said. "I think that we need to focus on the main reason why we came here."

Mary swallowed her fear, no longer feeling the rest of her body.

"Come on," urged Ryder and took her hand.

She passed the collapsed storefronts during the walk, skirted mounds of yellowed bones and empty bottles of Summoner of Sleep and Summoner of Chaos.

Pigs.

Mary's eyes narrowed at the gnaw marks on the bones. Flowers bloomed in the bloody cracks of the cobblestone. She strode up to one of the piles in front of the general store, but the stench made her vomit in the street. Then there were the beheaded monsters on stakes left deliberately in her path.

What happened here?

"Come on," Ryder said again. He tightened his grip around her fingers. "It's okay."

She headed toward the giant temple steps and climbed.

You can do this. Don't look behind you. Concentrate on reaching that door and stopping this madness.

The steep porphyry steps strained her legs, for the height of each one seemed fit for a giant, but what alarmed her the most was that her footfalls were soundless.

A thunderous shriek boomed from inside the temple just as they'd reached the top of the flight.

"What was that?" She jumped off the steps and into the thorny shrubs on the steep hill alongside Ryder and Claude.

Her eyes scanned the town behind her as she clung to the branches. Her arteries throbbed like deafening music and filled the whole forest.

They'll see me. I'm dead.

A silhouette appeared in the middle of the street below.

Whoever it was, they shook. Their clothes hung in tatters.

The person mumbled words that didn't make any sense and pointed a haunting, bloody finger at the gleaming temple.

Who is that? What are they saying? Can they see us?

Under the full silver moon, something approached the person on all fours from behind—A repulsive, yellow-eyed, brittle-haired creature that looked more dead than alive. The thing's white, rotted flesh melted so far down its sides it dragged on the concrete. It emitted an unexpected rattle that grew louder as it approached its prey.

Mary perked up. "We've got to help them," she whispered. "Before that thing gets them."

"No," Ryder said and pushed her down.

She tightened her muscles, "But—"

The creature sprang into the air and with a single claw punctured the person's neck in one fluid motion and ripped flesh and limbs. Then the same claw parted skin and muscle, skirted over rips, drew a liver from the torso, and swallowed it whole. Howls echoed through the air.

Tears rained down Mary's paralyzed face. Her eyes would not pry away from the unfolding horror as its claws sank deep into the person's scalp. Blood pooled on the pavement, sloshing down the street gutter like a river current. The fading screams were just as horrendous as the thing ripping the head clean off and sucking out brains in its toothy jaws.

Thick, fresh gore oozed down its throat and the creature lapped at it.

If that wasn't enough to make her blood run cold, it was the watch bound around the creature's leg—the same watch she had given her dear neighbor Charles for Christmas last year.

She drew in a sharp breath. Within seconds, a nerve-shattering scream would escape her. Ryder pulled her into him and muffled her mouth. She couldn't breathe, but she could still smell the remnants of his cologne. Her entire body went into a fit of panic. It twitched and convulsed and lost control.

"I know it's a lot to take in," Ryder whispered in her ear as he restrained her, "but you've got to be calm or we're all going to die."

The creature paused and Mary's heart stopped.

It's coming for me.

The thing screamed and then turned and scrambled toward the adjacent woods.

Ryder released Mary. "I know. Charles was something else not too long ago and now, well, I don't know what he is. I'm sorry you had to see that, but that's all the more reason we need to get into the temple—not only to destroy the potions but to get out of sight of any other creatures that might discover our presence. Can you keep going?"

Mary pursed her lips. She forced herself to push past the dizzy black spots that enveloped her vision, the ringing in her ears, and the violent pulsing in her body. She remembered the mission and took a deep breath. She turned to meet Ryder's black eyes and lingered there for a moment.

The world snapped back into focus. She nodded.

Ryder adjusted his backpack of supplies and motioned toward the temple. "Come on then. Stay low."

Mary returned to the giant temple steps and began the difficult uphill journey toward the door.

As she crawled along, feeling sick to her stomach the entire time, the temple changed and moved farther away in the shadows. Had it intentionally pulled away?

You're stronger than this.

Sweat. Blood. Dirt. Pain. That's all life was in those minutes it took to reach the top.

She sighed as she entered through the great ominous door.

Coldness ate at her delicate skin. It was just like the inside of a subterranean crypt. There was darkness on all sides. Ahead there was a narrow hall that led to a small balcony. Lights flickered below.

Mary entered the mezzanine behind Ryder and Claude. Her gaze swept the extravagant hall with thick shadowy Roman columns. Had she entered an ancient opera house or cathedral? There were rows of pews, a golden pulpit, a handsome organ with enormous silver pipes, and peculiar statues hung from every shadowy ledge. Tropical tones from pink stargazer lilies greeted her nostrils. She couldn't help but inhale a deep whiff of the intoxicating fragrance. The candles danced beneath red-stained glass windows.

She found herself grabbing Ryder's hand. Not out of fear, but out of amazement.

As lavish and fascinating as the room was though, she trembled upon sight of a large shadow in one of the golden pews.

Mary ducked. "There's someone there," she whispered. "I thought you said no one would be here."

Ryder and Claude didn't unglue their eyes from the figure.

The same high-pitched screech she heard outside wailed through the temple, and it continued in short, rapid screeches.

Mary's mind went wild. "What's going on? Is it some other creature that has come for us?"

Claude towered above her, his mouth agape. "No. It's Vern," he said, shocked. "I think he's crying."

Mary stood.

Vern wore a black coat, and his hair was auburn, long, and shiny like a woman's. He stared upward and then hunched over the high-backed pew and wept into his hands.

"This doesn't make any sense," she said. "I didn't sense his presence. I had no idea we weren't alone."

"Maybe you're losing your ability," Ryder said. "Maybe that's what happens after you survive withdrawals. Or it could just be that you've been distressed and that hindered your ability to sense."

Mary swallowed.

"What's that?" Claude pointed to a golden altar in the front surrounded by three enormous marble statues positioned together.

Mary glanced over. There had been so much luxury, color,

and detail she couldn't believe she overlooked the statues.

"It must be the different forms of the demon, *Trem Autem Somno*," started Ryder. "It first bestowed the plant upon my grandfather. Look," he pointed, "that must be the Summoner of Sleep right there."

Mary's gaze darted to the statue in the middle, which was taller than the others and draped in shrouds. Its face was half-man, half-devil; its marble eyes replaced with rubies, which watched over the temple. In the statue's extended human hand, it held a small cloud, and in the other hand, it held a tiny bottle of emerald liquid.

The second statue had a beautiful human female face. It wore an intricate crown adorned with a rainbow of jewels. She was half-naked and draped in fresh floral garlands. In one of her extended hands, there was a mirror and the other held an open white box.

"That must be Summoner of Youth," Mary whispered. She then turned her attention to the remaining statue, which was a shock compared to the other two, with darting tentacles, hooves, fangs, long flowing hair, and jetting ibex horns. Each of its six eyes was a different colored gem. The longer Mary studied the monstrosity, the more it appeared to inhale and exhale.

"Summoner of Chaos," Ryder said under his breath.

"I don't like this." Mary grasped one of the columns.

"Then let's do it now while he's at his most vulnerable," uttered Claude. He reached into his jacket and removed a pack of matches and a bottle of lighter fluid.

"What are you doing?" she gasped.

"What does it look like? I'm burning down the temple with Vern in it. I'm going to end this."

"Kill Vern? I never agreed to hurt him, let alone kill him. I agreed to destroy the shipment of the potions. That's it. Killing him was never part of the plan."

"As much as I hate to say it, Claude's right. We need to destroy the temple and everything in it."

"Well, I just can't. We must get him out of the temple first."

"We can destroy the potions, but it won't stop Vern from making them again. He knows the recipes," warned Claude. "It won't stop him from unleashing their devastation onto more innocent people and changing them. He's evil, Mary. Don't forget what he did to you. To us."

Vern sniffed and paused, then sniffed again. She froze. "Dear God. He can smell us. I forgot that he told me he can smell all sorts of things. He can smell our fear right now. What are we going to do?"

Footsteps echoed beneath the balcony.

"Shhh, someone's coming," Ryder said.

Mary darted into the cover of darkness. "Who is it?"

"A woman I've never seen before," Ryder said. "With long blonde hair. She's sitting next to Vern in the pew. She just kissed him on the cheek."

Her heart raced and she crept from her hiding spot. "That's my mother. Haley."

She cringed as her mother caressed Vern's face and asked, "Are you okay, my darling?"

"Of course," Vern said. "Why would you think I wasn't?"

"I thought I heard you crying."

"Oh, that?" he scoffed. "Those were tears of joy. Although I am a man with flesh, the beast within me also lives. I'm overjoyed and can't wait until we embark on our journey and spread the good word. There's power in this discovery. Everything else is wishful thinking. Just imagine the fortune that awaits us. Just imagine the incredible life we'll live together."

She rubbed his shoulders. "Good, I was afraid you were having second thoughts about your brother and Mary."

His laugh bellowed through the temple like a demonic wind. "Why would you think that? I told you. They're traitors. They don't realize the ancient evolutionary power captured within those bottles. They're both dead to me."

Haley smirked and said, "I know, I just wish it didn't have to be this way. I tried so hard to reason with Mary, but she wouldn't listen. She doesn't understand that the Summoner will save her mind, body, and soul. That it'll take away her pain. That it'll give her hope."

Mary recalled right then the most painful points of the quarrel they had about Vern and Summoner of Sleep a few days ago. Her mother couldn't be argued with despite the evidence that the potion was cursed, nor could her affections toward Vern be swayed even though Mary revealed that he had tried the same tactics with her.

Vern took Haley's hand and kissed it.

"I can't believe my daughter rejects this new life," Haley said. "Doesn't she know I know what's best for her? That's why I rejected that job out of town so long ago. It was best for her to stay put in Marble Woods where her family roots are. But her ungratefulness during all this has turned me. I'm ready to leave Marble Woods."

"And I can't believe my brother wouldn't listen and follow the same path as me. I looked out for him, protected him, and this is how he repaid me." Vern's face contorted and he slapped a hand against the pew.

Mary sneered.

"There's nothing we can do for them," Vern continued. "I hope they both rot down there in the basement."

Mary's mother nodded. "Me too."

A poisonous arrow punctured Mary's heart. Her mother had used her talents to her benefit, working her so hard that she created poor products to get it to stop. Her mother was domineering and judgmental and there had been a forced closeness between them since they were related. Mary wanted a stereotypical relationship, but her mother was resistant at every opportunity. Her mother's poisonous words confirmed her worst fears about her remaining family.

Mary clenched her fists and said with words as smooth as cream, "Let's burn it down."

Chapter 24

Ryder

Ryder dashed for the stairs. As he descended the winding stairwell, the solid concrete swayed like waves with each footfall, and he clenched the railing for support. He was a step or two behind Mary, but her little legs moved faster than his.

His stomach ached. When was the last time he had eaten or slept? He wanted to rest, but the long, tiresome descent into the bowels of the temple was met with a locked door.

"What do we do now?" Mary said.

The smell of damp wood wafted under the door crack. Ryder pressed his hand flush against it and pushed one of the planks. The aged wood gave a bit. "I think I can break through it."

"Won't they hear us though?" Mary asked.

"You said you wanted to burn it all down, remember? We need to light the belly of the beast."

She nodded as Claude remained silent.

Ryder pushed his palm against the black paint. It wouldn't give anymore. "Shit." He pressed both hands and his torso into its damp softness. The hinges groaned, just list the doors in ghost stories. The rotten wood buckled. He pressed and pushed and when the opening was large enough, they squeezed through.

Inside was a dank, suffocating crypt of bones with sharp scrawl upon the walls. He wrinkled his nose at their pungent odor of decay. He couldn't resist touching one of the skulls, then regretted it. It had been a human being after all. There was a shimmer of light from somewhere down the tunnel and he headed toward one of the dying torches on the cavernous wall.

Ryder took the torch and illuminated the unhallowed terrain. He squinted at the cryptic writing on the stone walls but was unable to decipher anything except for the crude loops and jagged symbols. At first, it was a bunch of circles and squiggles with thick lines, but upon closer inspection, he spied three distinct symbols intertwined into one. He made out a moon sliver, a compass pointing north, and a flower—perhaps a daisy. Something about the symbol made his stomach lurch.

As he crept farther down the passage and adjusted his heavy backpack, the painted scenes grew more detailed. The aerial view of Marble Woods in its glory days with beautiful, vibrant houses and cheery people sent a shiver down his spine. Then there was the town's gradual decay with derelict houses and streets; the erection of the monstrous temple; a strange new realm built upon the old town where the race was half-human, half-monster; and a peculiar creature with black wings and a bright yellow robe towered above the others without expression. Upon the creature's head sat an onyx crown and beneath its golden robes peeked out an assemblage of limbs. The collar of the beast's robe bore the same symbol of the moon, compass, and flower.

The forms of the people in this storied history appeared to change and the winged creature hovered above them. In this disturbing series of pictures, Marble Woods was reflected in the moonlight with crumbled walls around its people. The scenes were too idealistic to be believed. Ryder reached out to touch the pictures several times, his mind was never satisfied when his fingers touched stone.

The scenes depicted a slow descent of civilization, coupled with a growing devotion to Summoner of Sleep. While he viewed the vivid transforming creatures, some of whose faces and forms he recognized now as Emelda and Charles, among others.

"Grandfather, what have you done?" he whispered.

Ryder followed the pictures all the way down the narrow corridor as Mary and Claude followed. He approached an opening at the end and entered with caution.

The room expanded into a tall cavern adorned with intricate statues of the black-winged creature, golden altars, and wreaths and vines stretching across the ceiling. He cried aloud in amazement.

The crypt was nothing like the temple above, but a hidden world of the most magnificent and disturbing art. As Ryder turned, he illuminated the cavern with his torch. Stacks of golden wooden crates with fronts of delicate glass etchings towered above him.

"There they are," exclaimed Ryder.

Mary advanced toward the crates. "It's worse than I thought. And look what it says on the glass."

Ryder lowered the torch. Inside were dozens of bottles of sparkling pink liquid with the words:

Summoner of Youth

Illuminate Your Beauty

28 bottle case, 15.5 oz.

Wick Corporations, Inc.

"I don't understand," Mary said. "How did they accomplish such a feat so fast? How were they able to afford such extravagant cases or bottles? How did they do it? It's impossible."

"Don't be defeated yet," Claude said.

"But what if Vern and my mother stop the flames early enough and there are still tons of unburned crates remaining?

The shipments will go out and infect everyone."

"This is the only plan we've got so we need to believe in it," Ryder said.

Claude's wrinkled hand glided over one of the Summoner of Youth boxes. His age had accelerated during the trek and Ryder couldn't help but pity him. How would he feel if his hand looked like a leper's?

Darkness glimmered in the old man's eyes, which burned red and ominous like the reflection of fire.

"Claude?" questioned Ryder. "What's wrong?"

His neighbor tore into the crate with his bare hands like a ravenous beast. The wood crashed against the wall and clattered to the floor in pieces. Claude's shrieks pierced the air as he retrieved a bottle and tried to guzzle the entire contents of Summoner of Youth.

"Get him," Ryder called to Mary and dropped the torch.

Mary grabbed him and Claude stumbled and fell to the floor. The old man scrambled after the bottle. It took all his and Mary's strength to tackle him.

"What the hell do you think you're doing?" Ryder said. "We're here to destroy this stuff, not consume it."

Claude choked and wiggled on the ground with a renewed determination, all the while yelling, "Let go of me, you fools."

"Shut up. You're going to get us caught," Ryder snarled.

"Just one taste. One little taste," demanded Claude, whose skin now sagged and had turned a jaundice yellow.

"Snap out of it," Mary cried, unable to hold on to his flailing legs. "Remember what the withdrawals were like, Claude. Remember all the things you told me about regrets. That you shouldn't have taken the stuff. Do I need to remind you of the suffering and pain you experienced while chained in your brother's basement? Do I?"

Claude ceased movement and lay there motionless. "I'm sorry," he sobbed. The red tinge in his eyes dissipated. "Summoner of Youth seemed to weave a spell over me."

Ryder didn't lessen his grip even though Claude no longer fought back.

"I felt revulsion for the stuff one second and then the next all I wanted to do was ingest it," Claude said. "I wanted to make the pain go away and return to my youthful state. Can you understand? My youth and looks were stolen from me, but where did they go so fast? And my brother, he's young and handsome again while I'm old and ugly. Except now it's so much worse, and every time I see myself, I've aged even more."

"Claude, I understand you're hurting, but it's no use torturing yourself," Mary said. "There's so much more to life than looks."

He subsided for a moment, then went on. "You don't understand because you're beautiful, Mary, and always have been." Claude's gaze turned to Ryder. "And you, too. Both of you have been handed everything in your life because you're attractive and it's not fair."

"I see how much you're suffering, Claude," Mary said as she took his hand.

"No," Claude interrupted her. "I used to be like you. I used to be like both of you. Everybody loved me and thought I was beautiful. And now look at me. I feel disgusting and I can't stop its hold over me. That's why I was so fascinated by you, Ryder. I saw myself in you from the very beginning. I think I was trying to save you from a lonely life so you wouldn't end up like me."

The realization that they had both suffered alone when they lived a few yards away from each other for so long made Ryder's heart ache and he cursed himself for having ignored this friendship right in front of him the whole time.

"I don't know why this is happening to me," Claude muttered. "I know why it's not happening to you, Ryder. You're an Ashling and immune to it, but why me and not Mary?"

"I don't fully understand the potion either," Ryder said, "but you did take a lot of it. And you had your brother's potent version of it as well."

"He's right," Mary said. "Remember, I had that initial dose

of Summoner of Sleep from the tainted water supply. I haven't had any since then and went through my withdrawals. You've not only had a lot of Summoner of Sleep but lots of Summoner of Chaos too."

Claude's tears glided down his withered cheeks. They pooled on the concrete on both sides of his white hair. His flesh was the consistency of ice—wet and slippery—and it permeated a sick scent of unkempt old age. "I'm grotesque. I'm dying. I can feel myself rotting away as we speak. So please, just leave me here to die. I'll hold you two back."

Mary let go of his ankles and motioned Ryder to let go of his arms. She scooted toward Claude's head, cradled it in her lap, and stroked his thinning hair, avoiding the charred stumps.

"There's no way we're leaving you, Claude. And all I see before me is a kind man with a beautiful soul."

Claude's face softened.

"Please don't forget what you've been through." She fought back tears. "What we've been through. Remember I promised to be here for you, that I'd be your friend? Well, I meant it."

Claude's eyes shot to Ryder. He bit his lip before he said, "Of course, we wouldn't leave you."

"Thank you," he whispered with a smile.

Ryder turned away and strategized what to do next but caught sight of another enormous pyramid of golden crates lurking in the shadows behind the Summoner of Youth boxes. He couldn't believe they had missed it.

As Mary and Claude continued speaking, Ryder retrieved the torch and strode toward the other crates. The glass etchings upon these crates were of a compass and the label read:

Summoner of Chaos

Adventure Awaits

28 bottle case, 15.5 oz.

Wick Corporations, Inc.

A chill shot down his spine and he said to himself. "I can't believe Vern is doing this. What kind of person would seek to turn themselves into a conglomerate of animals with a patchwork of random characteristics?" He turned and yelled at the others right then. "We don't have much time." He dropped his heavy backpack to the floor. "We need to get to work." Ryder removed the supplies one by one and belted out orders. "We've got one shot at this. We need to light everything all at once and flee. If we hesitate for a second, we'll be ignited along with the boxes."

Mary wore grief on her face like a mask. "I don't know if I can do this anymore." She looked to him for consolation with Claude's head still cradled in her arms. "I don't think I can hurt anyone, let alone kill anyone. I still love my mother so much even after everything she did. I can't live with blood on my conscience."

Claude nodded in agreement.

"You begged me to help and now I'm helping." Ryder walked over to Mary and handed her an alcohol-soaked rag and match. "We both know this needs to be done and I'm going to burn it down with or without your help."

—

The great blaze illuminated the crypt in an instant, spraying orange embers and debris into the smoky air. Ryder covered his face from the intense wave of searing heat just in time.

Mary zipped up the collapsing stairs in a flash of yellow and white.

Claude took one step and wheezed. He looked more emaciated than a few minutes prior; his large murky eyes held a world of pain in their melancholy depth.

"I can't do it. Please, Ryder. You need to carry me," Claude said.

Ryder hesitated for a second, but there was no other choice. "Get on my back."

His legs strained like noodles under Claude's enormous weight. He tried to run as fast as he could, but the ache in his thigh throbbed and bled each painful step of the way. Sweat and blood drenched Ryder by the time he reached the top of the stairwell.

Claude's cries to move faster buzzed in his ears.

Shut up, you fat slob. I'm doing you the favor.

He traversed past the dark and disturbing art and the gloomy chambers of the temple.

Smoke suffocated his exhausted lungs. All around him was black, asphyxiating smoke.

He fumbled and groped about the temple. "I'm not going to make it."

Gloom shrouded him.

Where's Mary? Am I going the right way?

A plume of smoke buried his view. Ryder doubted if his strength would allow him to continue carrying Claude or even allow him to escape on his own.

His arms readjusted the weight. The spell broke. All at once, a fleeting spasm of energy passed through his fatigued body.

He reached the mezzanine and flew through the great temple doors. With a convulsive jerk, Ryder threw himself and his neighbor down the hill.

Chapter 25

Claude

A high-pitched hum swelled, then a deep bellow like the gates of hell prying open. The structure rattled and an insidious hiss percolated. The seconds ticked by. Why hadn't it exploded yet? Sunbeams broke through the dark clouds for a second, then a thunderous burst and rain of fire ignited the sky with gold and crimson. The hot red glare scorched the trees next to the temple as the sulfurous wind rushed past Claude's ears and blew the straggling hairs off his eyebrows.

He hoped that the burden of his extra weight would've slowed Ryder down inside the crypt and forced him into a state of total exhaustion where he could leave him for dead, but his neighbor proved stronger than expected.

Damn.

Still, he wished Ryder could've been inside when the temple blew. How he would've delighted in watching the fire ravage Ryder and turn him to ash. A smile wormed across his face.

"We did it," he said.

Mary's agleam eyes grew watery, her expression uneasy as she pointed. "No, we didn't. Look."

Time broke into a million pieces.

"Oh no," Claude whispered.

"I can't believe it. How could Vern and my mother have escaped unscathed? They were in the temple much longer than us and everything was ablaze. We barely made it out."

"It's impossible." Claude's mud-covered hands shook, and he prayed some act of God would sweep his brother into the bowels of hell right then.

"Is that the best you can do, brother?" Vern screamed into the foul, sulfuric air from the top of the temple.

Claude's stomach turned.

"I shouldn't have given either of you a fighting chance. I should've slit your throats when I had the chance," Vern shouted. "You risked our lives today. You risked the townspeople's lives. I'm disappointed in your actions. My brother betrayed me yet again."

Haley nodded; her long blonde hair blew in the wind like a phantasmal succubus. "I knew something was the matter with you, Mary," she began, "but I never would've imagined you'd stoop so low. When I agreed to tie you up in Vern's basement, I knew someone would come, that you wouldn't die there. But you tried to murder your mother. You can't imagine how I feel about you right now, and after the way you behaved, I have no more empathy for you." Her gaze turned to Vern in adoration, and she cradled his face with her hand. Two long white fangs protruded from her lips. "At least I've found true love now."

Mary sat back on her haunches, her face red and blotchy.

Claude's attention turned back to Vern, who still smiled at Haley as if lost in her radiance. Then he turned and shouted, "I was prepared though. I knew that you two might try something stupid like this—further affirmation that I was right to accuse you both of treachery in the first place." Vern descended one of the monumental temple steps and flung his arms out. "Ah, but you overlooked one important thing, dear brother. I told you that I improved the potion, remember? What you didn't know is that I made it so powerful, even fire can't destroy it." He laughed. "And I found a way to make indestructible bottles too. That's my next order of business. Seems just as many people want to buy those bottles as they do my potions."

Claude's mind recalled his moment of weakness in the crypt. Had he heard the bottle break when Ryder and Mary tackled him?

Haley mouthed the word "fool." Her age reversed so much that she and Mary could be twins.

Claude balled his fists. The world grew red. He would charge his brother again for the kill—horns or not.

Just then Ryder slapped a firm hand over his mouth. "No." Ryder's voice was a raspy whisper. "You have to be quiet. Don't provoke him and give away our position."

Ryder's touch repulsed him so much he gagged. He'd never forget awakening his neighbor in the puddle of urine, drool, feces, and blood, nor the overpowering smell of death. He would never forget the disrespect or Ryder's lack of appreciation.

Claude pried Ryder's hand away. "Don't touch me."

Ryder said nothing; just continued to kneel next to him.

"I do commend you on such a creative and volatile act though," added Vern. His face was set with the righteous look of a preacher. "I'm quite delighted that you fought back. I wondered when you'd get the courage to fight me one day and not grovel at my feet. It took you long enough, brother. And Ryder, don't think for a minute that I don't know about the little plan to intercept Emelda's Halloween cookies to dose everyone with a so-called antidote." His laugh bellowed over the hiss of the flames behind him. "You really must take me for a fool."

"How did he know I'm alive and hiding here with you?" questioned Ryder. "And how did he know about my plan?"

"What plan about cookies?" a twinge of anger tolled in Claude's voice. "Why didn't we try that instead of trying to burn down the temple? It would've been a hell of a lot safer."

Ryder shook his head. "It wouldn't have worked. The antidote was for the old potion—Summoner of Sleep. The new ones are too powerful. The chemistry is different."

"We could've at least tried," Claude said. "I'm sure people are still taking Summoner of Sleep."

"I'm telling you; it would've never worked. Everyone is hooked on Summoner of Chaos now. That creature we saw before, Charles, is proof. "

"But you've all conspired against me," continued Vern. He paced along the great step. "So, let me conclude with this. All of you are worthy opponents. But hear me now upon these grand steps of this still-glorious temple." He stopped and stared right at them in their hiding place. "You've invoked war." Vern's eyes glowed red. "Wherever you three hide know this. I will find and destroy you."

As Claude listened, his body not only burned from the withdrawals but also the effects of his brother's venomous words. The dark force inside him took hold of his flesh and he could feel deep valleys of wrinkles carve into his face. It pulled and lengthened the delicate skin underneath his eyes, turning them into big swollen sacks of fluid. His fingernails turned yellow and hardened like the fingers of a long-dead corpse. And no matter how much he had washed the broken horn stumps adhered to his skull, he smelled sour milk. Sharp. Pungent. Vile. There was an unnatural sense to scratch the acrid wounds which intensified by the second. He could think of nothing greater than to slip his plump fingers into an opening of his skull, scratch with his nails, peel back the skin there, and let the blood roll down.

Chapter 26

Mary

The shouts and screams of the townspeople echoed through the streets.

"They're coming," cried Mary from the thorny bushes. "We need to hide someplace they'll never suspect. Ryder, you said your grandfather lives in the woods. Let's go to him."

Vern and Haley strolled off into the town hand in hand as the sky rained ash and embers upon them. Intoxicated with despair, she shivered. Her hands and feet grew colder.

The temple shrieked and crackled; its flames clawed at the black clouds. She glanced at it for just a second. There was some gloomy magic within those temple walls—magic that terrified her and that she had to get away from. Then a devastating eruption shook the whole town, lit the dark sky, and cracked the structure in two.

Mary ducked next to Ryder and covered her head. Strewn across her bare and bloodied knees were the remnants of her favorite dress, which now resembled a grandmother's doily. The fragments of the clothing expressed the attitude of her spirit and the situation. She wanted to cry. To scream.

A moment later, she lifted her head. The point that drew her eyes next was Ryder's solemn expression. Even in his dismay, he was still elegant with dark, glossy hair and a face of depth and beauty.

"Ryder?" Mary shook his shoulder.

His deep-set eyes stared straight.

"Ryder?" she said again. "We need to hide. Can we go to your grandfather's house?"

Ryder's head was turned toward the temple. The corner of his mouth was agape like a black hole at the bottom of his face.

"Ry—?"

"I told you," he interrupted. "I never want to see my grandfather again."

"There is nowhere else to go. I heard my mother tell Vern the other day that they pushed your car off a cliff, and I don't have a car. The next town isn't for sixty miles. We'll never make it on foot. And if the townspeople find us, they'll kill us."

Something passed across the dark haze of Ryder's eyes. "I'd rather die than go back."

The ground trembled and heaps of earth slid from the crumbling structure right then. Smoke soaked into her skin and sank into the depths of her soul. Voices rose and fell nearby. Were they laughing or crying? Whose were they? The ground swelled and groaned beneath her. Terror filled her by the second. Steadier on her feet, but still feeling faint, she yelled, "We're all going to die. Put aside whatever petty grievances you have with your grandfather and help us, or you're just going to be a selfish asshole like Claude said."

"Petty grievances?" Ryder's face went white as snow and rotated to meet her gaze as if her words seared his soul. "You assumed things about my old life before, and now you tell me that my private dispute with my family member is petty," he scoffed. "My grandfather is just as evil as Vern. In fact, he may be even worse."

"Come on." She yanked his collar. "Your grandfather didn't try to infect everyone with Summoner of Sleep on purpose. It was an accident. There's nothing he could've done that was so—"

"He killed my father," Ryder interrupted and swatted her hand away as he rose to his feet.

Anxiety grew in her throat. She didn't take her gaze off Ryder even though the clamor of the townspeople grew louder.

"Ryder, I had no idea. I'm s—"

"No," he cut her off. "I think you've already said too much. I'll take you to him. I'll put my petty grievances aside for a moment and help you this one last time, but once you get there, I'm finding a way to leave for good. I've had enough of this place and its wicked people. Just don't come crying to me when you discover the truth."

—

Mary found herself unable to say anything to Ryder as she trailed behind him in silent embarrassment. She breathed with restraint as she stared at the back of his head, all the while her mind reeled with questions.

Although she swept her feelings about Ryder into a neat pile in the back of her mind, thoughts about him blew around in her head like skittering dead leaves sailing away from the pile.

Sure, Ryder was stern and odd, but that was what she liked about him. He was different from all the other men in Marble Woods. He had character and determination, and the more she learned of his former life, the more she fantasized about running away with him, hanging on his arm at extravagant galas, and visiting exotic places she always dreamed of.

But now that these tragic events had happened and everyone in her beloved town either changed or turned on her, she had nowhere else to go and no one else to go to. Ryder had been her one chance to leave Marble Woods and start anew and she blew it. She was careless to hurt him, and she was determined to make it right.

They walked for what seemed like hours, passing gutted animals and the remains of townspeople strewn about the forest floor like confetti. Blood splashed her boots and shins as she walked. The mutations from the tonics had granted the townspeople certain abilities all right but also latched onto an innate animalistic desire to kill. It made her want to vomit, but there was nothing left in her stomach, so she just endured the queasiness. At one point she passed the mutilated face and neck of Dr. Achilles. It was the only little bit of him that still looked human, normal even, compared to the gelatinous pink mass of the rest of his body.

A chill wind sang through the treetops, carrying the scent of bonfires.

Mary's knees ached. They wobbled and staggered with fatigue, but Ryder never slowed down or turned to check on her despite her whimpers. Claude hadn't said a word as they walked, and despair gripped her tight when she looked at his maturing body.

A few times she swore things watched her from the shadows. Some with blue eyes. Others gold. Were those red eyes too?

She turned her attention to the monstrous trees to distract herself. Their serpent roots twisted and sucked the life out of all surrounding vegetation. Some were like giant octopi with groping tentacles choked with blue and green fungi. As a child, she played in the surrounding woods every day—making forts out of felled branches and climbing to the tops of the trees. All the other children were afraid of these parts of the woods, claiming they saw devils and trickster spirits wandering about asking for odd items like their jacket buttons or old shoelaces, but Mary never saw such spirits. She always brought extra shoelaces with her just in case though.

Strange birds swopped overhead. She rubbed her bare, frozen arms. Her will was fading.

"There it is," Ryder said.

Her ears perked as she approached a tiny cottage with a single dim light twinkling behind a weathered window and smoke twirling out of the chimney. The quaintness of it melted her heart.

Why is Ryder so afraid of this place?

"Jesus. Shit. Oh, God. Shit." Ryder's gut-wrenching cries shocked her back to reality and she saw him keel over and stumble to the ground.

Mary froze, unable to see the cause of his agony.

Had one of those creatures attacked him? Am I next? Were there devils?

Her gaze darted from tree to tree.

"My ankle," screeched Ryder. "Shit. Help me." His face was slick with sweat.

Mary hurried to Ryder's side. A rusty animal trap had eaten his foot and a deep tide of blood formed around him.

"Oh my God." She staggered back.

"Hurry, I'll bleed out," Ryder moaned.

She put her hand on the back of his clammy neck. She wanted to tell him it was going to be okay, but she had never seen so much blood in her life. The forest floor was black and glistened like a mirror.

"You have to open the trap," instructed Claude who appeared at her side, or had he been there the entire time? "Age is getting to me. I'm too weak to do it."

Mary's head went light.

I need to vomit.

More and more warm blood spewed onto her. She couldn't help but think of everything on a cellular level. Millions and trillions of cells spewing around her in a great ocean of red.

"Mary, come on," screamed Ryder.

"I'll try." Her little hands grabbed hold of the big metal jaws and she yanked at them with an enormous grunt, but they didn't budge.

"I can't."

"You have to," cried Ryder.

She readjusted her grip and yanked again. Mary's face seared under the pressure.

"Pull harder."

"Come on," Claude shouted from behind.

Mary repositioned herself in the slippery, sticky ground again, thrust her weight, and pulled as hard as she could. The corroded metal teeth pried open.

Ryder flinched and moaned, then jerked his leg from the jagged teeth.

She surveyed the carnage. Ryder would die if she didn't stop the bleeding fast.

It wasn't much, but she tore a strip of cloth from the bottom of her dress and fastened it above the wound as Ryder squealed. The cloth seeped with blood. Her hands went numb from applying such pressure. Claude threw a piece of clothing at her and she tied it taut, but there was too much blood.

Ryder's face was the color of milk, and he struggled to keep his head up as he sat on the ground.

"Come on, Ryder," she encouraged, "Don't you leave me. Just a little bit more to the cottage. You must help me, though. I can't lift you and neither can Claude."

Ryder groaned. His head fell back, and his eyes rolled up to the whites. "I d-don't think I c-can."

"Yes, you can. You're a fighter." She placed his arm around her neck, steadied her weight in her thin legs, and pushed up with all her might. "Come on, you can do this. Now stand with me."

With shaky feet, Ryder found his footing and the two staggered along the path.

A tall, elderly man clad in a woolen robe stood at the threshold of the dilapidated cottage. The family resemblance was uncanny—his face had the same unique lean angles, the same dark eyes full of secrets, and the same wiry, towering height.

"What happened to my grandson? I heard screams." The old man's milky eyes swept to Ryder's injured leg.

Ryder mumbled and his body collapsed against Mary. She gritted her teeth at the extra weight.

"Please help us. He's hurt from one of the traps, and we need a place to hide."

"I see. Come quickly, I have something to help." The old man hobbled out of the cottage and made his way to a wheelbarrow stationed next to a bed of vegetables.

"Thank you," said Mary, out of breath.

They eased Ryder's unconscious body into the dirty wheelbarrow.

"Will he be okay?" she asked.

"Only time will tell," the botanist said.

In a fit of uncontrollable anguish, she leaned over the wheelbarrow and kissed Ryder on the top of his head before they moved him into the cottage.

Chapter 27

Claude

Claude couldn't set his thoughts straight. So much confusion had happened in just a few short hours. The burning of the temple. Escaping from a mob of mutations. His rapid aging. Ryder almost chopping his leg off. Meeting the legendary botanist. But the real surprise and perplexity came when he first entered the botanist's cottage.

The pleading eyes of his brother and Haley pierced him as they sat bound to a chair in the middle of the parlor. The light from the oil lamp shed a gleam on their panicked faces.

Had he lost his marbles? How had the botanist managed to carry out their capture or know that they needed capturing in the first place before they even arrived? And what weakness caused their enemy to capture them?

The botanist disappeared with Ryder and Mary into the back of the cottage and he was left alone with them for what seemed like an eternity. Claude exchanged a fierce look with each of them. Then he took hold of one of the kitchen knives on the counter. Every few seconds Vern or Haley would mumble through their gags and wiggle in their restraints, but Claude remained motionless, ready to stab them if they escaped.

When Botanē returned sometime later, he ushered Claude to another room with a quaint rocking chair and fireplace and insisted that he let go of the knife.

"Sorry for leaving you. I'm sure you're confused by what you saw, but I had to tend to my grandson and if I didn't do it fast enough, he would've bled to death."

"Will Ryder live?"

Botanē cocked his head. "If his body doesn't reject my medicine. It's up to him now." He removed a tiny bottle from his cloak and uncorked it. The smell of wet dog slapped Claude in the face.

"Here. This will help you slow the aging process."

"No, I couldn't possibly," Claude said in his most nonchalant tone, unsure if he was in the presence of a murderer as Ryder had accused. A huge chunk of white hair fell to the floor right then. The scent of sour milk glided through the air. His eyes stung with tears.

"If you don't take it, all your hair will fall out. Next, you'll become incontinent."

"Incontinent?" Claude accepted the bottle and huffed before he ingested the mysterious tonic that tasted like an old shoe. Within minutes he had an upset stomach and spent the rest of the night on the toilet.

The next morning, the botanist grinned at him as he sat on the bathroom floor and said, "Don't worry, it's normal to have that reaction. I have this for you next. It's topical."

Claude accepted the slippery, shiny substance to rub on his temples, but it stained his skin bright yellow and stung.

"You must rest as much as possible today to help your body heal. I recommend you spend your time in the rocking chair by the fire. It's the coziest place in the house."

"Okay," Claude said. "How's Ryder today?"

"Too soon to tell." The botanist headed toward the door. "I need to gather some more herbs and things and will be gone the rest of the day. Mary is tending to Ryder and your brother and Haley are fine where they are. Do not talk to them or go into the parlor. I'll explain later. It's urgent that I go now."

"What am I supposed to do until then?"

The botanist's white eyebrow arched. "I told you. Sit by the fire and relax." He exited through the door and left Claude with his thoughts.

Claude wandered to the rocking chair and eased into it. "Maybe this won't be so bad. I'll get the relaxation I've been wanting this entire time," he laughed.

A bang awoke him from a delightful nap several hours later. He sat up and wiped the drool from the side of his mouth. "Botanē?"

Silence.

Claude exhaled through his nose and closed his tired eyes.

Clink. Clank. Bang.

His eyes sprang open again. He couldn't have heard heavy chains dragging along the floor, could he?

"Mary is that you?"

He listened to the silence of the cottage and hoped to hear the rustle of her dress when she would pass by.

A deep, indiscernible voice croaked. It had come from the botanist's adjacent room. When had he returned? The craving to spy was unavoidable. The urge made his back tingle.

Just one little peek.

Claude rose from his chair and nimbly tiptoed toward the botanist's room.

Creak.

Time slowed to a crawl. He did not move or dared to breathe.

The voice resumed, and he supposed it was safe. As he continued at a much slower pace, he couldn't help but compare himself to an obese sloth. He huffed. Why hadn't the Summoner potions allowed him to lose weight?

When he arrived, he glued his ear to the door.

Not a sound.

He put his eye to the keyhole but could see nothing except darkness. He was just about to go, when a sinister voice said, "It depends on how much you want it. There are costs."

"I'll do anything," someone said.

A chill ran down his spine. Claude flew back to his chair with a pang of distress in his belly. He hadn't heard the voice before or seen someone enter the cottage, and this reason alone sent his heart into a perpetual state of alarm. Did Botanē have someone else tied up in the cottage?

Claude didn't sleep at all that night. Every creak and gust of wind sent his heart into a nervous flutter. When the botanist appeared the next morning, he flew past him in a great hurry, snatched up various books, dried herbs, and things, and stuffed them into his billowy cloak. Claude studied his face—trying to decipher his secrets. How could someone so much more decrepit than he have such energy and vigor?

"I'll be back late," Botanē said. "Mary is still tending to Ryder, so just continue your herbs I set out for you on the mantel and rest."

"I will. Thank you," replied Claude, hesitant to listen to anything the botanist said now.

As soon as the botanist left the cottage, Claude sauntered to the window, parted the drapes, and glanced out at the quaking gray trees.

The coast was clear for him to do what he did best. Spy.

Claude turned and headed to a big pile of old medicinal books on a shelf next to the hallway. The stained and yellowed pages curled at the end, but it was obvious that there was nothing of use in them. He shuffled to an old desk next where he hunted through the botanist's notebooks peppered with complicated drawings of sprawling plants and blooming flowers. One of the drawers was locked though. After several failed attempts to pick the lock, he searched for the key in every oddball hiding place he could think of but couldn't open the mysterious drawer. He gave up after an hour and headed toward the botanist's collection of strange-smelling bottles next. He made the mistake of opening a clear bottle of a gray liquid, which shot a whiff of vile air up his nostrils and made him sneeze.

With growing impatience, he mustered the courage to venture to the botanist's chambers. His hand trembled as it stretched to touch the solid reality of the door. There was an ethereal silence in the cottage. He pressed his ear to the wood. He inhaled and exhaled.

"Hello?"

Silence.

His heart thundered louder. He knocked.

Nothing.

He grasped the handle and turned. The tiny clicks inside the mechanism reminded him of an old music box.

"What are you doing?" Mary said from the threshold opposite.

Claude jumped.

Their eyes met. He released his grasp on the handle.

"Nothing."

She cocked her head. "Did you need something? I thought I heard you knock before."

"I was just curious how Ryder was doing. I thought this was his room."

She smiled. "He's coming around slowly but surely." There was something joyous in her pale face—a happy, pleasurable look like she was glad to be tending to him.

"That's good news."

"It is. He's still got a long way to go before we can even think of getting out of here. I still can't believe he didn't see the trap."

Claude's gaze dropped. The floorboards became visible in the dark. Every nail. Every scuff. Every crack in the grain. He felt her staring. Staring into the secret embedded deep within him. Did she sense that he saw the trap and didn't warn Ryder as he walked toward it? Did she know how much he hated Ryder and wanted him to suffer? Her silence added to his panic.

"Claude?" She touched his shoulder. "Are you okay? How are you feeling?"

He was embarrassed now to even think she had known. It made him grin. "I'm fine."

"Glad to hear. Well, I better get back to Ryder. It's time for another bandage change soon." She turned on her heel, then swung back around. "Oh, did the botanist feed Vern and my mother yet?"

"I'm not sure. To be honest I haven't seen them since we arrived. This whole thing is very strange."

"That's okay. I'll check on them in a bit."

"Don't you think it's all a little unnerving having them in the house? I mean, the botanist has yet to explain to me how he captured them and what his plans are. Did he tell you?"

"He did. Once they go through their withdrawals, they'll return to normal and will be released. The botanist assured me that once they can think clearly again, their desire to consume any of the Summoner potions, along with their belligerent need to share the potions with the rest of the world, will cease."

"How long will that take?"

She shrugged. "It may be a few more hours or in a week. There's no telling."

"Mary, um." Claude's head lowered. "Do you think that the botanist is, well...good-intentioned?"

She cocked her head as if it was an absurd question. "Of course. He's been giving Ryder all sorts of medicines to nurse him back to health. He's helping you reverse the aging process, and he's been an absolute doll to me. Like the grandfather I never had. I don't think that sweet old man is a murderer. In fact, I think Ryder may have misunderstood him."

"Whether he's trustworthy or not, what do you think happened to the shipments in the temple? If they didn't burn, what if someone else found them and shipped them? And what if the townspeople consumed them? If they have, what new travesties await us?"

"You're really worked up, Claude. Why don't you go lay down and relax? All this speculation isn't good for your health."

He inhaled. "Okay, maybe you're right."

"Good. I'll see you when I see you then."

Claude turned and drudged down the hall to his rocking chair and tried not to let his terrible fascination with the botanist and the mysterious voice seize him.

Chapter 28

Ryder

It wasn't the searing pain in his leg that woke him, but the cold, penetrating draft. Ryder opened his foggy eyes, stared at the wooden ceiling for a moment, and turned his head toward the open window to find a little blue bird pecking dispiritedly at an old tree stump.

He shivered, and his head rotated back to the middle of the lumpy pillow.

The room's familiar details appeared. Everything had a blue hue, and countless carved wooden trinkets lay in the shadowy corners. He discerned one of a bear, a turtle, another of a man's face, a mystical creature—and dozens of other animals. An earthy scent tickled his nostrils. Then there were the books. Hundreds of them lined the shelves.

His gaze swept to a big object draped with a sheet in the corner.

Tick. Tick. Tick.

Ryder's heart froze. Was this another nightmare?

"Welcome back," my boy.

He jolted.

"Sorry to startle you." Botanē set his coffee on the nightstand and hunched forward. "I thought the fresh air would wake you and I was right. How do you feel?"

"W-what h-happened?" Ryder rubbed his head.

"You had a bad accident."

"What?"

"Your leg got caught in one of my traps, but there's no need to worry."

"Worry?" Ryder cried. "This is your doing, isn't it? Are you trying to kill me? Are you trying to make another sacrifice for another bullshit dream?"

"Stop being paranoid. I wasn't even there. It was an accident. I've used some of my best medicines to heal the wound. The side effect is excessive slumber though, and a little dizziness. You've been out for two days."

"What the hell did you give me?" Ryder sat straight up like a reanimated corpse. "It better not have been Summoner of Sleep or some other weird concoction of yours."

"Relax. Nothing out of the ordinary."

"Tell me what you gave me."

"Well," the botanist mumbled, "it's my own combination of medicinal herbs I've been using on open wounds for decades now. Let's see if I can remember all of them. There's a bit of turmeric...that's for antiseptic purposes...umm, some fresh garlic for its antibiotic properties...hmm, a little bit of honey to dehydrate the bacteria. Some aloe vera to soothe. Shall I continue?"

Ryder flung off the quilt to survey the damage, but his foot was bandaged. He tried to wiggle his toes and a sharp twinge of pain shot clear up his leg and he yelped.

"I wouldn't do that. You're still healing."

Ryder ignored him and glided his fingers over the most painful point, but even the slightest pressure from his fingertips was too much, and once again he cried out.

"I told you."

"I don't care what you say, I'm not staying in this place another minute. I'm leaving."

He swept both legs to the side of the bed and positioned himself to stand.

"No. You mustn't." The botanist stood and nudged him down. "You can't walk, or you'll damage it beyond repair. I had to give you thirty-seven stitches. That, along with the ligament damage you sustained...you came close to never walking again." He repositioned his cloak and stared at Ryder's foot. "It's quite miraculous that you've healed this much already. We Ashlings tend to recover quicker than normal folks, thankfully."

"Then give me some crutches or your cane. I want to leave."

"Even if you did have a crutch, you'd never make it through the woods on your own in your current state. Are you forgetting the steep cliffs? The boulders? The earth floor covered in sharp needles and rocks? And let's say you did somehow manage to make it out, what are you going to do when the townspeople find you? They've probably all changed, you know."

"I'll figure something out."

"How would you get to the next town sixty miles away? On your injured foot, or do you plan to ask one of those creatures in town for a lift? I'm sure they'd be happy to oblige."

"I have a car. I left it by the entrance to Marble Woods."

"You mean the one they pushed over the cliff?"

Ryder brushed his hair away from his face. Hadn't Mary also reported this to him?

"Even if you managed on foot, it'll be damn near impossible to find your way to the road."

"Why?"

"Hard to explain," the old man grumbled. "The woods here have a way of...uh...how do you say...ah, yes...*transforming.*"

"Transforming?"

Botanē nodded. "Some say that the trees walk at night. That

they're enchanted with magic from devils. People who've lived here their whole lives can get lost if they're not careful. A lot of people have gone mad in these woods as a result."

"But I remembered how to get to your cottage."

"That's not to say that you wouldn't have difficulty next time. The woods are very particular. They have their favorites, but sometimes they like to play tricks on people just to have a bit of fun."

"I don't believe it," Ryder snapped. "You're trying to scare me to get me to stay here."

"Believe what you will, but it's the truth. I've lived in these woods long enough to know. And your friend, Mary, she even told me she'd gotten lost in these woods before. She said she played in these woods a thousand times, but never where my cottage stood. What do you make of that?"

"I—" he started just as a pale light glided through the door. Ryder's focus narrowed as Mary walked into the room carrying a stack of pillows.

The old man turned on his hip towards her. "He's back."

"Oh good," Her blue eyes lit up. Mary rushed to his bedside, dropped the pile of pillows on a chair, then grabbed his hand. Her softness was so delicate. Like a porcelain doll hand. "I was so worried about you. How do you feel?"

Ryder recalled his altercation with her earlier. It was her fault that he hurt his leg if she hadn't demanded that they hide in his grandfather's house in the first place. It was her fault he had to see his grandfather again. Her fault for keeping him in Marble Woods. He wanted to leave so many times and kept getting roped into doing things he didn't want to do.

"Are you okay?" She cocked her head. "You're not still mad about the other day, are you?"

Ryder huffed, lowered his head to his chest, and removed his hand from hers.

"I'm sorry, Ryder. I wasn't thinking. I was under so much stress and said something stupid. And we had no other choice but to come here. Will you please forgive me?" she said with a smile. "After everything we've been through."

The botanist laughed and slapped his thigh. "Good luck getting him to accept your apology. Ryder is just as stubborn as his father and me." Botanē moved into the light. "You'd have to move a mountain for him to forgive you for anything, even something trivial."

She turned to Botanē. "Really?" she questioned with an arched brow. "Why do you say that?"

"Ashling men are a peculiar mix of things, my dear. We were blessed with towering height and good looks, our names reveal our destinies, and we're incapable of forgiving. In fact, I remember the time that his father and I were playing in the lake when he was a boy. We decided to take a dip after a long, hot day of fishing. Oh, we had a wonderful time, but I surprised him by splashing him hard right in the face, then by holding him under the water for a bit. You know, the usual horseplay between father and son, but all in good fun."

Ryder's ears perked at the unheard story, but he refused to change his stern expression or break his gaze with the floor.

"Oh, it was hilarious to me. That boy thought he was so much better and stronger than everyone. He was such a cocky boy. I had to put him in his place. Sometimes that's what needs to be done as a man," snickered the botanist, "but of course, he didn't find it funny or learn his lesson. He hated weakness. Hated that I beat him. Then he played the victim and said it was cruel to have done such a thing to a child. Never forgave me after that, and any time we were ever close to water he'd take it upon himself to douse me right in the face or try to hold me under. Didn't matter how many times I apologized or where we were, he refused to accept it and chose to drench me at any cost. Goodness, the things that child did. We'd be at a restaurant and he'd thrust a glass of water right on my lap, he'd push me overboard if we were on a boat. The list goes on and on. It sure got old when he was still doing it even as an adult."

Ryder didn't remember much about his father, but he had pled with him on more than one occasion to let him go swimming. His father always refused. He would watch his friends hike off toward the community pool with their swimming gear in hand and their faces bright and smiling. He remembered watching them from his bedroom window as they returned with tanned skin and a look of contentment on their faces. So many nights he cried himself to sleep and never knew why swimming was forbidden—until now.

Mary's head swiveled back to Ryder and she ventured a slight smile. "Come on, please don't be like that. I'm sorry. Please forgive me and break the curse."

The pain of never knowing his father and the experiences that were robbed from him in his childhood now took precedence. Ryder huffed and turned away from them.

"Ryder?" she said.

"Leave."

She sat in silence for a full minute, then scurried out of the room.

Good riddance.

He listened to her footsteps run through the cottage and out the front door.

"What's the matter with you, my boy?" Botanē poked him in the arm with his gnarled cane.

"Let her go. I don't forgive her. Or you. I don't care if it's an Ashling curse or not. Once my foot heals, I'm getting the hell out of Marble Woods once and for all."

The botanist eased out of his chair; his cane teetered with the pressure. "I understand if you don't want to forgive me and I accept my punishment, but that poor girl has nothing but good intentions. She said something foolish one time in the heat of the moment, but she didn't do anything to harm you. She saved you by bringing you to my cottage. Don't you understand that?" He leaned forward just an inch with a wheeze. "That young woman has tended to you nonstop. In fact, she hasn't slept in two days and has been by your bedside this entire time taking care of you, dressing your wound, and waiting for you to wake."

"So?"

Botanē hobbled toward the door. "She's also the one who covered the clock. All she's done is try to help you, so I suggest you accept her apology and not bear the curse of stubbornness like all Ashling men."

"I don't care."

The botanist swallowed hard and loud; his wrinkled neck trembled. "Who knows, if your stubborn father had forgiven me over the water incident, I might've felt different toward him and not have been so inclined to do what I did. You know, it was that incident that unraveled our relationship—as stupid as it was. Things were never the same again between us, and I do regret it, but never in my wildest dreams did I think that he'd hold it against me to such an extreme degree. Don't let another Ashling curse ruin you like it did your father and me, and please remember that I'm the only family you have left."

"B—"

"Forgive her. And when you do, you must forgive her or it will eat at your body and soul." Botanē placed his hand upon the knob.

The cloak sleeve inched back. Curving across the withered flesh and protruding veins on the back of his grandfather's hand were the dark markings of a moon, compass, and flower. It was just for a second, but the tattoo was enough to add to Ryder's confusion and torment.

Chapter 29

Mary

M ary examined the vial in her palm.
I hope this one works.

She smiled at it and recounted Botanē's tour of the cottage and how she questioned him about the collection of mysterious bottles in the kitchen.

The old man's face had lit up. "They're my life's work. There's a bottle for everything you can imagine to achieve one's desires. My tonics are digestible and dermal. I have ones for truth-telling, curing disease, love, good luck, beauty, curses. The one for love is my favorite though, and the most dangerous since it doesn't wear off as easily. In some folks, the result of using it as little as one time will have a permanent effect. I've been able to make everything except a tonic for sleep. Sleep is the trickiest, you see, as it delves into one's subconscious, and from there things get messy. I attempted so many times to achieve my desired dreams with different ingredients and spells, but nothing worked."

Mary had remained quiet as the botanist explained his methods, and as she listened, she became convinced that the sweet old man wasn't a cold-blooded murderer as Ryder accused. But in all the detailed explanations about his potions, she hadn't forgotten the most important word he had said: *love.*

"How can you tell them apart without labels?"

"They're color-coded to my own system. Only I know which is which and the extent of their powers as I do not wish anyone else to know about them or use them—or we could have another dreadful situation on our hands."

She pretended to heed his warning and never expected him to leave the cottage so that she could be alone with his incredible potions. But, to her delight, he was away more than he was at the cottage. Claude slept in the den by the fireplace too; his bloodless, worn face snoring in the glow of the fire, so she had time to experiment.

She tried her first guess of which bottle was the love potion two days ago. It was a blue liquid with flecks of gold—each fleck reflected tiny yellow kingdoms of glory. The liquid was hypnotic, and its intoxicating scent of cocoa added to her enjoyment. She sprinkled a few drops on Ryder's forehead and rubbed it in as he slept. Then she said, "You will love Mary."

There were a few excruciating seconds that passed, and then she saw a noticeable change in him. Ryder started to mumble about clocks, demons, and running through the woods. His forehead crinkled and his lips shook in a panicked expression.

The effects wore off after an hour, so she attempted other tonics using the same methods as before and saw the things he said in his unconscious state. None indicated love though.

When he woke and still refused to forgive her, she began to step it up and use more tonics each day. Mary played with dozens of different tonics and doses as Ryder slept, but she grew more frustrated after each unsuccessful attempt.

The pastel pink tonic seemed too obvious, so she saved it for last since love was associated with pink.

She uncorked the pink vial. "Here goes nothing."

Mary held it to her nostrils and inhaled citrus. Her eyes danced with wonder, then she administered it to Ryder.

"You will love Mary," she repeated.

He stirred under the quilt and smiled. Within seconds Ryder muttered about blue eyes and gold hair. His mouth crooked and he said the name "Mary."

Her stomach fluttered.

It's working.

She hoped the botanist's claim that the tonic could have a permanent effect was true. She wanted Ryder more than anything in the world. His lips. His smell. His lean and pale body. The glitz and glamour of his life. Mary grabbed Ryder's cold hand and warmed it against her cheek.

His black eyes popped opened and panned up. "M-mary?"

"I'm here."

"I feel so—" He paused. "Wonderful."

Mary squeezed his hand. "I'm glad to hear it."

Ryder blinked and sat up. "Thank you for taking care of me. I'm sorry about getting mad before. I forgive you."

Her cheeks burned with warmth. "It's no problem. Can I do anything for you?"

He shifted under the quilt again and she heard his stomach grumble. "Maybe a bite to eat?"

"Of course." Her face lit up. "That's a good sign if you've got an appetite." She stood, walked across the room, and stopped at the threshold. "Be right back."

"Don't be gone too long."

Mary glided down the hall. She twirled and danced all the way to the kitchen. Mary giggled at the loud, pig-like grunts Claude made from the den.

She put together a simple meal of soup and a sandwich for Ryder and headed back to the room balancing the tray of food on her forearm as she continued to sway and dance to the music in her head.

Something large thumped in the botanist's room and she stopped in her tracks.

Her ears strained at metal scraping across what sounded like a chalkboard—a muffled, garbled sound of misery. It grew louder.

Mary tensed.

A hideous gurgle followed, then a tail darted from under the botanist's door.

Her eyes were two bright moons.

She jumped back. The tray crashed to the floor.

The tail disappeared.

Her stomach turned and consumed her with a mixture of fear and curiosity.

Claude appeared at her side out of breath. "What happened? Are you alright?"

"Oh, it was nothing." She dropped to her knees to clean up the mess. "Thought I saw something."

"What?"

"I think it was just a spider."

His nose whistled as he inhaled. "Are you sure you're okay? You look like you saw a ghost."

"Yes, I'm fine."

The cottage went silent.

Claude didn't budge. "You can tell me anything, you know."

"I know."

"I'll ask you one last time then. Are you okay?"

"Never better," she smiled.

"If you say so." He turned. His muddy eyes slid to the corner to watch her like a curious pigeon. A moment later Claude wobbled back down the shadowy hallway.

Mary allowed herself to exhale and wiped the sweat from her forehead. She continued toward her patient's room with the tray in tow. Her gaze darted once or twice back at the botanist's door, but she refused to let anything disrupt her victory of having captured Ryder's heart.

Chapter 30

Ryder

Whenever he awoke, Mary was there with a smile, ready to cater to his every need. Why hadn't Julie been more attentive during their marriage? Not only that, but their conversations were also thought-provoking and exciting, which passed the time so fast that hours seemed like minutes. Whenever Mary left the room, he was so anxious for her return that he listened to every creak and footstep in the cottage; his heart leaped when footfalls approached his room.

He had misjudged her. She would make a wonderful addition to his life since she didn't seem concerned with money. Why had he been so foolish to believe Julie when she said she loved him, that her smile was genuine, and that she wanted to start a family with him? Why did he look the other way when she started spending more of his money, inquired about grander purchases, or when she wasn't satisfied with the expensive jewelry? He wouldn't make the same mistake twice. Mary was different. She'd never leave him. She'd do anything for him.

The door skirted open and Ryder's stomach fluttered.

Mary entered in her white cotton dress with a chunk taken out of the bottom from the accident. She held a tray full of broken dishes and splattered food.

"I'm so sorry. I had a bit of an accident with your lunch. I salvaged what I could to no avail, so I'll have to make you something else instead."

"No." Ryder rolled onto his hip. "Stay."

She turned. "It's no trouble."

"Please sit."

She walked across the floor, set the tray on the nightstand, and plopped herself in the chair next to Ryder, putting her slender little ankles upon an embroidered footstool.

He took her hand in his. "You've no idea what it's like to have pleasant dreams for a change. Not to be plagued with nightmares of clocks anymore. Instead, my dreams are bright and cheery. They're all about you now."

Mary turned red. "Oh?"

"Yes. I feel better than I have in my whole life."

"I'm happy to hear that."

"I want to ask you something."

"What?"

"I've been thinking maybe we could leave Marble Woods together."

Mary's face brightened. "Really?"

"Yes. But I need a crutch. Can you find me something that'll work?"

"Do you think you can walk?"

He nodded. "I feel much better, thanks to your help. I've tested weight on my foot, and it seems to be holding up well. I feel a little tingling. I just can't put my full weight on it yet, but if I had a crutch, I could walk."

"Are you sure? Your grandfather warned that you needed a full two weeks of immobility to recover. There's no way that I could ever carry you or help you along, and we don't have a car."

"I remembered something while you were in the kitchen. When I was spying on the townspeople, I saw Doctor Achilles leave his car key under the front left tire. I forgot before. So, what do you say?" He stared into the depths of her turquoise eyes.

"I say yes."

"Good." He leaned forward to kiss the top of her hand, "but we need to do it fast. I don't want anyone to know."

Her smile vanished. "Not even Claude?"

Ryder sighed and leaned back onto the pillows propped behind his back. "I hate to say it, but I think we need to worry about ourselves right now. I have respect for him, but the reality is that he'll just slow us down. Besides, he's safe here and resting comfortably."

"To be honest, I don't think he has much time anyway."

"Why?"

"His health hasn't improved as far as I can tell." Her expression turned sorrowful. "The botanist told me in private that he should be much further along by now, but there appear to be some complications with the anti-aging potions. They stopped working. And even if he wanted to take one of the Summoner potions, it wouldn't work anymore. His body is too far gone, so I hate to say this, but it would probably be better to let him expire in comfort than in the cold, dark woods."

"I feel terrible about it, but I'm glad you agree."

She stared at him with a luminous face, and said, "I think I know the perfect thing to use as a crutch."

An abrupt squeak of the door spooked him.

At the threshold stood Vern and Haley.

Blood rushed to his face. He flung the tray of food on the end table at the intruders. "Run, Mary," yelled Ryder. He grabbed hold of the lamp next to the bedside and flung it at Vern.

The lamp smacked Vern's forehead. The force sent him stumbling backward, but Haley caught him before he fell.

Vern stood, wiped the blood from his brow, and took a step

toward the bed.

"Get away from me, you bastard." Ryder grabbed whatever was within reach and flung it at him—books, teacups, food—all the while hurling curses.

Somewhere in the panic, Mary cried out, "Stop. Stop," and wrestled Ryder back into the center of the bed.

"What are you doing?" Ryder pushed Mary off his torso. "Don't you remember what they put us through?"

"It's all right," she said. "I released them. They passed their withdrawal stage and have returned to normal. They're on our side now."

Ryder stopped his struggle and lay unconvinced with his bad leg hanging off the bed, Mary on top of him, and his hands curled around the end of the table.

"Remember our plan about getting them back to normal?" she said.

He vaguely recalled Mary telling him about the botanist's plan, but that was when he was sedated, and the details were fuzzy.

"Incredible," scoffed Vern. "You sure have an arm on you for a cripple."

"What the hell is going on?" demanded Ryder.

"We're on your side," Vern said.

"What do you mean?" snapped Ryder.

"You've tried to kill all of us...multiple times. You're crazy. You worship a plant."

"Ryder, please stop and listen or you'll hurt yourself further." Mary repositioned herself next to him on the bed. She turned to Vern and Haley with a scornful look. "I wish you two had given me some sort of warning that you were going to come in here instead of scaring Ryder half to death."

"I did. I told Claude to tell you," replied Vern.

"Well he didn't," she said.

Ryder sat up and took a deep breath. "Will someone tell me what's happening?"

"It's simple. We realize the error of our ways," Vern said. "I understand that distribution of my Summoner potions was unethical. Having been through the withdrawal stage and coming back to my former, normal human state, I see my mistakes."

Ryder studied Vern's skin. The clear slippery sheen was gone.

"I'm sorry for any pain I've caused you, and you too, Mary. It all got out of hand," Vern continued.

"Out of hand? That's all you have to say? You bound your brother and Mary in your basement and left them to die. We found Belinda dead in your house. You took my grandfather's plant and changed it so that it makes people less human. There are creatures out there hunting and killing. You think this is out of hand? Out of hand is a fucking understatement."

"I know you're hesitant to believe us, but at least let us try to explain," Haley said and stepped toward the bed.

Ryder flicked his hand, and she stopped. "Explain away, but that won't change what you did."

"The Summoner potions are a diabolical drug that grabbed hold of us," Haley started. "It has the power to destroy us—body and soul—but now that they're out of our systems, they've let go of our minds. I can only compare it to being drunk. It's like you're not in control of what you are saying or doing. You're not thinking and when you wake up the next day with a hangover, all the regrets rush back when you remember what you did."

"Even so. That doesn't excuse it. Drunk people do stupid shit and they still have to pay for it." Ryder studied their faces and the slight signs of aging that hadn't been there before. "And why don't either of you look like Claude? He stopped taking the tonics too, so why don't you look like corpses?"

"I honestly don't know," Vern said. "I figured you of all people would know since your grandfather is the creator."

Ryder shrugged.

"Well then, if I had to guess," Vern said, "I think the reason we don't look like Claude is that the Summoner potions affect people in different ways."

Haley nodded. "And now that we're free from the effects of the Summoner's hold, Vern and I want to help. We're sorry for the unthinkable things we did. Vern and I want to stop what we started."

"How?" Ryder barked. "Claude is almost dead thanks to your potions. Besides, those shipments have probably already gone out. What do you expect everyone is doing down there? Sitting around and twiddling their thumbs? I don't think so."

"We're doing the best we can," barked Vern. "We just need to go into town and investigate."

Ryder turned to Mary. "Are you buying any of this shit?"

Her gaze darted around the room. Her mouth was open. "Yes."

Ryder sat there contemplating what to believe while Haley cleaned Vern's injuries. A dark shape under a bald patch of Vern's skin caught his eye. Perhaps it was a birthmark that had been covered by his hair, but upon second glance, it was a tattoo of some sort.

Ryder couldn't quite make out the shape until Haley moved out of the way to clean his arm wounds. One of the teacups he had thrown broke on impact and there was a large shard still stuck in his forearm.

He squinted hard at the shape—it was a blotchy tattoo about the size of a silver dollar. Although some of the symbol was still covered by Vern's hair, he was able to identify three distinct markings. One of a moon, another a tiny flower, and a circular symbol. Perhaps a compass? It was the same symbol Ryder saw in the temple and the same mark his grandfather bore on his hand.

Ryder almost swallowed his tongue.

After Haley cleaned Vern's arm, she made her way back to his head. She forked her fingers to cover the spot with hair and then shot Ryder a contemptuous look.

He forced a quick yawn, turned to Mary, and said, "This is a bit too much for me too soon. I'm still weak and my bandage needs changing. May I please have a few minutes alone with Mary?"

"Sure, we can give you some space," replied Haley and retrieved the tray from the floor. "We'll just go and prepare some food for all of us."

"Thanks," Ryder said. Did Haley suspect he hadn't breathed for the length of their conversation? "Would it be too much trouble for a sandwich and some tea?"

"Of course not."

As soon as Vern and Haley's footsteps disappeared, he turned to Mary and whispered, "Bring me that dictionary on the shelf."

Mary furrowed her brows. "A dictionary?"

"Shhh."

"Why on earth would you want a dictionary at a time like this?"

"Just bring it. Quick."

She got up, walked to the shelf, and grabbed the large brown book. As soon as she handed it to him, Ryder thumbed to the N section.

"What are you doing?"

He found the word he was looking for and felt the warmth drain from his cheeks. The words shuddered on the page, soaked in the sin of secrets.

"Oh no." He pushed the book away.

"What is it?"

He closed the dictionary in a daze and set it on the nightstand. "It's just as I feared." He groped for Mary's hand. "This is terrible. His name. It means *traveler*."

"Whose name?"

"My father. His name means...meant traveler."

"So?"

"Don't you see?"

She shook her head.

"Ashling men are part of a trifecta. It binds us all together and refuses to be buried. This curse lives here in this hideous town. When I saw those strange symbols in the temple basement and then on my grandfather's hand, I realized it's meant to symbolize us. It means we are at the nexus of some sort of larger strategy and it all has to do with that symbol."

Mary cocked her head, her face was as grim as he had ever seen it. "You're talking about the symbol of the moon, flower, and compass, right?"

"Yes. It's all been right in front of me the entire time." He gestured to the dictionary. "I feel so stupid for not seeing it before."

"I'm sorry. I don't understand. What strategy?"

"My grandfather's name, Botanē, means botanist. He's the one who created Summoner of Sleep and his symbol is the flower. My name, Ryder, means messenger of sleep or dreams. I'm the one meant to deliver the word about it and my symbol is the moon. And my father, his name was Nestor, which is Greek for traveler, symbolized by the compass. He's the one intended to distribute Summoner of Sleep. I think we're all connected in this and that we each have our different roles. I think there's some ultimate plan at work here."

"Well, I do remember Botanē said how Ashling men had names that revealed their destinies. But how would a plan like that even work if your dad is dead?"

"I don't know."

"Maybe that's why Botanē has been helping us," continued Mary. "It also explains why he stopped Vern and my mother from distributing the potions. It's the job of the Ashlings."

"So, Vern's my father's replacement." Ryder's face twitched and he forced a breath. "Everything my grandfather has said to me, to us, is a lie. Even the whole scheme to put the antidote in Emelda's cookies for everyone to eat on Halloween. I wonder what was in that pot we stirred for all those days? Colored water scented with some herbs?" He smacked his fist against the bed. "So stupid."

Voices approached.

"They're playing us, Mary," he whispered. "I saw a tattoo of the same symbol on Vern's head just now. They're working with my grandfather somehow."

"What? Are you sure? How do you know it wasn't a birthmark or something?"

"Because your mother saw that I noticed it, and when she did, she covered it with Vern's hair."

"Did my mother have the tattoo?"

"I don't know," replied Ryder.

Mary went quiet for a second and then turned scarlet. "If what you're saying is true, my mother lied to me, and she chose Vern instead of me *again*. That would mean your grandfather also lied to us about the withdrawals and going back to normal. That would mean my mother and Vern are still the same. They're monsters, and I'm the one who released them."

"I tried to warn you not to trust him. There's wickedness going on here. I can't shake the feeling of a dark presence."

"What do we do? We're trapped in the house with them and with God knows what in the botanist's room."

"What?"

She watched the door for a moment. "I saw something sticking out of Botanē's room. A tail. I don't know from what kind of creature. I heard a horrible sound coming from inside too. That's why I spilled your food. I saw it and was so scared I dropped my tray."

He squeezed her hand tighter, "Do the others know?"

"I don't think so."

Footsteps approached.

His heart never beat so fast. "I have a plan. Take this and hide it." He handed her a wolf figurine from the nightstand. "Promise me you'll throw it without hesitation when the time is right. Can you do that for me?"

Mary's eyes teared. "I t-think so."

"Good. Just remember. No hesitation. Our lives may depend upon it. Now wipe your tears."

Chapter 31

Claude

Claude's body was nothing more than a sack of sharp, decaying bones covered in sores. He could ingest nothing but coffee with a dollop of milk. What kind of a pathetic existence was that? He was always cold, so he rubbed his legs for warmth every chance he got. The worst part was that he couldn't draw a full breath without liquid rattling inside his lungs.

One afternoon he found himself in an argument with his wife debating over who ate the last chocolate-covered cherry truffle. He turned to say something, but where had she gone? Claude hesitated a moment. Wait a second. Hadn't she been dead for years? Who was he talking to then? He cursed his mind for playing another cruel game on him.

A strange metal tapping reverberated through the den, and he pondered if it was his imagination again.

He eased out of the chair and stole down the hallway to discover that his brother and Ryder were getting ready to enter the botanist's room. He had heard commotion earlier when

Vern and Haley entered the room and frightened Ryder, but he was perplexed to see the two of them getting along so well now—especially in a joint endeavor of breaking into the room.

Shit.

Another one of his sabotages against Ryder hadn't worked. He for sure thought that if he sent Vern and Haley in the room unannounced a brutal fight would follow and Ryder would be beaten due to his handicap. But here they were working together.

Claude's scornful eyes fell upon Ryder. He hadn't seen him in the past few days and his neighbor's corpse-white skin gleamed, as did his icy gaze. He looked eternal. He leaned on one of the botanist's gnarled canes with one hand and held a big kitchen knife in the other.

"What are you doing?" Claude said with a wheeze.

Ryder pressed his lips together and tightened his grip on the knife. "My grandfather isn't here. We heard something inside. We picked the lock and now we're going in to investigate."

Vern's brows pinched together, and his eyes shone with an apprehensive gleam. "Have you heard anything coming from inside, brother? Your chair is so close."

Claude fought the urge to ask how the two were now friends, to scream at Vern for abandoning him in the basement, or to reveal the sounds and strange voice that had shaken him to his core. Everything was awkward and befuddling.

He shook his head.

The cottage went silent except for Mary and Haley's heavy breaths who stood in the threshold of the adjacent room.

"Brother, you should go back to your chair. This doesn't concern you."

His words dug into Claude's heart like a miner tilling for gold. That's all he had to say after everything? If his brother had turned back to normal as Mary and the botanist claimed, he wanted an apology and it seemed that Vern could care less about making him feel better. A flash of red sliced through his vision.

Calm down. Don't show you're upset.

"I think I'll stay and watch," Claude said through gritted teeth. "But I think you should go first though on account of Ryder's leg." He brushed a strand of remaining ghost-white hair from his eyes.

Vern's head swiveled to meet his gaze. "Are you sure you want me to go in there first?"

"Yes, brother. You'll be fine. I don't think there's anything to be afraid of."

Vern inhaled. "You know I've changed back to normal. That I'm on your side."

Claude nodded and searched his brother's face and body for any sign of a shimmer. "I do."

Vern bit his lip. "You know I'm doing this for you, right?"

"So many times you called upon me to trust you, brother. I'm asking you to do the same. Trust me that there's nothing to be afraid of. If anything, it's just a rat and then we can all go back to our day. But like I said I haven't heard anything, and I've been sitting here the whole time."

Vern looked at Ryder. "Do you agree that I should go in first?"

"It makes the most sense," replied Ryder. "Besides, Claude's right. It's just a rat or something. And don't worry, I'm right behind you."

Vern swallowed, turned, and placed his hand upon the door handle. "All right. Here we go. One, two, three."

The door squealed open.

The cottage went cold.

Inside it was pitch black.

With a heavy heart, Claude watched Vern take a breath, hold the kitchen knife in front of him, and step into the room. When his brother and Ryder crossed the threshold, a little grin wiggled across Claude's face.

Chapter 32

Ryder

Ryder hobbled into the dark, bone-chilling room. "Well, do you see anything?" he whispered to Vern.

"No. Where's the damn light?"

"I think it's on the wall over there on the right."

Vern crept deeper into the room as Ryder leaned on his good foot, but the slope from the floor shot a pulse of pain up his leg. He bit his lip and directed his gaze to a shadowy spot in the corner.

His breath stopped.

The light from the open doorway fell upon it like an iridescent veil. His brain couldn't understand the leering face—the face with eyes as red as blood. It stood motionless, tall, and erect. Its mouth formed a painful toothless grin. It sniffed out of the jagged slits that zigzagged down its stitched face. Then something else moved next to it. Ryder's heart thudded in his temples and his gaze turned to a little bald figure. Its head crooked to the side at an impossible, unnatural angle.

Dear God.

"Mary, throw it now," he yelled.

The wolf figurine hurled into the center of the room.

Vern jerked and stumbled into some furniture, which caught the attention of the creatures. Their ominous gazes flickered back and forth with hunger panes and anticipation.

Vern pressed himself up from the floor, but Ryder lurched forward and gored Vern as hard as he could with the tip of his cane. It was too dark to tell, but Ryder swore he had gotten him right in the spleen.

"What are you doing?" Vern groaned and thumped to the floor.

"Giving you a taste of your own medicine."

There was a cold chill behind him.

They're coming.

His jaw chattered and his legs shuffled toward the door, just missing the creatures that descended upon Vern.

Something popped, snapped, and grinded. Warm fluids and blood rained upon his back, but he didn't turn around. The ground was a slick sea of black. He couldn't get his footing.

Oh, God. I can't get out.

His heart hammered. So much blood. So many screams.

He flew through the door, slammed it, held it, and waited.

A second later Vern banged on the other side. "Open the door. Let me out. They already got my fucking arm."

"No. You're one of them," Ryder shouted.

"You don't understand," screamed Vern. "Your grandfather promised me immortality. I had a terminal disease. I had no other choice."

"You're a lying bastard." Ryder's fingers throbbed like boiled hot dogs from his grip on the handle's edges.

His head spun; his eyes remained welded shut as sweat poured down his face—a carousel of anxiety brewed within him to a blinding level.

His grip slipped more with each dreadful, pleading pull. His plan was failing. He couldn't hold on a second longer. Vern and those things would get out and it would all be over. Why had he stayed this long already?

Something touched him.

Ryder opened his eyes to discover Claude's gray, wrinkled hands upon his. His neighbor grabbed part of his hand and the handle, shifted his weight, and pulled to help hold it closed. Ryder marveled at how his neighbor had found the strength to hold the door.

There was blood in the door jam. So much blood.

Haley cried and pounded her tiny fists on their backs, but Ryder didn't break his gaze from Claude's. It was as if they both exchanged a magnetic power in that unbroken gaze.

"Let me out. Please." Vern banged and scratched like an animal on the other side. "There are demons in here. The botanist conjured them, not me. Please."

"If you knew there were demons in there, then why did you agree to go and investigate in the first place? You were going to leave me in there, weren't you? You were going to do the same thing to me, you bastard."

"You don't understand. I'm bleeding to death. My arm. You've gotta let me out now. There's more. So many more. They're coming. Jesus Christ, they're coming."

Steps approached the door and Vern's dreadful cries screeched to a childlike pitch. For a moment, things went quiet and then a voice wailed through the halls—a thin, haunting voice. The voice split the atmosphere with its eeriness.

Shadows gathered beneath the threshold. And then obscure, infantile singing floated through the air like a distant lullaby. The floor by the door turned blue with a dim aqueous light.

Glass shattered and violent thuds shook the cottage. Dishes and knickknacks plummeted and smashed on the floor. The thuds sounded like a great drumbeat and with each forceful beat, the ground grew shakier. He focused all his attention on the melody. In a matter of seconds, the drumbeat turned into a seamless animalistic shriek that kept perfect time with the strange beats.

"They're going to kill him since Vern isn't the magician who conjured them," Haley cried from somewhere behind him. "Stop—for God's sake, stop."

"It's too late now," Ryder said, as he pressed his ear to the door.

Vern cried out again and then ripping replaced all other sounds.

Ryder continued to hold on through all of Vern's dreadful pleas and screams. And he continued to hold on even when enormous amounts of warm blood seeped out from under the threshold and soaked his shoes and filled the hallway with a revolting stench.

The horrific screams and noises stopped.

The old man sobbed.

"Don't cry," Ryder said. "You're free now."

"I k-know. These are happy tears. T-thank you," heaved Claude. He raised his head. "How can I ever t-thank you?"

Ryder swallowed, speechless. His entire being softened.

They stared at each other for a full minute without a word.

"You can come with us," Ryder said.

"I'd love to," Claude started, "but we both know this is where I leave you."

Ryder nodded.

"I'm sorry for all the pain I caused you. For all the stupid things I did. Thank you for everything you've done for me. I was wrong about you and it's a shame it has to end like this now."

Ryder let go of the handle with swollen, shaky hands and wedged his cane under the doorknob. He teetered for a moment, leaned forward, and embraced his neighbor.

Although Ryder couldn't see Claude's expression, his neighbor's smile shone through him like the sun slicing through the clouds.

Chapter 33

Ryder

Twelve slim, square towers connected the giant, thin walls made of bronze. Small windows scattered across the walls in an asymmetrical pattern. A heavy gate with thick wooden doors stood at the top of the steps. Lush trees surrounded the temple walls, all swaying under the full moon.

"That can't be," Ryder gasped. "I watched it burn."

Ryder inched closer. The branches snapped around him as he fought through the trees, which tore and scratched his hands and arms to shreds. His fingers were already numb, and the wind had slashed his face like razors. His nose tickled from the faint stench of death.

His gaze swept to the rest of the town. Most of the homes were torched. Mounds of bones were piled high in front of the general store. All the other businesses in Marble Woods had been ransacked and charred. Overturned signs, shards of glass, and piles of blackened wood littered the streets. All doors had been ripped off the buildings.

There was a noise from below.

Some poor creature roamed the street. Its broad shoulders were covered by a mass of hair. The rest of its wet flesh fell away in crimson shreds and oozing green liquids, which revealed two bloody, gaping sockets in place of eyes, yet it still avoided obstacles and maneuvered with precision. Its huge black nostrils sniffled like a rabbit's.

Ryder drew back a cry as the abrupt sound of a light, frail voice floated out over the night.

He leaned against the side of the tree while the moon shone on him through the branches. His gaze shot to the resurrected temple below in search of the voice and found a black silhouette.

There in the moonlight that flooded the gray woods was one cloaked figure. The hood slid back to reveal Botanē's perturbed face.

Ryder's first impulse was to charge down the hill and dump the contents of his homemade potion on his head. It had taken him hours to concoct it and he never would've known it was a weakness of his grandfather's had he not seen the old man's skin bubble and blacken upon contact, but Ryder wanted to see what his grandfather would do, so he continued to watch him walk across one of the great granite steps.

A second cloaked figure appeared from the temple despite no visible door. Had it moved through the wall?

Half gliding, half floating, the crimson-clad figure approached Botanē. They bowed to each other in a ceremonial way and Ryder inched forward from his hiding spot.

He strained his ears.

"They've gotten to Vern," his grandfather grumbled. "Trapped him in my chambers with the new demons. Those demons weren't supposed to interact with other humans, just help us make more potions, so naturally, they killed him. It's a shame, but it's a good thing that this happened to Vern. He was too hungry for power. He should've never built the first temple without us. But now that he's out of the way, we can focus on the task at hand."

The cloaked figure nodded.

Ryder shifted from behind the tree to get a look. Ryder's fingertips were sticky from the sap of the rough bark, but he didn't care. There was a dark silence, like the silence of a wicked, lifeless world.

"I'm ready to get started. Are you?" the botanist asked.

The second figure eased back the crimson hood. "Yes."

Ryder's knees weakened.

It must have been some kind of illusion. Some trick. How could his father, Nestor Ashling, be standing next to Botanē?

The world spun. He blinked a few times. Something pressed against his back. He jumped and turned.

Mary.

He forgot she had been beside him the entire time. Her pink mouth was agape, and her hair splayed like white branches against a black sky.

"Ryder?" Mary whispered. "Is that who I think it is?"

Ryder nodded, unable to catch his breath. "I don't understand what's happening. How my father is standing down there. How my grandfather knows about Vern when that just happened. How the temple is still standing after we saw it crumble."

"I don't either, but I'm scared." She paused and turned white as snow. "Did you hear that?"

"Hear what?" Ryder spun around.

The branches danced.

"It sounded like footsteps. Do you think it's my mother? Do you think she came back after running away?"

Ryder shook his head. "I think she's long gone."

Mary froze. "What is it then? Did those things get out of the cottage?"

Before he could respond there was an unmistakable, low-pitched gurgle. Branches cracked and claws sank into his injured ankle.

He took one step forward and screamed.

The pain was indescribable. He staggered a few steps, then lost sight of Mary in the blinding agony. His soaking wet legs buckled, and he fell to the forest floor.

Chapter 34

Mary

Mary wiped the saliva that had collected around her open mouth. The stale cold air made her shiver. She reached for the thick marble wall supporting her, beholding its strange texture—like cold stone mixed with grease—but a sudden blast of pain shot up her arm. She retracted it and held it at her chest. Her gaze swept the barren room. Upon one of the walls was the familiar symbol—moon, compass, and a flower—all encapsulated in an enormous circle. On the other side of the room, there was a slow, steady stream of water that tumbled down the wall and disappeared below. In the alcove across from her, a slender figure stood with its back to her, illuminated by a torch.

Mary straightened.

She slid onto her hip, but a whimper escaped her.

The shadow turned and floated toward her.

She was trapped in a broken, petrified body, and watched the figure in dumb horror as it approached.

"Please don't hurt me," she cried.

"It okay. It's just me."

Relief swept over her in a tidal wave of emotion, and she sobbed.

"Oh, Ryder," she squealed and raised her arms for a hug. There was so much pain inside her that she couldn't feel his embrace.

She slumped back against the wall. "What h-happened?" Just speaking those few words made her exhausted, and she wanted to return to sweet slumber.

"Don't move your arm. It's broken." His eyelids lowered, and his mouth lengthened into a smile as if he had just enjoyed a pleasant breeze on a hot summer day. He ran his fingers through her hair. "I'm so glad you're awake now. You can't imagine how scared I was."

"W-where are w-we?"

"Please don't be scared by what I'm about to tell you." He gripped her shoulders with both hands, his expression never sterner. "We're in the temple. They've captured us."

"What? I d-don't understand. How did...how did we get here?"

His chest heaved before his head sank to his chest. "After we left my grandfather's cottage, we walked for quite some time through the woods. We were going to try and poison my grandfather."

"I remember that."

"Then we saw that the temple had been rebuilt. But before we could do anything, they ambushed us."

"A-ambushed us?"

"Yes. I have no idea how they did it. We watched them in front of the temple one minute and then they were behind us the next."

"Who is t-they? The townspeople?"

"No."

"Who, then?"

"I can't believe I'm saying this." Ryder inhaled and shook his head. "My grandfather, and, well, my father."

She cocked her head, but her view of him was narrow and telescopic. Everything looked strange. She went to touch her tender eye with her uninjured arm, but Ryder stopped her.

"No. Don't. Your eye is hurt too."

"My eye?"

"Well, you fought back, Mary," Ryder smirked. There were those dimples she adored again. "I've never seen anyone fight like that."

"Really?"

"Yes. You managed to slug Botanē right in the face. Got him good," he laughed.

"That's so cool of me. I've never done anything like that in my life."

"I wouldn't be surprised if you broke his nose even." Ryder held out his bruised and bloodied hands. One of his fingers had sliced in two.

Mary bit her lip with disgust.

"I tried to fight back as well, but I'm afraid we were no match for the two of them. We've sustained many injuries as a result."

"That must be why my head hurts. I don't remember t-that." Mary rubbed her head and touched the cloth wound around it.

"Yeah. You hit your head pretty hard in the scuffle. It happened so fast, but I think you smacked it on a rock." He stood and gazed at the stone walls. "While you've been unconscious, I've tried everything to find a way out of here, but it's all sealed." Ryder dipped his fingers into the stream of water. "It's so peculiar that this water doesn't look like it's coming from anywhere. There are no cracks or holes in the ceiling at all, yet here it is."

She stared at the point on the ceiling Ryder watched.

"I just can't stop thinking about my father. I don't understand it," continued Ryder. "He's dead. I don't understand how I saw him. Are you sure you don't remember anything?"

The trickling water made her want to urinate, but her gut ached too much. She shook her head.

The vault door sprang open.

In walked the botanist and a man who looked just like Ryder.

Botanē locked the door behind them with the most complicated key she had ever seen, and then it vanished somewhere within his cloak.

Mary staggered to her feet, but the pain and dizziness were too great, so all she could do was cower against the wall.

"I'm not doing it, so don't waste your time." He threw up his fists and walked up to them. "I figured it out and I want no part in your sick and twisted plan to distribute Summoner potions to the world."

As Botanē studied Mary, she was stuck dumbfounded that such a sweet and innocent-looking man would do this to her and Ryder. What about all the deep conversations they had shared in the cottage? All the meals they had together? She had trusted him.

The skin underneath the botanist's eyes was black, and his nose had a large, painful-looking bump in the middle—no doubt an injury from their scuffle.

Ryder exchanged heated words with Botanē, all of them buzzed like bees in Mary's ears.

Her head was going to crack open like an egg. Somewhere in the mix, Botanē uttered, "I've come to offer you one last test, my boy."

"Test?" Ryder asked. "What kind of test?"

"A test to prove yourself as an Ashling or accept your fate inside this room."

Mary's blood went cold.

The old man's milky eyes shot to her. "You must kill her."

Chapter 35

Ryder

"You can't be serious," cried Ryder. "I'm not going to kill Mary."

"But this last test will allow you to prove yourself," Botanē said.

Ryder shook his head. "Last test? There were others?"

"In a manner of speaking," Nestor said.

His father's voice sent his heart into a nervous hammer. He didn't know where he had been those last thirty-something years, but he looked well preserved, like a marble statue in a museum. Before he had the chance to ask him one of the hundreds of questions that tumbled over each other in his mind, he erupted, "Asshole."

Nestor smirked.

The pit of Ryder's stomach ached. "You've been in on this too? What did you do?"

"We had to," Nestor said. "We've been testing you since you were a child by presenting hardships to see how you'd respond.

To make sure you could fulfill your duty as messenger in the family, as such a task isn't for the weak, unwise, or faint of heart."

"Tell me what you did," screamed Ryder.

"At first, they were smaller tests to see how you'd persevere," replied Nestor. "There were tests like not having a biological father around to test the importance and value of family, and then the nightmares of clocks and sleepwalking to see how you'd respond to persistent struggles, which you would no doubt face when it came time to fulfill your sacred duty."

"So, it was all intentional?"

Nestor nodded. "You showed tremendous strength throughout adolescence, but we had to be certain that you wouldn't falter and could complete your duty as an adult."

Ryder crossed the room and socked Nestor. "Asshole." Ryder walked away, shook his fist, then he turned, and walked back, ready to hit his father again.

Blood trickled from Nestor's nostril, but he didn't move. "I get it. You're mad at me. It's to be expected. Go on. Get it all out."

Ryder stopped in his tracks, out of breath. "Did my mother know?"

"I don't know if she did."

"What else? Tell me everything," Ryder demanded.

"Well, when your grandfather and I were almost certain it was time for you to come to Marble Woods, we presented one big challenge to see how you would react, and you passed."

"Is that why my life went to shit all at once?" He scoffed and reflected on how the whole scenario of losing his wife, home, and all that he valued had been orchestrated down to the day. Ryder glanced back at Mary. Blood gushed from her head, a squalid look in her eyes.

"I know it's painful," Nestor said, "but these tests...it's what you were born for."

Ryder spun around and spat.

"You showed tremendous promise with your messenger duties," said his grandfather. "In some sense, you're a hero for having advanced so far. Things progressed nicely. You followed the cues that your dreams sent you. You found Marble Woods. You were on the right track until things went awry when you met Mary. Everything changed, my boy."

"We feared you were losing your focus as a result," Nestor said. "That whole business with the antidote was a devil's advocate experiment to see just how deep Mary's impact had on you. We needed to see what you were willing to do to stop the Summoner potions from spreading to the world, and you gave up so easily. To think that if you were truly on our side and wanting to share the gifts of Summoner of Sleep and were met with an obstacle you would've given up so easily. Too easily. Once more, you became vengeful toward your own flesh and blood, and family is the most sacred thing."

"If family is so sacred to you, why did you punish me?" snapped Ryder. "Why wouldn't you show me a shred of care and abandon your son like that? When I was an innocent kid?"

"Oh, but I did show you I cared about you," Nestor said. "Remember the poetry book in your mailbox?"

"How did you know about that?"

"I put it there. Your stepfather didn't approve, and I wanted to show you some little way that I cared." Nestor smiled with identical dimples. He stepped forward and went to touch Ryder's face, but Ryder slapped it away.

"If you cared about me, you wouldn't have left me for some test."

"That's just it. Because I care about you, I had to leave you." Nestor's black eyes welled. "I didn't want to abandon you like that, but I needed to give you space and time to learn and grow on your own, to follow the signals, to become strong, to prove yourself as an Ashling, and now I'm so happy to have you here with me, my dear son. I've missed you."

"Don't give me any of that bullshit. You set me up. I never

wanted this, but you forced me to do it, you tricked me into coming here. You've puppeteered everything in my life, and now you want me to kill somebody on top of it?"

"I'm sorry it has to be this way," Nestor said, "but this is who you are."

"No, it's not."

"This is your destiny, and I'll prove it." Nestor inched up his shirt to reveal the mysterious symbol tattooed upon his hip. "This is mine, but you also have a tattoo of our sacred family symbol."

"I don't have any tattoos," laughed Ryder.

"Please let me prove it to you." Nestor extended his hand, but Ryder slapped it away. "You asked for proof, so let me prove it. I'm not going to hurt you."

Ryder stood motionless. "Go ahead but you won't find anything."

Nestor's hands pulled on Ryder's neck and his fingers fluttered through his hair and stopped at a spot on the back of his skull. "You see. It's right here."

"That doesn't prove anything," Ryder said. "Am I just supposed to take your word on something I can't even see?"

"Then ask Mary if there's a tattoo there."

"Fine," complied Ryder.

Nestor turned Ryder's head in her direction, "Do you see anything there, my dear?"

Mary leaned forward and gasped.

"There, you see. You have the tattoo."

Ryder pulled away and stared at his father, un-comprehending.

"We gave you lots of chances to prove yourself, Ryder," added his grandfather. "Some you passed, but some you didn't. For example, don't think for a second that I don't know what's in your pocket. Your potion won't work by the way. Haven't you learned by now that Ashlings are immune to these types of things? It might as well be water."

"But I saw it burn your hand that day in the greenhouse."

The old man sighed. "Another test. It was a charade to see what you'd do if given the chance to hurt me. You saw that opportunity and once again tried to hurt your flesh and blood."

Ryder frowned.

"Because you've been unsuccessful with several of these tests that we created for you," Nestor said, "and your mission has been compromised by your feelings for Mary, there's no other choice in proving yourself to the Ashling name than by killing her here and now in front of us."

"I won't do it. No." Ryder's stomach lurched. "I'll have no part in spreading your potions or being your stupid messenger. I won't let any of those potions out of Marble Woods."

"It's too late for that," Nestor said. "All of Marble Woods has turned. And Vern already explained how we've sold the formula."

"But the side effects. Once they see what happens to them and what happens when they stop taking it, then they won't want to take it anymore. The entire town is riddled in bones and carcasses for God's sake. You've created monsters. You're ruining people's lives for nothing."

"All I can tell you, my boy, is that people don't care if something is bad for them so long as it makes them feel good, or they think it's making them better," his grandfather said. "Look at any drug or beauty product on the market and the side effects that go with them. They cause allergies, liver damage, cancer. People still use it or take it. They don't care. They just want to feel good. Look good. Summoner of Sleep offers them something better, new."

"But they're not humans. They're monsters."

"Survival of the fittest, my boy," replied his grandfather. "I know you're upset, but you must see the good in all of this. You're the messenger of genetic perfection. What started as a quest to reunite with my beloved in my dreams has led to accelerated evolution. Moreover, we've found a way to improve upon it. It's so exciting that we've found another way to have dominion over God's creatures and to adapt the incredible characteristics from these creatures."

"Why do you even care about any of this if Ashlings are immune to it?" Ryder asked.

"It's our creation, my boy." He waved his arms beneath his cloak. "We've made the perfect humans. Don't you see? We're gods."

Ryder shuddered.

"And the initials S.O.S. are no coincidence," continued the botanist. "We're saving the world. Helping them improve. A life free from disease and death. A life of perfect genes. Genetics that adapt and change at a profound rate and like never before."

Nestor took a step forward. "We're offering you this final chance to prove yourself, dear son," he said, holding out a black vial with a smile. "All that's needed is one drop upon her skin and she'll die. It'll be painless. We just need you to do this one little thing and then we can be a family again."

Chapter 36

Mary

Mary covered the back of her head and neck and formed into a tiny ball. She shivered beneath her blood-crusted clothes and stared at the missing spot at the end of her dress she had used as a tourniquet to save Ryder. As her body grew colder, icy despair gripped her heart.

Boom. Boom. Boom.

Her head was going to detonate.

"This is your destiny, son," Nestor said.

Her heart pounded the more Ryder paced.

She knew firsthand what it was like to grow up without a father at home, and how all holidays and birthdays were torturous occasions, filled with unrealistic, drowning hope that her father would walk through the door and everything would be okay again. Since her father wasn't involved in her life either, she pondered what she would do if she met him now. Would she embrace him and forgive the past like she always did with people who had wronged her or slap him across the face for the misery he caused; for leaving her alone in the wretched town of Marble Woods.

Her muscles tensed and she sank tighter into the ball.

This can't be happening.

"And if I refuse?" Ryder asked.

"If you don't kill her right now, we'll be forced to kill you both," said his grandfather. "We would have no use for you or her if you were both alive. But you, you still have a chance, my boy. A bright future awaits you. A future with a real family."

Silence filled the vault.

She peeked out to find Ryder holding the vial. The stubble on his chin shined dull silver instead of black. He stared right at her with a look of acceptance plastered across his ashen face.

"How could you?" She scrambled around the vault floor even though there was no escape. The back of her eyes ached with malaise and the thumps in her head grew furious with each breath.

Ryder advanced. "I'm sorry, but I hope you know it's nothing personal." He bent to kiss her on the head, but she slapped him.

He looked down and paused.

Mist sprayed her face, and she couldn't help but look at the mysterious water cascade behind him. In her peripheral, Nestor surveyed it too with a look of fury. The sight triggered something in him. One last hope.

"Wait." A touch of energy jolted her body. "Before you kill me, I have a question."

All three men stared at her.

"Why are you staring at the water, Nestor?"

Nestor cleared his throat as if surprised that she had spoken to him and with such a ludicrous question. "It's the lifeblood of the temple. Without it, our temple would cease to grow."

"I understand its importance. Memories are also important. Do you remember when your father splashed you in the lake and held you under the water when you were a child?"

Nestor took a step back from the cascade, his eyes black as

space. "How do you know about that?"

"Doesn't matter how I know. Do you remember that your father held you under the water?"

"You want those to be your final words?" Nestor scoffed with crossed arms.

"I know you know the answer. I just want to hear you say it. Did he hold you under the water?"

A few spasmodic muscular motions followed, and then an eye twitch. There was audible breathing from his chest. Nestor closed his eyes. His lids flew open a second later to reveal stewing silver eyes.

"Yes. I remember. Happy now?"

"Well, this water here reminded me of that story, and I was just thinking how cruel it was for Botanē to do that to you," she said with forced sympathy in her voice. Mary met Ryder's gaze. "Wasn't that a mean thing to do, Ryder?"

"Yes. She's right. What a cruel thing to do to a child. Imagine doing something to make your own child hate water for the rest of his life. Imagine almost drowning your child to prove that you were the alpha. Why would a father do that to a child he loved?"

"It was a test, my boy," the botanist said. "Just like the tests, we gave Ryder. They made you stronger."

Ryder cocked his head and locked his eyes with Nestor's. "Who's to say he wouldn't perform such a test again? And from the sound of it, all this test business was Botanē's idea, to begin with."

Botanē swallowed.

A malicious gleam flickered in Nestor's eyes.

"It's true," chimed in Mary. "He's doing it now even with bringing you into this very room. This temple is huge. There must be hundreds of rooms. Why else would he choose a room with running water to hold us of all places? He's sticking it to you."

Water rushed through the room.

Nestor let out a small, high-pitched cry as if a floodgate

within him opened. He glowered at the botanist. "They're right. I've always wondered why you did that to me, Father."

"I told you." The botanist took a cautious step back toward the wall. "Don't listen to them. They're trying to distract you from the task at hand. To make you turn on me. Don't be fooled."

"I've hated water my entire life as a result of that incident." Nestor's face was the color of fire. For every step, the botanist took away from him, Nestor took two.

"You'll get over it. Just be strong."

"How does someone afraid of water stay hydrated? Did you ever think of that? How does someone who shudders at the sight of water stay clean?"

"Listen to me, my son. I was just trying to teach you a lesson," the botanist's voice cracked.

"No." Nestor exploded in a nerve-shattering scream. "I remember now. I remember how you held me under the water. I couldn't breathe. I heard your laughter above the surface. Why? Why would you do such a traumatizing thing?"

The old man was flat against the vault wall. "Please, just listen to me. I've apologized a thousand times for it. Don't forget why you are here. Don't forget the sacred bond of family."

Nestor's nostrils flared. He lunged and tackled Botanē to the ground, then punched him square in the face. A crack of bones reverberated through the vault, but Nestor didn't stop. Nestor stuffed the botanist's cloak sleeve in his mouth, not withdrawing it despite the old man's desperate attempts to wiggle free.

When the enormous keyring flew out of the botanist's cloak, Ryder intercepted them and fiddled with the lock.

The rest happened at such tremendous speed that all of a sudden the room was rumbling, and Ryder was scooping her up and ushering her to the door. Before it slammed shut, she shuddered at the sight of Botanē lying motionless on the floor, his bashed bloody face unrecognizable.

Ryder maneuvered her down a dark and winding labyrinth comprised of prodigious slate blocks that towered over them. At one point she reached up to feel the wide cloth wound around her head; it was wet and heavy with blood.

"Stop," she panted to Ryder as she tried to struggle free.

"We've got to keep moving or they'll catch us."

"N-no. I'm not going anywhere with you until you tell me if you were really going to k-kill me back there."

"Of course not," he laughed, still holding her up.

"I-it certainly looked like it," she jeered.

"That was a diversion. I had a plan too. Not as good as your plan though."

She blinked. The gold and red world spun around her.

"I was going to pretend to give you the potion, hoping you'd play dead while I attacked them."

Mary studied his face. "Why wouldn't you choose your family over m-me?"

"Are you crazy? I would never hurt you, Mary. Nor would I ever follow their insane plan. What they did is unforgivable, so please trust me that I'm telling you the truth. I don't know what I'd do without you here with me."

Her face softened beautifully as her mouth twisted into a smile. "Y-you mean that?"

"Of course."

She smiled just as Ryder leaned forward, grabbed her waist, pulled her flush against him, and pressed his lips to hers.

Chapter 37

Ryder

He struck the matchbox, which illuminated the soaring tomb-like walls that disappeared into the shadows above.

"Look at all these symbols." Ryder ran his finger over the crude circles, sharp lines, and jagged arrows. He strained his eyes to try and decipher the effaced markings.

"How did they carve all this? None of this was here before," Mary said.

"I don't know, but it's creepy," Ryder said and lit one of the torches sticking out from the wall.

Footsteps approached.

He grabbed the torch and took a deep breath of cold, damp air. "We've got to move quicker."

Mary groaned and hitched her arm on his.

They moved through a tangle of dark stone mazes. Every muscle in him ached. His hands burned. His leg throbbed. He was afraid to see what his ankle and thigh looked like under his clothes. Images of raw meat danced in his head and he swallowed the nauseating thought. He had the wretched feeling that they were trapped in the temple until he discovered a triangular-shaped door at the end of one of the tunnels.

"Maybe this is a hidden passage." Ryder reached out to discover that the handle was just a life-like painting. "Dammit."

"Hurry. They're coming," cried Mary.

They went back to the original tunnel they had come from.

Mary's bandage had thickened with so much blood it was more red than white, and he cringed every time she looked up at him with those big hopeful blue eyes.

After another few minutes, the stones thinned, and the walls now oozed with a sticky gelatinous substance.

"Eww." Mary plunged her fingertip into the auburn goo. "What is this stuff?"

"I don't want to stick around and find out," Ryder said.

Footfalls echoed through the unhallowed temple.

His heart leaped to his throat and he navigated the stone maze for what seemed like an hour. As they progressed, the gooey substance became bright yellow and clear to the point he could see through it. When touched, though, it was solid like glass.

The air grew cooler as Ryder continued to navigate through the network of underground tunnels. After a solid thirty minutes of nonstop dead ends, the cavernous lair of dark secrets led to an unlocked door with a working door handle.

"Should we go in?" Mary asked. "Or do you think it's a trap?"

Ryder scanned the tunnel behind them. A heavy mist obscured most of the tunnel. Despite his fatigue, he found himself saying, "We don't have a choice."

Her face was as white as milk. "Okay," she whispered.

Ryder twisted the doorknob and poked his head inside.

"W-well? What do you see?"

"Just a desk and a chair."

"G-good."

The warmth of her skin surprised him when he helped her

to the chair next to a row of windows covered in the clear goo.

"How do you feel? Are you okay?"

"N-not great," whimpered Mary as she studied the desk in front of her, her thin pale fingers fiddled about the little cubbies and drawers. "Look at all these bottles of Summoner of Sleep, Summoner of Youth, and Summoner of Chaos. T-this must be Botanē's study."

Ryder set the torch in the holder on the wall. "It probably is. That bastard is full of tricks." He darted to the door and locked it. "I think we'll be safe here for a little while, but we have to find a way out of the temple."

"I'm scared, Ryder."

He paused, wanting to tell her he was scared too, but he refused to show weakness. "Don't worry. We'll get out of this."

He limped over to the row of windows. Far below sat the dilapidated and charred fragments of the once-thriving town. Mary's house smoldered in the wreckage. Mounds of gnawed up bones lay in front of Belle's General Store. Blood stained the concrete. Then there was Emelda's home which looked toppled from a tornado—the cookie recipe lost forever.

"Can you s-see anything?"

"Just the town. We must be in one of the temple's towers."

"How's that p-possible?" Mary held herself at her stomach. "We haven't been ascending."

"I don't know. Maybe we made a wrong turn." Ryder couldn't recall if there had been turns in the tunnel or not. He couldn't recall much about their journey at all now, or where he had made a mistake—only Mary's bright red blood infusing into her golden tresses like a fine brewing tea. He glanced at the ground in search of some miraculous clue.

"The building must be more complicated than we thought."

"What'll we do?" she asked.

"I don't know. Maybe there's something that can help us in the desk or this room. Like a map or a cure."

A strange gargle of maddening sounds emitted from outside

the temple.

"What was that?"

Ryder peered out at the town once more. A dirty plume of smoke darkened the sky, and at the edge, a line of shadows gathered.

Shit.

He turned toward Mary. He opened his mouth, but no words came.

"W-what?" She hunched over and groaned. Oww. I...oh, God. Ow. I d-don't feel so good." A moment later she raised her head. A line of blood dribbled from the corner of her mouth making her resemble a little vampire.

He didn't know whether to tell her about how bad the bleeding was. He didn't know whether there was any hope. He didn't know what to do. He turned to stare out at the town again. How would he solve this horrible dilemma?

A few yards from the edge of the woods a legion of monsters loomed. The moon illuminated the slimy, chaotic horde of abominations drudging toward the temple. They were a mass of impossible shapes. He recognized most of their faces hidden within the greasy, gelatinous flesh, but the worst victims were the children and their bloodless faces. The deformed anatomies, the scales, claws, liquefied heads. All their attributes were spread among the bodies conceived by Satan himself.

"They're coming and we're trapped," he whispered and let the tears he had held back for so long come.

"L-leave me. Save yourself."

"There's no way I'm leaving you," Ryder said.

She swiveled around and hunched over onto the desk in one swift, violent motion, which knocked over one of the bottles of Summoner of Chaos.

It smashed open, spraying the tonic everywhere, scenting the room with magic.

Ryder screeched and jumped back.

"Oh, no." Mary sat up with a start and breathed in the

shimmering particles of chaos. It was all over now.

It became clear to Ryder that her entire dwindling presence was already morphing into something indescribably preternatural. Her face went from a sick yellow-gray to taught, glowing skin. After another second, her flesh was hard and liquid at the same time, melting like candle wax down her neck.

"What have you done?" he moaned. "You're turning into one of them."

She remained still and silent as he staggered to look out the window again.

His ankle was a dead weight, his injured foot the size of a watermelon.

Their groans sang louder in his ears. The creatures were puffy and hideous, sprouting and bubbling bluish-green flesh everywhere. Some were headless, throwing their arms in a gesture of desperation as if the nerves were recalling their lost humanity. Some jumped, others flew, but most of them drudged toward the temple as if in a funeral procession.

He punched one of the strange windows, which splintered in a star shape around his busted knuckles. The moon cast a green hue upon the abyss circling the temple. Scaling the fifty-foot vertical wall with an obsidian sheen to reach the lower level of the temple was impossible. Even if he jumped through the window, he wouldn't survive the fall.

He tilted his head to examine the wall once more and spotted a narrow row of black stairs—his eyes were experts now in identifying the weird caches of the temple and followed their path from the solid black door some fifteen feet away around the front side of the temple. Whether the stairs were real or a painting he didn't know. There was no telling if they reached the bottom, or if there were any other doors along the way with monsters behind them.

If he dared to try the mysterious staircase, he'd have to jump a good five or six feet to the tiny landing below, walk ten feet across the narrow ledge, and descend the stairs. Just the thought of that much pressure on his ankle from the imagined jump sent a shockwave of pain through his fatigued body, but it was his only chance for survival.

Something soft touched his side, and he jolted.

"There's no hope for me, Ryder," Mary said. "We both know there's no cure and that Vern and my mother were somehow faking their recovery."

Her fingers touched his cheek as if groping in the dark to know that he was there. He felt the heat from her chest against his as he drew her close to him.

Ryder didn't see the monster before him. Only her beauty, and as he went to touch her, his fingers slipped through her skin and into her rib cage like a hand through water. It was warm and wet inside.

He found himself saying how beautiful she was despite her disintegrating flesh and pressed her into him. She was so fragile in his arms, her bones so delicate like a bird's. He breathed her faint flowery, ghostly scent and the cotton of her dress.

A sob rose in the back of his throat.

Stupid immunity.

In his peripheral, the horde approached—all skin and muscle stripped from the bone.

All rot. All blood.

"I'll miss you," he whispered.

"I'll miss you too." She lifted her eyes to meet his. "I hope you understand this is a good thing. I've wanted nothing more than to be free, and now I will be."

"Mary, I—"

"Don't tell me you're sorry for me. There's nothing you can do. All you need to do is be strong, Ryder."

Ripples of shrieks and cries burst through the hallway outside. He held her tight, his heart knocked against his ribs, one eye on the door.

This is it.

"You must go before they come. Before I do things that I

don't want to do."

The unmistakable sound of slippery appendages and claws beat against the wood. A slender black arm crawled underneath and headed for Ryder where it swelled into a great, palpitating mass.

He released her.

The arm smacked the torch from the holder, then hit the desk, and everything ignited. Within seconds the room was a snow globe of embers whirling together into a seductive dance of oranges and reds.

There was nowhere else to go but down.

Ryder punched the window until it broke. Warm blood ran down his arm.

The ledge was too far away, the ground implausibly high, his ankle too weak.

"Go," she yelled, her eyes now black and full of darkness. "You have to."

Horrid grunts emanated through the tower followed by incessant bangs against the ancient wooden door. And with each thrust and splintering of the boards, Ryder summoned all his strength to jump.

—

The sun was rising—a ruddy disc floating in a sea of hazy orange and pink above the mist-clouded tress. He had camped the night on the thorny ground of the forest floor, trusting the leaves and branches he used to cover himself would provide enough camouflage while he slept. Every few minutes the searing pain in his ankle woke him, but he didn't dare look at the state of it. The burning had spread to his calf and thigh.

He cut his rest short and groped the tree as best he could with a vague recollection of which direction he was traveling.

He soon found himself once more fleeing for his life, but the softness from the soil slowed him like traveling across quicksand—each step heavy and agonizing.

Every hiss of the wind and movement in the bushes made him think he heard the monsters and he paused and turned every few seconds toward Marble Woods.

Mary?

The odds were bad, but he had successfully scaled the temple staircase and traveled on foot through the gray woods without being caught yet.

Ryder trekked for what seemed like another hour, using up his energy and forcing him to pant and wince the entire way. The trees thinned and a faint overgrown dirt path lay ahead.

He tripped over rusty car parts sprinkled along the tangled auburn grass. The curvature of the trees screamed familiarity. The dilapidated gate hung on rusted hinges. In the distance, the church bell chimed, and for once, the sound of a clock made him smile.

He knew where he was.

The road was just up ahead.

He could go home.

A car zipped across the road in the distance.

He limped faster. When he reached the road, his car was indeed gone, but the sight ahead jolted him to his core.

On the other side of the road, there was a billboard of a gorgeous smiling woman holding a fancy pink bottle bearing the words Summoner of Youth. A hundred questions overtook him, and he trembled with acute fear, unlike anything he had experienced before.

Another car loomed in the distance.

His heart jumped into his throat.

Ryder darted into the road.

"Stop. Please stop," he waved, his throat feeling like an open sore.

The car honked and swerved. Dust and debris pelted him. Ryder spat and brushed himself off.

He stood there frozen until a truck approached a few minutes later. Ryder waved and yelled, "Please help me. Help.

It's an emergency."

The truck rolled down the driver-side window and out hurled the words, "Get out of the road, you damn bum."

They were right. No person in their right mind would stop and help him looking like this. Even if they did stop, what would he tell them? A horde of monsters was after him? That their potions would take over the world and change everyone, except him because he was immune? It sounded delusional. No one would believe him until it was too late.

For several minutes he stumbled, cried, kicked, and flailed. The wind made him realize he was cold, and his clothes were wet.

His hands and knees shook so hard that he collapsed in front of the billboard. It was all right there laughing at him the whole time. The smiling woman who resembled Julie. The blatant name *Wick Corporations* plastered across the label. The emblem of the flower, moon, and compass as the logo. All of its swirling madness would prevent him from ever sleeping again.

He sat there for a long time, hands wrapped around his knees, and as the sun faded, a great fiery layer spread upon the horizon which stretched far into the heavens that he would never reach.

Acknowledgments

I am deeply thankful to the following people for their encouragement and support: Bruce and Jane Arnold, Jennifer, Tim, and Marcia Bridwell, Nancy Colby, my family in New Zealand and Australia, Stefanie Fenrick, Fabiana Nardi, my parents, Diana Ruybalid, Paris Snyder, Liz Swan, and Mike and Jim Young.

Thank you to Susan Brooks at Literary Wanderlust for welcoming this project and supporting me along the way.

Lastly, I send gratitude to everyone who has read my books. Without your thoughts, feedback, and encouragement, this book would not exist.

About the Author

A.I. Winters is an award-winning author known for her works of horror and fantasy. She is the author of the young adult fantasy novels Strange Luck, The Nightmare Birds, and A Darling Secret.

She currently lives in Los Angeles. When not writing books, she enjoys breaking a sweat in Jiu-Jitsu class, baking, and traveling.

She would love to interact with you on social media:

@AmieIWinters
http://www.facebook.com/aiwinters
http://www.instragram.com/aiwinters_author
YouTube http://bit.ly/2NwnAYd